# INTENT TO DEFRAUD

Sue Carol Nussbaum

PublishAmerica
Baltimore

© 2004 by Sue Carol Nussbaum.
All rights reserved. No part of this book may be reproduced, stored in a retrieval system or transmitted in any form or by any means without the prior written permission of the publishers, except by a reviewer who may quote brief passages in a review to be printed in a newspaper, magazine or journal.

First printing

ISBN: 1-4137-1980-5
PUBLISHED BY PUBLISHAMERICA, LLLP
www.publishamerica.com
Baltimore

Printed in the United States of America

*For my husband, Kenneth.*

## *Acknowledgments*

I would like to thank my husband, Kenneth Ragland, without whose encouragement, suggestions and support this book could not have been written.

I would like to thank, also, the members of my writers' workshop, participants in the Creative Retirement Center at the International College of Naples, Florida, who listened to my readings of various chapters in this book and who gave me their opinions and suggestions. I started this book as an exercise in writing an opening chapter. It was their interest in the story and their prodding that kept the book going.

Special thanks go to my dear friend and fellow writer, Sarah Gwynn, who persuaded me to finish the book and who read it when it was complete. It was because of her encouragement that I pursued having it published.

# Chapter One

Barry left the bank building on his way to meet Dan. He was thinking about last night's *All In The Family* and was laughing to himself at the genius of the writing. Boy, things had really changed. All that talk about "jungle bunnies" and "fags." The show was certainly on the edge. He always had enjoyed a good laugh, and now that the Bellows case was over, he had allowed himself a night, free from preparation, to just relax and watch television. Soon, it would all start again and he knew he wouldn't be able to allow himself too many of those nights. Nineteen seventy-eight was going to be his best year ever, but with the success came the price. Oh well, he was still young and he didn't mind the price. At least, not yet. He knew he wouldn't be able to keep the pace forever, so he had to make it now.

As he crossed the street, he suddenly had a weird feeling. He didn't know what possessed him to look back at the second floor window, but look he did. He couldn't believe his eyes; staring at him through the glass was a beautiful woman, clearly looking at him, without reserve or shame. It was a long way from the street, but shadows from the sun had not yet obliterated the form within. There was nothing to diminish the view and there was no question that she was looking directly at him. He couldn't make out the color of her hair, it could be red, or perhaps brown, nor could he see exactly what she was wearing. It appeared to be a white blouse. That meant she probably worked there, or she'd have had on a jacket. He shaded his eyes to get a better look but when she saw him look back at her, she stood her ground, not retreating from the frame. It was almost a challenge, not exactly brazen, but confident. Yes, confident was the word, but about what?

Barry was determined to find out who this mysterious person was, but he was in a hurry. He had promised to meet Dan at the Premium Diner at eleven. He knew that it would take half an hour to get there in city traffic. His mystery woman would have to wait.

He reached his car and, without looking back at the window, made a mental note of the floor and the number of windows from the corner. If she worked in an office, he would find out who she was—and if his luck with women held—he would find out why she was staring at him.

He pulled his new Mercedes slowly away from the curb determined to return the next morning, if for no other reason, out of curiosity. He told himself he would make no obvious attempt to find her but that he would casually go up to the second floor and look around. He clearly remembered her face, if not the details. He was particularly good at seeing and remembering what people looked like, especially beautiful women. He searched his brain to think where he might have seen her before, but came to the realization that he had not seen her, ever.

He was sure that if he had, he would have remembered. No, this was someone he had never met; still she had watched him. He was sure of that. *What did it mean?* he wondered.

Oh well, maybe he should just forget it and take it as a compliment. Maybe, at forty-two, he still looked pretty good, but as the day wore on he found himself thinking about her and the way she had stared at him. It was more than a passing interest; he could see that. Her look was almost predatory—intense and concentrated. He felt as though she looked at him through the sights of a gun, that somehow he was her quarry, and it made him uncomfortable.

He arrived at the diner and found a space right in front of a window. He noticed that Dan's car was in the next space, on his right. Dan was already inside; it was unusual for Dan to be on time. This must be important. And why here? Dan didn't usually frequent diners. He was used to more elegant dining, even for breakfast. He generally ate at the Johnson Club, where he had a membership, and would be greeted with familiarity, and obsequious courtesy. Dan ate up that kind of treatment, so why here, on the outskirts of town? Did Dan have a secret? Not like Dan at all. Not at all.

Barry smiled at the thought of the Johnson Club. It was an exclusive club, for men only, and Barry often teased Dan about its name. "Fitting," he would say, and fall into gales of laughter. Dan always smiled and shrugged it off good-naturedly. He pondered these matters as he carefully put up the roof on the convertible and turned the key. He opened the door carefully, so as not to hit the car on his left. He had waited too long to afford a car like this, and wasn't going to damage it the first week. This was his baby, bought and paid for with hard work, and he intended to take care of it the way it deserved to be taken care of. It was his way of telling clients and colleagues alike, that he had "arrived." He had won his first million-dollar case, and he knew that clients would be flocking to his door when the word got out. The car, besides being a well-deserved toy, was his way of telling the world that he was a success. That's why he chose red. Barry had never been flamboyant, but now, well, why not?

He stepped out and depressed the master lock button. He hoped Dan had chosen a booth near the window so he could keep an eye on this baby. On the other hand, if Dan came all the way out here to see him, then he would probably have found a dark corner in the rear.

As he entered the diner, he looked around. It was filled with workers getting coffee to go, women with little children, and old men meeting friends for breakfast. He looked in the rear and spotted his brother in a back corner booth. *Uh oh, this does not look good. I wonder what's up.*

When Dan saw him, he got up and shook his brother's hand. Dan always got up when someone approached him—force of habit.

"Thanks," he said. "Thanks for coming way out here to meet me and on short notice. You know I never would have asked you if it wasn't important." He looked around nervously and then sat down.

"What's up?" asked Barry. "What's so important? Jeez, you look jumpy."

Dan had not shaved and the gray stubble aged him about ten years. Barry was shocked to see his older brother so unkempt. He had started to thicken around the middle several years ago. Barry guessed that he stopped going to the gym because of his busy schedule; a surgeon's life is not easy. He knew that his brother usually got to the hospital about five-thirty every morning, and that was not counting emergencies; and there were plenty of those. The life of a neurosurgeon was very demanding.

He had been urging his brother to take in a young partner to help with the emergencies, but Alex, Dan's wife, was a high-ticket item. She needed a great deal of maintenance, not just with attention, but also with high priced clothes, jewelry, the latest fads, and constant redecorating of their house. He knew when they bought the "castle," that Dan would have to hustle to pay for it.

Barry always thought the financial burden of his marriage would break his brother and he worried over him, almost as if he were the older brother and Dan the younger, instead of the other way around. Barry had never seen his brother sweat, but Dan was actually sweating. One thing about Dan—he was good in an emergency. He always had the cool head when there was a problem. *Good old Dan. You could always count on him to have the solution when others were just beginning to realize there was a problem.*

"I'm in trouble Barry."

"You look like hell."

"Hell would look good after this mess."

"What's going on?"

"I screwed up. Badly."

"What do you mean?"

"I mean that I'm being sued for malpractice."

The waitress came and Barry ordered coffee. Dan's cup was empty, and he asked for another cup. His plate had crumbs and nuts on it, and some little flakes of icing, no doubt the remains of a Danish pastry. Barry ordered a buttered roll; he sensed this wouldn't be over quickly.

"It's not the first time. Didn't you tell me it goes with the territory, with neurosurgery?

"Well, yes it does, but that's not all."

"I'm listening."

"I'm not covered."

"What do you mean, you're not covered? How could you be not covered?"

"It's a long story."

"I'll cancel my appointments, I'm your brother."

"Well, not that long. Remember when we bought the house?"

"Yeah."

"Remember I told you that I really didn't have the money to buy that kind of house, and you gave me a hard time about not living within my means."

"We had quite a discussion over it. I thought you were crazy."

"Yes, well there were reasons that I never told you, but I don't want to go into that now. I just had to find a way and I did. Some guy came into my office one day selling medical malpractice insurance. At the time, I was paying an arm and a leg for it, so I took the time to sit down and talk with him."

"And?"

"And I bought it from him. I canceled my other carrier and bought it from him. His price was about two-thirds what I was paying, and with those high rates, even a third less counts for a lot. I was buying the house and Alex needed all new things, and I was really afraid I couldn't swing it all."

"So you went out and bought crappy insurance, just to pay for that ridiculous house."

"Yes." Dan dropped his head, embarrassed.

"Were you out of your mind?"

"Yes, I guess I was."

"Okay, no sense in giving you a hard time over what's done. So what's the problem? They say the contract doesn't cover you for this particular type of episode? Or are the coverage dates not right? What are they saying?"

"Nothing."

"What do you mean nothing?"

"I mean I can't find them."

"Can't find them?"

"Right. They're based in some God forsaken place—Nevis/St. Kitts or something—and, either they never existed and I was scammed, or they're out of business. I called the insurance commissioner in Nevis/St. Kitts, and—can you believe it—they had a goddam answering machine? Can you believe it? They had an answering machine. I mean the insurance commission. Where were they, at the beach or something?"

"Barry I'm out of my mind. I've been calling every day and I can't get a real person on the phone. And, on top of that, I'm too upset to work. I mean I've handed all my cases over to Jim Casey. I'm afraid in this state of mind, I'll do it again."

"What did you do?"

"I was doing a laminectomy, something I could almost do blindfolded and I cut the cord. The patient is a twenty-two year old boy and I made him a paraplegic. I just cut it at L-3 and now, well, he's in a wheelchair for the rest of his life."

Barry did the math quickly. *Jesus*, he thought. *A twenty-two year old, lifetime expectancy, now about seventy. Present care and rehab, retraining, not to mention lost earnings. Uh oh, this is catastrophic. We're looking at millions, here.* Finally Barry spoke.

"This is serious."

"I know, I know. It'll wipe me out."

"Yes, probably, and that's not all."

"What do you mean?"

"It's worse than that."

"How?"

"You'll have to spend years paying off what you can't pay, now. I mean this boy is the partner you should have taken in. He'll be your partner for a long time to come. Does Alex know?"

"I've been afraid to tell her."

"She's your wife, for God's sake."

"I wanted to know how bad it was before I told her."

"I can't lie to you, Dan. It's not just bad; it's a real calamity."

Dan started to cry. No, not so anyone would see, but Barry knew his brother and saw the tears.

"Listen Dan, give me about twenty four hours to think this through and maybe we can find a way out. But you'd better tell Alex. You'll need all the support you can get."

"Yeah, from Alex? Like she'll be supportive. I sometimes think she just thinks of me as a cash bull. I wonder how long she'll stick now, if I lose it all."

"I never realized it was that bad a marriage."

"Oh, it isn't, really. I mean we go out, we have fun together, but it's all based on a certain lifestyle. I don't know how good she would be in a pinch. I was never really sure she loved me." Dan paused for a moment and then said, "I guess I'm going to find out, now."

Barry didn't say a word but solemnly nodded his head. When the waitress dropped the check on the table, Barry reached for it, but Dan grabbed it and said, "Not yet. Maybe someday you'll have to take them all, but for now, it's on me." He smiled the smile of a man condemned.

## Chapter Two

Tilden Jennings realized that he had seen her. She walked away from the window, and went over to the conference table where she had books stacked up. Tildy, as she was called, had graduated from law school last year after a brief career as an elementary school teacher. She knew that she was not cut out to spend her life in the classroom with eight year olds and, following in Grandpa's footsteps, she decided to be a lawyer.

She had just turned thirty and was finding that it was much more difficult to land an interesting job just out of law school, even with Grandpa's connections, so she took a job with Wright, Landwehr, and Cummings, as a ground level associate. She was assigned to work with Jason Kraus, the hotshot medical malpractice defense lawyer in the firm. He had immediately asked her to research the legal and medical issues on a number of cases he was working on. Tildy found the work interesting.

Jason had the reputation of being a tough litigator and appeared to have all the charm of a lizard, but he was decent to her and seemed to appreciate her work. She loved the law, and even began to like her job, but felt she was on the wrong side of it. She had envisioned herself representing victims of negligence, not defending against them. Nevertheless, she was determined to learn everything she could.

Grandpa had told her that civil defense attorneys were all sleaze bags. Nevertheless, it wasn't a bad idea to see the practice from this side, before she took her rightful place at the bar, as a plaintiff's lawyer.

She knew Grandpa was right. She could never be happy seeing the big companies stiff deserving victims. However, she was lucky to get this job. Many of her classmates were still scrounging around for employment, or doing *per diem* work for other lawyers.

Jason was unusually grumpy this week, since he had just been trounced with a huge jury verdict against his client in the Bellows case. She knew that Barry Chandron was the victor in this four-year battle to get justice for his client, who had been misdiagnosed with a rare form of lung cancer and, after going through a regimen of radiation and chemotherapy, found out he had never had the disease.

When Mr. Bellows was first told of the diagnosis, he went into a deep depression, costing him his marriage and his job. After two years of "therapy," he sought another opinion.

Tildy had not worked on the case; all the research, as well as the discovery, was over by the time she came to the firm. The news of the beating the firm took, however, became a great subject of office gossip. That's how the name of the famous Barry Chandron first came to Tildy's attention. She had asked some of her colleagues to point him out to her and, one day in the courthouse not too long after, she got a glimpse of "The Great Barry," as some had come to call him. She had even walked into a courtroom where he was trying a case, but couldn't stay long enough to watch.

She was impressed. Clearly older than she was, although he had the leanness of a younger man, he had a slightly receding hairline, with graying temples. He was about six foot two; but it was his erect bearing that gave him a kind of invincible look. She thought he must have been in the military to carry himself so tall. He was not so much handsome, as elegant, a term she had never used to describe a man before but even the way he reached for things or waved at the court clerks, had an air of "presence," something she couldn't define, but which piqued her interest.

After his big win, she knew he was someone she would love to work with, to learn from and, eventually, to have the respect and acclaim that he commanded. As she looked out the window, she spotted him crossing the street. She knew that his office was on another street, not in her building, but she had seen him several times before, crossing to go to the bank, no doubt.

She had watched him enough to notice that he had a new car. She smiled when she realized where the money came from, but he had never looked up before. It was almost as if he could sense her looking at him when, today he looked up, catching her in the act. She took a deep breath when she realized he had seen her, but she stood her ground and hoped he would wonder about her. She was sure that he had gotten a good look at her by the puzzled expression on his face. Yes, she was sure he had seen her and realized she was watching him. *But what now? What happens next?*

She put it out of her mind and returned to her work on the Sanding file. She didn't know who the plaintiff's attorney was yet, but hoped it would be Barry Chandron. Maybe she would get a chance to meet him at depositions or something.

## Chapter Three

Dave awoke to find the sun streaming in the window. The shutters were wide open. He looked at his watch and couldn't believe it was only five o'clock. The sun was too high in the sky to be so early. *My watch must have stopped*, he thought. He shook it, but the second hand continued to work its way around the dial. He looked around the room. He was confused. *Where am I?* he wondered. He put his head back on the pillow and remembered. They had left Costa Rica late yesterday. Of course, that must be it; Nevis/St. Kitts must be on Atlantic time. There's a two-hour difference. He reset his watch to 7:00, got up and looked out the window. The sun was bright over the ocean, and made little dancing diamonds where it reflected on the deep blue water, way out to the horizon. He could see the wakes of the boats on the water, bright white streamers against navy blue, but the boats were too far away to see what kind they were. Now and then, there was a flash, as the sun reflected off one of them. The sky was clear and bright. It was going to be a beautiful day. A busy one too, he thought.

Dave went into the bathroom and relieved himself. He looked in the mirror and saw that his eyes were bloodshot. He thought about yesterday and his flight with Lindy. Lindy was a great guy—lots of laughs. He tended to drink a lot, but this only made him more fun; he was a happy drunk. Lindy had only two rules that he lived by, one, to have a good time whenever and wherever possible, the other, never to fly drunk. That's probably why Lindy was still living at the age of forty-eight and, more important, still flying. Dave knew that Lindy was fearless. He would take off in almost any kind of weather, and had no fear of night flying. When required to do so, he could fly low, under the radar. Although people considered him a daredevil, Lindy was cautious in his own way. He was an excellent flyer and, what might have been risky for others, Lindy knew he could handle. If he wasn't sure, he had to be paid very well and, even so, he was known to have refused some jobs. Lindy was no fool.

The best thing about Lindy was that he knew his way around these islands. He had been living on one or another of them for the past twenty years. He was a good friend and an even better companion, but mostly Dave liked him because he could be useful. Lindy had friends in most of the island governments, many of whom were corrupt enough to sell almost any kind of favor or, if that wasn't possible, to provide valuable contacts who could arrange for most anything. If you needed a favor, Lindy could get it for you. He had told Dave, more than once, that if he needed a new passport, Lindy knew where to get it. Lindy also knew that Nevis was a good place to stash your money, with no questions asked. Yes, Lindy was a handy guy to have as a friend.

Dave smiled as he remembered his first meeting with Lindy in San José. He was drinking alone at a bar and Lindy just walked up to him and offered to buy him a drink. Dave always did wonder why Lindy did that but, of course, he returned the favor and soon they were buddies. Lindy offered to take him flying the next day, and Dave heartily accepted. When he arrived at the airfield the next morning, he understood why his new friend was called Lindy. He was wearing a leather jacket, a leather helmet with goggles, and a long white scarf. Dave laughed as Peter Hunziker introduced himself, again.

They spent a couple of hours looking down on the mountains and forests of Costa Rica and ended the day, again at a bar, drinking the night away. Lindy was full of wild stories. Dave never doubted for a moment that they were all true. However, he noticed that Lindy never, ever mentioned names. At least he was discreet, Dave thought. Lindy told him that he and his Cessna were always for hire and it never mattered what the job was. He was paid well for his services. He had contacts all over the Caribbean, and could be useful to anyone—for a fee.

He and Lindy took off last night about seven and, within a few hours, had landed here in Nevis. When they landed, they went right to their hotel, had dinner, and headed straight for the bar. *What in the world was that whiskey we were drinking?* he wondered. *Boy, it only took five or six to level me. I kind of remember Lindy helping me to my room, but the rest is a haze.*

As he tried to remember the events of the evening, his headache grew worse. *Hung over! Can you beat that? Me? Hung over! That hasn't happened in a lot of years. I must be getting old or it was that whiskey, what the hell did he call it?*

Dave dressed quickly and went next door. He knocked on the door, but there was no answer. He went downstairs to the lobby, and there was Lindy, sitting in a large wing chair, reading a newspaper. Naturally, he was out of uniform, so to speak, just a pair of khakis and a green knit shirt. He looked fresh and crisp, as if he hadn't had a single drink the night before. But of course, that's the mark of a long time alcoholic, which he was sure Lindy was.

When he saw Dave approach him, he jumped up and said with a big grin, "I thought you were going to sleep till noon. We have a lot to do today." Dave looked at him sheepishly.

"Uh, have you had your breakfast?"

"Only coffee." Lindy went back to his chair and picked up his newspaper. Together, they entered the dining room. Dave wasn't sure just how much breakfast he wanted.

## Chapter Four

*What an idiot my brother is,* Barry thought to himself as he hit downtown traffic. *Jesus, for such a smart guy, he sure is dumb. Actually, isn't that what he often thought of the doctors who were defendants in his malpractice cases? Weren't the ones most likely to get into trouble the ones who were first in their class, but never learned how to talk to patients?*

In his experience, doctors who had a good relationship with their patients seldom got sued, even those who committed the most egregious errors. The others, the ones who adopted a superior attitude, often got nailed. Well, it usually served them right for not developing a little humility along the way. He always took pleasure in bringing down some arrogant son of a bitch who thought that he was above it all. Dan wasn't like that. Barry had to admit, though, that he did have some feelings for the little guy who made one bad mistake and had to pay the piper, but that's why they carried insurance.

He tried to tell his doctor friends—and surprisingly he had a few—that malpractice was like running a red light, getting into an accident and hurting someone. It didn't mean you were incompetent, only that for one second, maybe while you were hung over, or overly tired, or worrying about your kid's college expenses, you failed to do that which you were supposed to do—take the necessary care.

But all the doctors he knew seemed to take it as a personal affront if they were sued and became impossibly hostile to him from the start. Well, it was a rotten job, protecting the victims of a doctor's carelessness, but someone had to do it. He knew he was remarkably well suited to it.

Now the shoe was on the other foot. He had to think about how he could defend his brother. *What an idiot! If only he had spoken to me first,* he thought. Yes, but that was the same thought he had when Dan said he was going to marry Alex. *What a bitch! I saw it right from the start. I knew there would be problems but, frankly, I didn't think Dan would be that dumb to go along with her every whim.*

"What a wimp! I'm so mad at him, I could kill him," he said out loud.

Barry had to slam on his brakes to stop for a red light he almost didn't see. Gee, I'd better pay attention. A few minutes later, he arrived at the office, just in time for his first appointment.

For a second—but just for a second—he thought of Tildy. *I'm going to have to find that woman and find out why she was staring at me. I know it wasn't just an idle glance; she wanted me to know she was looking because she didn't turn away. Now, what the hell is that all about?*

## Chapter Five

Dan went back to his office not feeling any better after his conversation with Barry. He entered by the rear door, so that his staff wouldn't know he was in. *I can always count on Barry*, he told himself, and he was right. *I'm an idiot. He didn't say it, but he thinks that I'm really a jerk to put up with Alex. Maybe he's right. I probably should have laid the law down years ago. I do know why I married her, though. She was beautiful. I could never believe that she would marry a guy like me. She could have had anyone she wanted, but she wanted me.*

*Sure, she wanted me but not for me. I know now; she wanted to be Mrs. Doctor. Yes, it was very important to her to be a doctor's wife. I guess I was the only doctor to come along.*

*Oh well, why she married me is really not so important. And why she stayed with me is probably not worth worrying about; that's a no-brainer. I gave her everything she ever asked for and more. I know Barry thinks I'm a fool to give in to Alex's every whim. Maybe that's why I have two beautiful children and he doesn't have any. He seems happy enough. God knows, he always has a stunning woman on his arm. I wonder if that's enough for Barry. Maybe he likes it that way; Barry always put his career first, just like me. Oh God! What the hell am I going to do?*

Dan put his head down on the desk and wept softly. He didn't want the nurses to hear him. He was glad he hadn't turned on the light when he opened the door; he really needed a few minutes to himself. Dan was not one to sit and feel sorry for himself, but he had never really been in this much trouble. A few minutes later, he picked up the phone and dialed his home. *Better get this over with.*

"Hello," he heard. Dan quickly hung up the phone. He hadn't really expected Alex to be home, but there she was, and he just wasn't ready. He'd call later.

## Chapter Six

Tildy left the office at noon to grab a quick bite of lunch. She had just found the book she was looking for and was anxious to get back. She went to her usual luncheonette, the one frequented by other law clerks. This time, though, she didn't look around for a familiar face. She thought she might be on to something in her research and wanted to get back to it.

She ordered a tuna sandwich and a cup of coffee, fully intending to go right back. Tildy ate her sandwich quickly and suddenly had an idea. *A little walk will do me good*, she thought. She was in the habit of strolling by the courthouse after lunch, hoping to run into friends.

She didn't deceive herself, though; she knew that today was different. He had seen her, and he knew she was looking at him. Yes, no doubt about it, he saw her. It would be more accurate to say he sensed her, because he turned around to look in her direction and caught her staring. He definitely knew she was looking at him and seemed quite startled by it. She was sure that women stared at him from time to time; he was a very attractive man, but he felt her stare and turned around. She knew this meant something; just by the look on his face; she knew that his curiosity was aroused.

Tildy mused about what would happen if she suddenly met him face to face. Would he acknowledge her? One way or another, she thought, he would find a reason to talk to her. Though she didn't admit this to herself at first, she was walking around the courthouse hoping he would emerge, see her and speak. She even imagined the conversation:

*"Hi, have we met?"*

*"No, I don't think so."*

*"But surely, I've seen you around the courthouse. Are you a secretary for one of the judges?"*

*"No."*

(Tildy knew that men always thought of the professional women around the courthouse, first, as secretaries.) She would stay very cool and not tell him at first that she was a lawyer. She would let him find it out and then be embarrassed when he found out. That would put her at an advantage.

Tildy laughed at her imaginary conversation. She knew she would meet him, but it would probably be through an introduction as Jason's law clerk. Still, he knew she had watched him and that would pique his interest.

As she walked by the courthouse, she didn't run into any of her usual acquaintances, probably because she had taken a short lunch break and had finished early. She turned the corner and headed back to work.

## Chapter Seven

Tildy returned to the office satiated by lunch and her amusing little fantasy. She started to pick up a book on obstetrics when she noticed a note from Jason. He wanted to see her. She took off her coat and called Jason's secretary, Betty. Betty told her that Jason was still at lunch. Tildy asked if she knew what Jason wanted to see her about but Betty had no idea. Tildy went back to her obstetrics research in the Anderson case.

Joan and Robert Anderson had a six-year-old daughter who was born with shoulder dystocia. Either her arm had been damaged during the forceps delivery, or this was one of those rare cases where children are born with this deformity. It was important that they find out which. They would need to call their expert, Dr. Steinberg, who usually testified in birth trauma cases. Dr. Steinberg could always come up with some theory that would exonerate the doctor, but Jason wanted Tildy to do some of the preliminary research herself.

Her research had turned up nothing so far, except to find the doctor responsible for the injury. She knew Jason would not be happy. She guessed that's why he wanted to talk with her. Just as she began to get more deeply into the subject, she got a call from Betty. Jason was back and wanted to see her immediately. She quickly got up and walked through the corridor, past the row of secretaries' desks, toward Jason's office. The law office had ten outside offices around the perimeter of the space. Each office had an outside window overlooking the city. Even from the second floor, most offices commanded a view of the river on one side of the building and the hills of the suburbs on another side.

The senior partners, naturally, had the large corner offices, which were beautifully decorated. The other partners and associates, had offices decreasing in size only as their names appeared lower on the firm's letterhead.

The firm was an old negligence defense firm. Mr. Wright and Mr. Landwehr were both deceased. The largest office, a corner with two big windows, was now occupied by Jason, who had been with the firm for ten years and who was now the senior trial partner. Mr. Cummings, who had occupied that office for about ten years after Mr. Wright died, had graciously given up the space when he retired. Mr. Cummings was now eighty-two years old, but still came in twice a week, mainly to take care of personal correspondence and, as he said, to keep his hand in.

Mr. Cummings' old secretary, Donna, who was now sixty-seven years old, continued to work for him part time at his request. Donna would have retired when Mr. Cummings did, but he asked her to stay on, so long as he was able to come to the office. He relied on her for so many personal things now that his wife had passed away. Donna came in for a few hours every Monday and Thursday. She paid all of his personal bills, and typed what little correspondence he had. As Tildy passed his office, she thought of Mr. Cummings, who had been a friend of Grandfather's. He always acknowledged her and exchanged a few pleasantries with her when he was in the office, often repeating some anecdote about her grandfather.

Mr. Cummings was a sweet old man and a perfect gentleman. He always came to the office wearing a three-piece suit, impeccably dressed, albeit with a tie that seldom matched. Tildy always wondered if the old man was colorblind, or if he had relied on his wife, now gone for several years, to put his outfits together. Although he no longer had any power in the firm, Tildy always enjoyed these pleasantries and was disappointed when she passed the office and he wasn't in. Today it was dark, no Donna outside either. She then remembered it was Tuesday.

When she reached Jason's office, his door was open and Betty motioned her to go right in. Jason didn't get up when she entered, nor was it expected. He was in his shirtsleeves, with his suit jacket partially sticking out from behind the door where it was hanging from a hanger. The hanger hung from a hook, the only addition that Jason had made to Mr. Cummings' office.

The carpet was a beautiful old Persian, which had been bought in the days when the firm needed to impress their insurance company clients; it was now a little threadbare. The desk had many scratches and a couple of burns, which Tildy surmised had come from Mr. Cummings' cigars, which he still smoked. The sofa was a burgundy striped Sheraton, and had been recovered by Mr. Cummings about two years before his retirement. Although it was slightly soiled by the many files that Jason had dumped on it during his tenure, it still looked elegant. The room had an air of old reliability, and Jason had preserved the look, in the off chance a new client might come to visit. Jason's success rate, particularly with medical malpractice cases, though, spoke for itself. Most of the new work came totally on recommendation from other carriers.

Jason motioned for Tildy to sit down. "How're you coming with the Anderson case?"

"Still haven't found anything of value. The O.B. text seems to indicate that the majority of the incidences of dystocia come from the doctor yanking on the baby's arm."

"Hmmm. We might have to pay on this one, but I had a similar case and Dr. Steinberg got us out of that one. May have to bring him in."

"I could look further. I could go to the medical library."

"No, Tildy, thanks, I've got something else I need you to work on. Have you ever worked on anything with head injuries?"

"No."

"Well, we have a sixty-year-old woman, who fell in Robinson's Supermarket. The report indicated there was some lettuce or something on the floor. Woman hit her head and now she's claiming everything from headaches and confusion to bad breath. I want you to go over our investigative report, and then interview the store manager. See if you can get anything more that might help us, especially about the lettuce on the floor. Then I want you to look into the woman's medical history. The signed authorizations are in the file. See if there's anything, other than the fall, that would account for her symptoms. Look carefully; after you finish with that, I want you to screen the medical reports to see what, if anything, her doctor says is responsible for the symptoms. Oh yes, better do some research on closed head injuries. Come up with some good stuff and I might let you depose the lady."

"Do you have any surveillance on her? I mean, if she's driving or going bowling or something we should know it."

"Good thinking, Tildy. First, I want to see what the medical turns up.

Might go with the detective after we get some more medical info."

"What about Anderson?"

"First we'll depose their expert. See how good a witness he is. If he holds up, we may have to pay on that one. Bring the file back and I'll follow up. Now get to work on this new one, okay?"

"Uh, who's the plaintiff's attorney?"

"What? Uh." Jason looked at the file and answered, "Looks like Chandron, again. Barry Chandron. Know him?"

"Only by reputation."

"Oh yeah, he's good. You'll have to be on your toes on this one. He doesn't like to settle anything, especially if he thinks there's good bucks in it. Keep good track of your hours on this. I expect you'll put in a lot of time on it."

Tildy asked if that was all, and Jason said, "For now."

Barry glanced at his watch. No wonder he was hungry. It was nearly two-thirty and he hadn't eaten since his breakfast with Dan. *Dan, that schmuck! I really can't believe what a jam he has gotten himself into.* Barry had been busy since he returned to the office. He had insurance adjusters to call, clients to see, one of whom he had to prepare for depositions.

*This client is a real loose cannon,* he thought. *He almost always confuses the facts and gets himself twisted up. If this happens in depositions, the opposing lawyer could have a field day and get him to agree to anything. His words would preclude even a small settlement and, if I have to go to court, this guy will make a real mess of his case. No, best to coach him again, and again, until he gets it right. In his case, settlement is the best way. He'll never withstand a good cross-examination, and Reisinger's good. He'll make mincemeat out of him. Oh, why do I have to suffer these fools, just to make a buck?* As if in answer he thought, *I chose this profession and it's not all bad. There are a lot of good days, too.* He smiled and thought of the Bellows case and his new red Mercedes.

Again, he turned his thoughts to his brother. *What can I do to help him? First of all, my turf is the other side at counsel table. I am always for the plaintiff. I could do a great job on behalf of that poor kid, the victim. I don't think that there's any defense that I could make to excuse what Dan* did. At least, not that I know of. I'm going to have to research the hell out of this one. I have to get an investigator on this St. Kitts thing, too. An answering machine, can you believe it? I know they're a little loose about things in the islands, but malpractice insurance, what was Dan thinking?

*I remember that case I had where the guy ran a stop sign and my client had three broken vertebrae. No carrier that we could find in that one, but luckily, the defendant had lots of assets and my client got paid a little. It was too bad; the case was worth a lot more. I don't think this kid's family will settle for very little. Nor should they. They'll have enormous expenses, to say nothing of his pain and suffering. I wish I didn't see their side so clearly. It won't help my brother to feel sorry for the victim. I can't even call one of my colleaguess, since I don't know who will be representing him. Best to work the insurance angle for now. I'll worry about a defense later.*

Barry left the office to grab a quick bite. No long lunch today. He walked over to the luncheonette across from the courthouse and ordered a cheeseburger. As he passed the bank building, he looked up at the second floor. No beautiful woman. Barry was disappointed. Realizing what he was doing, he laughed. *For all I know she was looking at something else. No, I really have to meet her, just to be sure. There was something curious in the look. I'm sure she was looking at me, but why?*

*Wait! Isn't that the office of Wright, Landwehr, and Cummings? Of course it is. I was in such a hurry to meet Dan, I didn't realize it. Barry had been there a few times, most recently to pick up the check in the Bellows case. Of course. She must be one of the secretaries there. She stared because she knew that I had just scored a big one off them. She noticed the car. That's all it was. Gee, what a jerk I am. Am I so shallow that I think every woman has the hots for me? No, I just never saw her there. I would have recognized her. A woman like that is not so easily forgotten. No, I never saw her. She must be new, or working for one of the other partners. Guess I don't have to nose around up there. Maybe one day when I'm in the building anyway, I'll just pay them a visit. Wow, she works for the enemy. Got to check out if we have another case with those guys. It'll give me an excuse to go up there.*

Barry finished his burger and walked back to the office. It was a beautiful day. He walked slowly, thinking about his brother and what the next move should be. He sometimes solved the worst problems by getting out of the office and walking. Today, the problem was a little closer to home. Suddenly, he found himself going past the bank building again. He had walked a block out of the way; but here he was again, looking up at the second floor.

What in hell was driving him to do that? *Well, at least she isn't there, so I don't have to think about that. I can concentrate on Dan's problems. Who am I kidding? Until I meet that woman, I'll probably find myself here again and again.*

# Chapter Eight

Rinaldo's was the most expensive restaurant in town. When they entered, all Dan could see were little flickering lights from the candles on the tables; it was the only lighting in the room. They created a surreal effect. Dan's nervousness added to the perception, making him dizzy. The room appeared to be swaying with each flicker. When he had called Alex, all he said was that he needed to speak to her and that he had made a reservation at Rinaldo's. He knew it was her favorite restaurant.

Alex loved to eat at Rinaldo's. In fact, when Dan called, she thought this might be just the opportunity she was waiting for. She had just become friendly with Ruth Cameron and this was a real coup for her. They had met recently in a game of doubles at the club, and Alex had been itching to make a date with her and her husband. Jack Cameron was a manufacturer of some kind of electronic systems used in commercial airplanes. Alex didn't understand exactly what it was, but she knew that Boeing was his biggest customer.

The Camerons also had myriad real estate interests and they were the largest patrons of the arts and other philanthropies in town. Being friendly with them meant being invited to the best parties and getting to know, intimately, the most important and wealthiest families.

Alex had been trying in various ways to meet and cultivate the elusive Ruth. She had tried to talk to her many times at the club, and finally she had been paired with her in a doubles match. She invited Ruth to lunch and Ruth had graciously accepted. Since that time a month ago, she had tried at every opportunity to engage them as a couple; it just had never happened. When Dan called her to meet him for dinner, Alex naturally thought of asking the Camerons to join them. Now that she had actually had lunch with Ruth and talked with her, it might be the right time to push the relationship a little further.

Ruth's husband might be the richest man in town, but her husband was no slouch, either. He was a very prominent neurosurgeon, a reputation greatly enhanced by Alex's mentioning that fact discreetly and at appropriate moments, whenever she had an opportunity. She had used his position as a foothold in her upward climb to social prominence and she had had to remind her husband of his own social standing on more than one occasion.

Dan, while generally sociable, was quite shy with strangers. She always had to coach him to be charming when meeting someone new. His natural diffidence usually made him appear—at least in Alex's eyes—as a social nonentity and that did nothing to enhance his position, or at least the persona she had created for him.

Alex was very annoyed with Dan for never wanting to go out with other people. She knew that he always preferred her company alone, to the company of "those phonies from the club," as he called them. Dan was really becoming a social liability. She would just have to work on him some more. Why couldn't he understand how important it was to be with the right people? For some strange reason, he just couldn't grasp this fact. She was not surprised when Dan turned down her idea to invite the Camerons, but she was very miffed, to say the least.

In spite of the darkness, Alex had the eyes of a jaguar searching for prey. She recognized people at various tables, stopping to exchange a few words or kisses with more than a few, depending on the amount of headway she had made in cultivating them. Finally, they reached a table in the corner, set up in a way to afford the most privacy. Alex asked the waiter if they had a better table, but Dan stopped her.

"I requested this table." I need to speak to you about something very important.

Alex sat down reluctantly.

"I'm all ears."

"Let's have a drink first."

Dan ordered a double martini.

"For God's sake, Dan, what's this all about? You're being so mysterious; you'd think our very lives depended on it."

"Why don't we relax and have our drinks? Our lives may depend on it."

Alex looked at him with a puzzled expression? Dan was not given to exaggeration; this must be serious. Now she was concerned.

"What's the matter?"

Dan took a gulp of his martini and ordered another, even before he finished the first. This shocked Alex because Dan wasn't much of a drinker. If anything, she was the one who liked to drink and—if not for his disapproving looks—stood a greater chance of abusing the stuff. She was truly mystified.

Dan began, "Remember that case I told you about, the one where I made a mistake and cut the spinal cord?"

"Yes, you said you would have to call your insurance company. Let the insurance company worry about it. You get so defensive when something like this happens. It always turns out okay, doesn't it?"

"Yes, sweetheart, I was always able to work it out and I always knew that my carrier would pay if there was no way out. You know it happens with neurosurgeons because the surgery often entails greater risks."

"Yes, I know."

"Well, I thought I just nicked the kid's dura, but it turns out I cut the cord and he's now a paraplegic."

"No one at the club knows about it, do they?"

"Alex, it's not the club I'm worried about. Will you realize that there's more to life than the club? I can't get that boy out of my mind."

"Dan, when will you grow up? You can't worry over every patient you have. You do the best you can, and if you can't make them whole, you have to move on. It's not the first time you had a patient become a paraplegic because of an accident. What makes this one so special?"

"First of all honey, he's not just any patient, he's a twenty-two-year-old boy. More important, it was not an accident that made him a paraplegic. It was me. It was my fault. Not the fault of a collision. If he had another doctor, he would have walked out of that hospital two weeks ago. Now, he'll never walk again, and I did it."

"Dan, you can't beat yourself up like this. Even if it was your fault, that's why you have coverage, isn't it?"

Dan hesitated for a moment. Alex looked at him, questioning.

"Yes, but that's the problem."

"Dan, you do have coverage, don't you?"

"I don't know."

"What do you mean you don't know?" By now Alex had raised her voice and, as soon as she did, she looked around the room and saw that people were looking at her. She quickly lowered her voice and repeated her question in a low whisper.

"Darling, I can't get in touch with my carrier. I bought this offshore insurance and the company has fallen off the face of the earth. I can't find them."

"When did you buy this offshore insurance?" she said, now panicked.

"When we built the house. I thought I could save some money."

"I don't believe this! I can't believe you put our whole lives in jeopardy. What were you thinking?"

"I was thinking how much you wanted the house and how I could save some money by changing carriers."

"Did you think I wanted the house and wanted to jeopardize it and everything else? Did you think about me, the kids? Oh my God, Dan, you're unbelievable!"

With that, she started to cry. "Does this mean we'll lose the house?"

"Probably."

"How can I stay at the club if we lose the house? Everyone there will know."

"Alex, everyone will know as soon as we give up the club. That's the first thing that will happen."

Alex began to cry as she looked at Dan, stupefied. Of course, she hadn't even thought about all the ramifications. "What about the kids, will they have to go to public school?"

"Probably."

"But, but," she stammered. "Did you talk to Barry about this?"

"This morning."

"When did you find out about the insurance company?"

"Last week."

"And you waited till this morning to talk to Barry?"

"I thought that I would be able to reach them. I think, now, that maybe they don't even exist."

"How in the world could you be so selfish? You didn't even think about me. You know the house and the club mean everything to me."

"What about me? Don't I mean anything to you?"

"Oh Dan, how could you?" Alex got up abruptly and started to leave the table.

"Where are you going?"

"You don't expect me to stay here and let everyone see our shame, do you?"

"Don't you want to eat dinner?"

"I couldn't touch a bite."

Dan quickly stood and motioned for the check. He knew that it would raise a lot of eyebrows to see them leave so soon after arriving and Alex didn't hide her emotions very well. *Well, these people don't mean anything, at least to me. I don't give a crap for what they think. I can't understand why they've become so important to Alex.* He followed Alex out, gave the ticket to the valet and waited with her for the car.

## Chapter Nine

It was 7:30. Barry always got to the office early. He lived alone, didn't even have breakfast at home. He often stopped off at Dunkin' Donuts for coffee and a doughnut and when he did, he always brought doughnuts to the office. That way he could get a jump-start on the day. He was going through the newspaper, but his mind kept wandering. He was trying to develop a plan for attacking Dan's problem. He had found out years ago, that next to walking, sitting in the office before anyone else came in was probably the best time to think about strategy.

He figured that there was no reason to continue to call Nevis/St. Kitts. Clearly, they were not going to answer their phones at the Department of Insurance. There was a strong possibility that if this insurance company ever existed, it wasn't even in Nevis/St. Kitts.

He had called the New Jersey Department of Insurance, yesterday, and found that Adelphia Security insurance was not registered to do business in New Jersey. This was not a good sign. Everything pointed to a swindle and, if this were the case, Dan is left holding the bag.

Too bad the claim is not spurious, but it looks as if Dan really did do the damage he says he did. No amount of good defense work is going to get him out of it. The first line of defense would be to find the sons of bitches that scammed him. To that end, Barry had put in a call to the Attorney General to see if there were any other complaints. He was waiting for a call back from his old law school classmate, Jake Sommers.

Jake had gone with the Attorney General's office right from law school and had had to pay his dues before they let him handle the tough cases. In time, however, he became a well-respected prosecuting attorney. He had made a reputation prosecuting white-collar criminals and had a very high success rate. Barry was sure that if there were anyone to give him advice,

Jake would be the one. He was hoping the state already had a line on these crooks and that some of the investigative work would have been done.

While he was wondering what the call back from Jake would reveal, he thought of Tildy.

"Damn!" he said out loud. *That girl has invaded my mind. I'd better do something about that and soon. She really has me obsessing about the way she looked at me.* With some conscious effort, he put Tildy out of his mind and started thinking again about Dan's case.

Barry realized there was a county bar dinner that week and—though he never went—he thought he would nose around and ask if anyone knew anything about this Adelphia Security insurance company. He thought about getting his investigator to look into it, but decided that there were things to do first. He could always do that. If there was a dead end with Jake, he might go that route. Finally, a strategy was beginning to take shape. He didn't have much time. He was sure that the boy would be filing his suit against Dan soon, and he wanted to have the insurance company lined up as a third party defendant.

Yes, he had better find these scam artists and see what, if anything, they had in assets. Barry heard rustling outside his office and knew it wouldn't be long before the phone started to ring and his day began. He was glad he wasn't in trial this week, so he could have the time to work on Dan's case. He would get one of the young associates to work on trial prep for some of the other cases that were beginning to heat up. He knew that whatever they did, he would have to review it, but that would be easier than taking on the whole job. In fact, Ray, his senior associate, was coming along really well. Bright kid! This would be good experience for him and give Barry a chance to see what the kid was really made of. He made a mental note to call Ray in later today.

Dan didn't go in to the office. He had turned most of his cases over to his friend, Jim Casey, and he had no new patients to see, so he just decided to stay home today. He and Alex didn't say a word to each other from the time they had left the restaurant until now.

She had gotten up early and left without a peep. He had pretended to be asleep, but he saw her dress and heard her leave. She didn't have breakfast, so he surmised she would be eating at the club.

*The club. Since we joined the club, Alex has been extremely happy. She's even nicer to me,* he thought. *Yes, I finally delivered on her investment in me. With her world about to fall apart, I guess she just wants to go on playing Mrs. Doctor while she still can. Oh, what a mess I've made! She'll never forgive me if she has to give up that membership. Think, think, there must be a way out of this. Maybe Barry will come up with something. I don't want to bug him; I'll wait until this afternoon, and then I'll call him. Jeez, if ever I needed him, I need him now. If anyone can pull a rabbit out, it's Barry.*

With that, Dan turned over and went back to sleep. He had hardly slept at all last night. Now that he decided to wait until the afternoon to call his brother, he fell into a deep sleep.

## Chapter Ten

Barry arrived at the county bar dinner a little late. He seldom went. He had little patience for the political chitchat that went on at these things. He really could care less who was in line for the next judgeship or who was screwing whom. He didn't want to hear what a great trial attorney each thought himself to be. He knew that there were few there who were as good as he was, and he wasn't too terribly interested in the inflated egos of the others. It was one thing to be a good lawyer and it was another to bullshit your way in a crowd who knew better. *Don't they realize that they make themselves look foolish,* he asked himself? He looked in the room, nodded to a group of colleagues clustered around one of the judges, who looked his way and nodded to him as he entered.

Barry made straight for the bar and ordered a double scotch. He intended to stay around long enough to make a few inquiries about Adelphia Security and then he figured he would skip out after the first course. By ordering a double, he wouldn't have to fight his way back to the bar, where the crowd usually congregated.

The room was packed with his fellow trial lawyers, as well as those others who did real estate, divorce and other areas of specialty. These were the lawyers from whom many of his referrals came. He really should make more of an effort to attend these things, he thought, as he stepped away from the bar and sipped his drink. He told himself that after two scotches it probably wouldn't be so bad.

He wandered over to the cluster of men that he first nodded to and joined the conversation.

"Hello, Barry," said Ted Jernow, a fellow plaintiff's lawyer whom he ran into at the calendar call every Monday. Ted was a good lawyer and hardly ever spoke about his victories. The two admired and respected one another, although they never saw each other socially. Each had the attitude that they dealt with lawyers too much during the work week to cultivate them as friends, although the latter thought was never spoken.

"Hi Ted."

Judge Rowland acknowledged his presence with another nod, as he listened to another fellow haranguing him about a case, already tried before another judge. Judge Rowland was one of those judges who brooked no nonsense in his courtroom, but who was the most polite gentleman socially. He would never have thought to cut the other fellow off, but Barry could see that he was being held captive by the talker.

Barry didn't know the lawyer talking to the judge. He was considerably younger than Barry and had still to learn the protocol of not talking cases with judges on social occasions, even when there was no conflict. The talker was still in love with the law and—by all appearances—with himself as well.

Barry went over to the judge and asked Judge Rowland if he could have a word with him when he and the young man were finished. Judge Rowland introduced them and then excused himself. As Judge Rowland and Barry walked away, the judge looked relieved.

"Barry, do you really have something you want to ask me, or were you astute enough to see that I needed rescuing?" he said with a laugh.

"No Judge, I don't know if I'm that astute. It was pretty obvious. Glad to be of service."

"Thanks. What's new with you? I really thought you were in trouble with that Bellows case. Jury surprised me."

"Judge, frankly, I thought I was in the crapper with that case, but I guess the obvious merits of my argument won them over." He said this with a grin.

"I've seldom seen a bad case won on final argument."

"But it was a good case, Judge."

"Well, you made it a good case and, I guess the jury was able to see through all the smoke that Jason was blowing. Sometimes they amaze me that they can see the light in those hard cases. It always renews my faith in the system."

"Mine too."

"And your pocketbook, as well," the judge said with a wry look.

Barry smiled and said, "I have no complaints."

"I didn't think so. I saw that new car of yours. BMW?"

"Well, no. It's a—a Mercedes. You know, until that case I never thought I deserved something like that. Now, I feel it's time."

"Good for you Barry."

As they were talking, Barry turned away for a minute to view the room. He was wondering whom he could find to ask about Adelphia Security. As he turned, there she was. Barry couldn't believe it, but suddenly there she was. That woman. The woman in the window. God, I wasn't wrong about her; she's really stunning. He saw she was tall, about five feet nine inches. She had beautiful copper colored hair, something he couldn't see through the window. Her skin was tawny, not the usual pink freckled skin of a redhead. Tildy was wearing a conservatively cut navy blue suit with a red blouse. *Nice*, he thought. *Very nice.*

She was with a very attentive group of men. She was one of only three women at the meeting. Even though there were many more women practicing at the bar, they almost never came to bar meetings. They had formed their own women's bar and met at another time. Barry never understood it, but he knew that they were never made to feel welcome here. But this one, he had never seen anyone so comfortable in an alien setting before. Good for her! I guess she's a lawyer. Boy, it shows where I'm coming from, I never even thought of that. Shame on me.

Tildy looked up and saw Barry. She smiled, turned to the others and excused herself and started to walk toward him. When she reached him she extended her hand.

"Hi, I'm Tildy Jennings."

"Hi, Barry Chandron."

"I know who you are."

"You do?"

"Yes, I work for Jason Kraus at Wright, Landwehr, and Cummings."

"Oh, I just finished a case with him. Bellows."

"Beat his ass, too."

"Not too bad a judgment." He smiled, so she really did know who I am.

"So I heard."

"Yes, well, I guess you would have. Did you work on that case?"

He thought to himself, damn, she was just curious. Then he saw her eyes. They were soft green. He had never seen eyes like that before.

"No, I just joined the firm last month."

"Oh, what did you say your name was?"

"Tildy, Tildy Jennings."

"Tildy? Short for Matilda? I like Tildy better."

"I guess I would too, if my name were Matilda. No, my name is Tilden. It was my mother's maiden name."

"It's different. And very pretty. Jennings? I clerked for a Roger Jennings, when I was first admitted."

"He was my grandfather."

"No kidding? Your grandfather? He taught me everything I know. What a great trial lawyer he was. I still wish he was around so I could ask him things once in a while, when I need help."

"I wouldn't have thought you needed anyone to ask anymore."

"Tildy, you always need someone to bounce things off. In this business there's always something new to figure out. Old Roger could get to the heart of the problem faster than anyone I ever knew, before or since. I loved that man. He was very good to me and really showed me the ropes."

"I wish he were here today. I could sure use his advice and help."

"Every new lawyer feels that way. It gets better with experience, but it's still good to have a neutral person to ask. Speaking of that, how's old Jason treating you?"

"He's okay. Not too much warmth, though. Very businesslike."

"Well, Jason's like that. He's not exactly Mr. Warmth, but he's decent. Unlike some others I've dealt with. Some are really unethical, and pull some amazing stunts. But I guess by now I've seen them all. Say, what are you doing working for the enemy? Your grandfather would turn over in his grave."

"Unfortunately, he wasn't around when I got out of law school, and it was tough finding a job."

"Tough? I'll bet you did well in law school."

"I was in the top ten percent. But you know, too many lawyers getting out of law school these days. I didn't want to go with those corporate firms. Requires too much dedication; I want to have a life besides my career. And besides, I want to know how the defense side operates when the time comes to change sides."

"Not too bad an idea. But don't stay too long. It'll warp you." With this, he laughed and took her arm. The others were beginning to scramble for seats for dinner, and he didn't want to lose this charming woman.

"Are you sitting with anyone?"

"Well, Jason couldn't come tonight, so I guess I'm free to sit where I want."

"Come with me, we'll find some seats." Barry looked around and spotted Judge Rowland waving at him. He was pointing to some empty chairs at his table and Barry nodded yes. He wondered if Judge Rowland had spotted him with Tildy, or whether he was just paying him back for being rescued. He seated Tildy with Judge Rowland, and told her he would be back in a minute. He had just caught a glimpse of Ted Jernow and wanted to speak with him privately before he sat down.

"Say, Ted. I have a client in a bit of a pickle. Could I have a word with you?"

"Sure, Barry, what's up?"

"Ever hear of a medical malpractice carrier named Adelphia Security insurance?"

Ted scratched his head, "Can't say that I have."

"Well, I think they're non-existent. Sold a doctor some insurance and now he needs the coverage."

"Big liability?"

"Could be. Haven't really looked at the claim."

"What do you mean? Don't you have the plaintiff?"

"No, the defendant. He's my brother."

Ted looked at Barry, sympathetically. "God, Barry, I hope you find them. What's the injury?"

"Bad, cut spinal cord."

"Where?"

"I think around L-2 or 3, but still don't have all the facts."

"I guess it could've been worse, it could've been higher up. You brother's an orthopod?"

"No, neurosurgeon."

"Oh. Tough. Adelphia Security?"

"Yes"

"I'll ask around. Wonder who has the case for the plaintiff."

"Don't think the claim is filed yet."

"Better get on the stick and find them before the claim is filed. And Barry, if they see me, I'll call you right away. You know I don't play games."

"I know that, Ted. Thanks."

Barry returned to Tildy and was happy to see that she was totally engaged in conversation with the Judge. It was easy to see that Judge Rowland was enjoying himself. He might have worried if the judge were a different man, but he knew Rowland's wife and that they had been childhood sweethearts. This is one man he could vouch for, one who always went home to his wife.

Judge Rowland looked over at Barry. "Did you know this young lady is Roger Jennings' granddaughter?"

"Yes, Judge. I just found out. Did you know I clerked for him?"

"No, I didn't. You weren't with him when I first met you."

"No, I was out chasing ambulances by then."

They all laughed and started on their nondescript fruit cup. Barry stayed through the whole meal and found any number of things to talk to Tildy about. She was not only attractive, but she was interesting to talk to. *Very interesting*, he thought.

Just before the speaker started, he told Tildy he had to leave, and asked her if she needed a lift home.

"No, I have my car."

Barry thought about asking if he could see her again, but thought better of it. He knew that he would see her again and, if it didn't happen accidentally, he knew where to find her. There was no question in his mind that he would call her, but he wasn't sure how long he would wait.

## Chapter Eleven

After his first cup of coffee and some toast, Dave felt better. He finished his meal and he and Lindy each smoked a cigarette. Breakfast finished, they left the hotel, hailed a taxi and headed downtown. In twenty minutes, they were in front of the office of Oliver Hemmings, Esq. While Dave paid the driver, Lindy entered the ground floor office of the esteemed lawyer, Hemmings. Dave quickly followed. A receptionist met them and Dave said, "I'm Stephen Graham, I have an appointment with Mr. Hemmings." This was the name on Dave's passport, the one he had used to get into Costa Rica, and the one he intended to use should he want to return home.

The receptionist answered, "Mr. Hemmings is just finishing up with his 10:30. He'll be with you in a moment." She then picked up the phone and announced Dave's arrival. Dave sat down and picked up a magazine. He held it in his hand, but looked around the room, instead. The room was painted a soft mustard color, not too appetizing. The chairs were old and straight-backed, and very uncomfortable. They were all covered in brown leather that was worn and cracked, showing extreme age. There was a stale smell of cigar smoke in the air.

Had this been an office in the States, it might have had a look of failure about it, but Dave knew what the business of this place was about and he surmised, correctly, that it had the look of a very old, very busy office, one that nobody had the time or interest to spruce up because it wasn't necessary.

Just as he opened the magazine a door opened and two men appeared. They shook hands and one of them left. Still in the doorway, in a three piece suit tailored to perfection, was a man about five foot seven with thinning white hair and a very ruddy complexion. His suit coat was open, the only relinquishment of formality. Dave saw that he was wearing a very heavy gold watch chain, attached to what he imagined was a gold pocket watch in his vest pocket. There was an enormous watch fob dangling from the chain. Dave felt as if he had just entered a law office in 1920s England.

Oliver Hemmings looked at the two men questioningly, as Dave stood. "Mr. Graham?"

Dave walked over to the lawyer and held out his hand as he said, "I'm Stephen Graham." Turning to Lindy, he introduced the two men. Lindy discreetly remained outside while Dave and Mr. Hemmings walked through the door.

As Dave entered the office, he was struck by the fact that the inner office was also designed in what can only be referred to as "early tawdry," much the same as the outer office. The same mustard color on the walls, only inside the office it was peeling in places. The desk was massive, but hadn't been dusted in weeks, and the visible remains of cigars were in the ashtray on its top. The place stank from cigars. The only thing that was in seemingly good condition was a couch on the side wall, also covered in brown leather. Dave surmised that it was never used, because no one ever stayed long enough to sit on it. Even Mr. Hemmings seemed too busy a man to take the occasional nap. The only thing that was smart and clean was Mr. Hemmings himself.

Mr. Hemmings opened with, "It is my understanding that you wish to deposit a sum of money in Nevis. Is that correct?

Dave, almost hesitantly, said, "Yes, that's so. I understand that any matters I discuss with you will remain confidential, and that I can rely on you to take care of the entire matter."

"Certainly," replied the lawyer, in a very proper British accent. "We are in a position to take charge of your funds and place them on deposit, which you may call upon at any time. Furthermore, the institutions in which you place them are pledged to the utmost secrecy. We have had many years experience in transacting this kind of business and, I assure you, Mr. Graham, that no one, not any person, can discover the amount deposited or the identity of the holder of the account. Additionally, Mr. Graham we, as your agent, shall handle any fund transfers that you wish to make, either by telephone, or in person. Now, I understand that you wish to deposit a considerable sum. Before we get to that, I must say that, although our financial institutions are totally reliable, I, as your agent recommend that the funds be placed in more than one account depending on the sum. Now, Mr. Graham, um, exactly how much do you wish to deposit?"

David said, barely above a whisper, "Two million, four hundred thousand dollars."

Hemmings did not register any response, but appeared to be filling out a form. As he wrote, he said, "Ah, yes, two million, four hundred thousand dollars." He looked up from his desk and said, "U.S. of course. For that sum of money, I would recommend two separate places of deposit. I will make all of the arrangements for you. Of course, there is a fee for our services. As long as one million dollars is the minimum left on deposit, there will be a fee of five per cent, annually, payable monthly from the day of deposit. Naturally, there will be interest on your account of three per cent so the cost is somewhat offset. If your balance should go below one million dollars U.S., the fee increases to seven per cent. Is that satisfactory? It is our experience that the amounts tend to increase with time." He looked up at Dave and smiled. Dave returned the smile and said, "That will probably be the case, here."

"Mr. Graham, will you be delivering the funds personally in cash or do you prefer to wire them? As long as you do not wire them from the States, there is no reason why you cannot do so. I will give you the wire transfer instructions before you leave."

Dave answered, "I prefer to wire them."

"You will wire them directly to our trust account and we will make the deposits for you. We will send you a receipt and, as soon as the deposits are made, we will send you the receipts from the bank.

"And Mr. Graham, when may we expect the funds for deposit?"

"Within the week, Mr. Hemmings."

The lawyer handed David a paper with the instructions, made a few more notations on his pad, and got up. He walked around the desk and put his arm gently on Dave's shoulder as he ushered him to the door.

"It's always a pleasure to do business with clients from the States, Mr. Graham, and if I can be of any further assistance to you, please feel free to call upon me. I shall expect to hear from you within the week." With that, Mr. Hemmings opened the door and ushered Dave out. As he emerged from the office, he noticed that several other people were in the waiting room. He and Lindy walked out of the office, just as he heard Hemmings say, "Mr. Evans?" They walked out into the bright sunlight.

"Everything go all right?" asked Lindy.

"Yes, thank you, quite all right"

Lindy replied, "Well, that's done, anyway."

Dave nodded, thoughtfully. *Yes, the first step is done.* He wondered if he should tell Lindy of his plans, but thought better of it. *He's a great guy and seems to be discreet, but what I don't tell him can't come back to bite me. After all, a dollar is still a dollar, and who knows when the right offer may just loosen his reserve.*

The two men found a taxi and went back to the hotel. They went to their rooms, gathered the little they'd brought with them and went back to the airport. They returned to San José.

The next day, Barry was in early, as usual. Jake still hadn't returned his call and Barry called him again. This time he found out that Jake was just finishing a trial and was expected to be in his office the following day. He reiterated that he wanted his call returned as soon as possible. He thought, *Gee, every day that goes by, those bastards are covering their tracks.* But there was nothing he could do about it.

He was just finishing his second cup of coffee, when the buzzer rang.

"Yes, Eleanor?"

"I have a Miss Jennings on the line."

"Put her through."

He couldn't believe his ears.

"Hi Tildy."

"Hi. I really enjoyed meeting you last night."

Barry wasn't used to this new way of doing things. He was usually the first one to make the call in a situation like this, but he was sure she was interested when he left her last night.

"Yes, Tildy. I enjoyed meeting you too."

"I'd like to see you again, that is, before the next bar dinner."

"Oh yes, Tildy, I'd like that too."

"Can you meet me for a drink after work today?"

*Boy, this girl doesn't waste any time. But why not? It's better without all that mating ritual he was used to. Direct approach. Okay.*

"Sure, Tildy. Uh—are you buying?"

"Only if I have to," she said laughing. She asked, "How about Jerry's at seven?"

"I thought you said Jason isn't working you too hard."

"Well, we have a new case in, so I have to spend some time on it."

"One of mine?"

"You never know."

"In that case, how about dinner?"

"Sounds great. By the way, I hear you're interested in Adelphia Security insurance."

"Do you know anything?"

"I might have something for you. See you at seven."

"I can't wait." Barry hung up the phone. So much for my day. Now I not only have to think about spending an evening with her, but I have to wonder what she knows about Adelphia Security.

Barry sat back in his chair and put his hands behind his head and his feet up on the desk. It was his pondering pose. Wonder how she knew I was asking about Adelphia Security? He picked up the phone.

"Eleanor, I'm going for a walk. I'll be back in about a half hour."

"Got some heavy thinking to do?"

"You know me like a book."

Tildy hung up the phone and smiled. Well, she knew he would ask her out, but she thought perhaps first a drink then the next time, dinner. He was certainly interested in her, but she knew he would also be very interested in what she knew about Adelphia Security. *Isn't it strange*, she mused, *how fate takes a hand? I happen to have information at the exact time and place that I want to know him better and it's information he needs to know. Funny, too, how everything fell into place last night. I had heard of Judge Rowland, but what a charming dinner companion he turned out to be. And he knew Grandfather too.*

*And what about those sleazebags, trying to hit on me? I pretended I didn't know what they were doing, but I almost vomited when they were trying so hard to flatter me. Compare them to Barry. He's direct, and a real gentleman. I don't think anything would ever happen with him, unless I start it. He doesn't have to be aggressive or pretend to be interesting. He is. I really like this man.*

*Imagine, he clerked for Grandfather. I would have been about thirteen years old. Wonder what kind of impression I would have made then.* She laughed at the ridiculous picture this made in her mind. *Oh well, back to work on my lettuce case. He still doesn't know that I am working on his case. That'll be interesting.*

## Chapter Twelve

Dave had been back in San José a few days when he got a call from Lindy.

"Wanna go up today, Steve?"

Having nothing better planned and having taken care of his money business, Dave readily agreed. When he got to the airfield, the Cessna was already warming up and Lindy was at the controls. Dave climbed aboard, said a few words to Lindy and they were off.

Lindy took the plane through a few maneuvers and headed east toward the coast. When they approached the city of Limón, he started to circle an airfield. The next minute Dave realized they were coming in for a landing. Lindy said, "Steve, there are some people I think you ought to meet. Let's have some lunch first, and then I want to introduce you to some people I sometimes do work for." Dave thought it strange that Lindy hadn't told him this before they took off, but he sat quietly and let Lindy land the plane.

It was obvious to Dave that Lindy had this meeting in mind for some time. It didn't look at all spontaneous. Dave wondered what was up. Lindy taxied the plane down the runway, brought it to a halt, and cut the engine. They both got out and it was evident to Dave that Lindy came here often. He was greeted by name by everyone he met. He waved back and answered in both English and Spanish. He led Dave to a small restaurant across from the airfield and they sat down for lunch. There was no air conditioning and Dave became uncomfortable in the heat. The ceiling fans were running but they didn't seem to lessen the heat. He looked up and saw flypaper covered with dead flies hanging from each fan. *Quaint,* he thought. Other than that, the place seemed clean enough. Lindy ordered chili con carne and Dave had the same. Dave noticed that Lindy chose a table, way in the back, away from the other diners. Dave looked at him quizzically.

"Steve, I don't know where you got the money you wanted to stash, and I'm not asking how much you have, but it seems to me that you're a fairly enterprising guy. I also get the impression that you might be willing to take a few risks."

Dave didn't answer. He had a hunch that this was coming from the last time he saw Lindy.

"The truth is, Steve, that there are people who've had their eye on you, since your arrival in Costa Rica. They're in need of some assistance and they think you might be able to provide it. Of course, there'll be an opportunity to make some money, here. I told them that I believed you'd be interested. Was I right?"

"I'm always ready to listen to a deal."

"I thought so."

"What's involved?"

"I think I'll let them tell you themselves; we're going to meet them after lunch."

Dave sat there quietly and finished his lunch. He knew that Lindy was up to his eyeballs in all kinds of nefarious enterprises, and it could be anything from drug dealing to any number of fraudulent enterprises. Whatever it was, Dave thought, it was surely something illegal and therefore, a chance to make some real money. Dave was never opposed to making money, legal or otherwise, and illegal had higher payoffs. He also thought that he was getting fat and lazy without something to do in San José. He was first attracted to Lindy because Lindy always seemed to be busy with something, and he had rather hoped that Lindy would bring something to him one day. *A chance to do something, and especially something profitable.* His hunch wasn't wrong.

When they finished eating, they left the restaurant and walked a couple of blocks to some wooden buildings very much in need of repair. There were boards missing from the side, and in places, there were actual holes in the building where some storm or other had blown it in. They were across the street from and directly facing the docks. It was a normal day in Puerta Limón. Stevedores were loading and unloading ships, shouting to each other in Spanish. It was a warm day and the men were sweating, so that each had large oval sweat stains on the backs of their shirts. Dave had a fleeting thought: *There but for the grace of God go I.* He knew that he was lucky he was born with brains. Brawn is not the best way to earn a living. By the time they reached the office of Reina del Mares Shipping, Dave too was perspiring. It was a hot day, but Dave realized that it was the tingle of anticipation that first made his armpits wet.

They entered a hot stuffy office, just large enough for a small desk covered with stacks of paper. Dave imagined these were bills of lading, having to do with the official business of Reina del Mares. Behind the desk was a small man, talking excitedly on the telephone. He spoke into the phone in Spanish, too excited and rapid for Dave to understand. Lindy just stood there smiling until the man finished his phone call. The man finally looked at them and said to Lindy, "Hola, amigo."

Lindy shook the man's hand and asked, in perfect Spanish if Tino were in. It appeared that Tino was expecting them as they were ushered quickly into a back room. Dave followed Lindy into the back room where there were two men sitting at a small table. There was a noisy air conditioner running in the window, and while it cooled the room and made it comfortable, it was hard to hear anything above the din. Nevertheless, the men, wearing knit shirts and khakis were looking at Dave and Lindy expectantly. There was no doubt in Dave's mind that this meeting had been planned, and probably for some time.

Introductions were made—surprisingly—in English. Tino was tall with dark straight hair and olive colored skin. From his features, Dave was sure he had some Indian blood in him. By contrast, the other, Hugo, was shorter, and somewhat overweight. He had light sandy hair, and very pink skin. Dave was surprised to hear Hugo speak English with a heavy German accent. Dave thought, *This looks interesting.*

Tino, however, seemed to be in charge. He spoke first. "Mr. Graham, we have been watching you for some time. We know that you checked into the Santa Maria hotel on March 4th, this year. We know that you are, ostensibly, a lawyer and businessman from New Jersey. You appear to have sufficient cash not to be doing anything in particular, yet you do not leave San José, except for one very short trip to Nevis. This could mean—from our point of view—that, perhaps, you are not able to return to the U.S. and that you have some money to—shall we say—protect. Am I on the right track?"

"You might be."

Dave thought that those little seeds he had planted with Lindy might be paying off.

"Be assured that we are not interested in knowing why you are here, or what your plans might be. We see you as a person who might be interested in a business proposition, which we can assure you will more than compensate you. Unfortunately, the authorities frown on this kind of activity, but we have assumed that you might be willing to take some risks for a large return. Naturally, we wouldn't approach you with a deal for which there was not a sufficient amount of money to be made. Mr. Graham—may I call you Steve?"

"Certainly."

"Steve, we have large sums of cash coming to us from certain sources, which I'm not at liberty to reveal. These sums come largely from the United States and need to have a change of, uh, status, if you know what I mean. We have to find a means to introduce them back into the U.S. so that they may be utilized without any fear of tracing them."

"I think I understand perfectly what you're talking about. However, I'm not sure how I can be of any help."

"Lindy told us that you are a lawyer."

"Yes, that's true."

"We are looking for someone, such as you, to take care of certain business for us, using your abilities and your knowledge."

Attempting a joke, Dave said, "Well I didn't think you wanted me to fly an airplane for you," smiling broadly.

Neither of the men smiled. Dave looked at Lindy who looked at the ceiling for an instant. Dave understood the look to mean that this was not a time for jokes. He changed his tone when he spoke next. "What do you gentlemen have in mind?"

Now Hugo spoke. "Steve, we need someone to travel for us. We want to set up corporations and make contacts with local bankers and business people in several countries in the Caribbean. We know that Lindy took you to do some private banking. We would like you to do the same for us. We will not need you to carry sums of cash for us; those can always be wired. However, we will need someone to open accounts, perhaps some with your name on them, and to perhaps buy and sell various items to, uh, shall we say, to make our trades legitimate."

"Mightn't that be somewhat risky for me?"

"We are prepared to pay very well for your services. Say seven per cent of all monies that you can sanitize for us. I'm sure that you realize that one needn't do business with bankers and lawyers, such as your Mr. Hemmings, in all transactions."

Tino broke in, "We would like you to be our Mr. Hemmings, shall we say?"

Dave could only guess at the amount of money he might handle for them. He knew it had to be in the millions.

He was quite prepared to take all the risks necessary to make that kind of money. He had no doubts about it being derived from selling drugs, but it didn't matter. It was not only a chance to make big money but, more importantly, it was something to do. The main thing about not being in the States was the boredom, and here was his chance.

He assured them that he was very interested. He told them they had come to the right man.

They shook hands and Hugo told Dave he would be in touch.

Both men stood, indicating the meeting was over. Dave and Lindy left the office. Lindy waved to the small man behind the desk who was on the telephone, again. "Luego," said Lindy as they left the building. Now, Dave was perspiring in earnest. He could feel his shirt sticking to his chest and back, and wished for nothing so much as a nice tepid bath. Dave knew it wasn't caused by their sudden emergence from the air-conditioned room; his heart was beating just a little too fast.

## Chapter Thirteen

Dan decided that he ought to start seeing patients in consultation again or else when this nightmare passed, he wouldn't have any practice left. He had called his receptionist and told her to call some of the patients he had canceled last week and see if any were available today. These would be just the non-emergent cases, since all emergencies were already being taken over by Jim Casey. He arrived at the office around eight, his usual time after his hospital rounds. Since he had no hospital rounds, he was able to sleep in a little longer.

*Why do I need so much sleep*, he asked himself? He knew very well why. After all, he had had some psychiatric training in medical school. If it had been someone else, he would have clearly recognized this symptom of depression. He seemed to want to sleep all the time. He had forced himself out of bed, shaved and dressed this morning and—while it was a great effort to do so—it made him feel a little better to be trying. He knew his depression had a very real basis. His world was really about to collapse. But he also knew that if the cause were dealt with successfully, the symptoms would go away.

He expected his first patient, someone with chronic headaches, to arrive about nine. This would give him some time to review some of his files, gather the papers that Barry needed, and show his staff that he was back in harness, even if it was a charade.

Alex had not said a word to him since the fiasco at dinner the night before last. *Oh well, she'll come around eventually,* he thought with a wry smile. He knew that he wasn't sure if she would ever come around, but it helped to believe all his troubles were temporary. He wondered when and if he should tell the kids. Would they sense something was wrong or were they too oblivious, as centered as they were on their own social lives?

*Well, that's natural at their age. I wonder if I was that way when I was a teenager? Times were different then,* he thought.

He went to the file drawer and pulled out the insurance file. For the first time, he noticed the fancy paper that the policy was written on. The whole border was engraved like a stock certificate. *I guess that was meant to instill confidence. Why didn't I read the signs before I transferred my insurance to them?* Now, everything he looked at shouted "scam" at him. *What was I thinking?* Dan felt like a prize chump. *Wonder how many other dopes like me were caught in this?*

He saw all his patients, and it was now three o'clock. He hadn't stopped for lunch, but he usually didn't have lunch while he was working. It was more efficient for him, and it helped to keep the weight down, weight that he started to gain when he stopped going to the gym.

*Well, I managed to get through that.* He was beginning to feel a little better and even a little more hopeful. After all, he had Barry on it and Barry was the best lawyer in town. At least, he thought so anyway.

He left the office with a few instructions to his staff. Even his step was a little lighter. As he walked to his car, a man approached him, and said, "Doctor Chandron?"

"Yes?"

"I have something for you."

The man handed Dan an envelope. The man walked away quickly. *Uh oh, here it is already.* He opened the envelope, and saw the word, "Summons," in bold letters on the top. *They're suing me. Well, it's not as if I wasn't expecting it.* He let his eyes read down the page and wondered. He didn't notice the words "Chandron v. Chandron" at the top. When he turned the page, he almost fainted. Alex was suing for divorce. He couldn't believe it. His eyes misted over so that he couldn't read the complaint, but even without knowing the allegations, he felt betrayed. *What am I, the Titanic? I really thought better of her.* He stuffed the envelope in his pocket and got in the car. He sat there sobbing before he could even put the key in the ignition. *Nothing like being kicked when you're down.* He started the car and pulled out onto the highway. As he turned into traffic, he felt a squeezing pain in his chest, which radiated down his left arm. He became suddenly nauseated. *Oh my God! This can't be happening*, he thought with his physician's knowledge. He pulled to the curb a minute before he slumped over the wheel. A passerby ran to a local drugstore and told the pharmacist to call 911. He then opened the door and found Dan unconscious.

Barry walked around the block several times. He wondered what information Tildy had for him. It was a brisk October day and the leaves had turned to shades of tawny orange and gold. Barry always loved this time of year. At the curb in front of each house were green plastic bags stuffed full of leaves already fallen and raked up by the homeowners. They stood as sentinels, guarding each house, as far up and down the street as he could see. *God, how ugly they are,* he thought. *It's like a village under siege, with troops at the ready, just waiting for the attack. Today must be pickup day.*

Oh how he missed the smells of his childhood this time of year, when people used to burn their leaves at the curb. He loved to watch the leaves as they curled up in the flames, trying to spring free from their fiery doom, only to turn into ash and then nothing. He thought of Dan trying to spring free of his own folly, trying to escape a fiery hell of his own making. He could feel his tears as if the smoke from the earlier time had gotten in his eyes, knowing that it was his brother's agony he was really feeling.

He thought again of his childhood and how he always wanted to pluck the leaves from the fire to save them. When he closed his eyes, he could see his father and hear him admonish, "Don't get too close, son." Barry realized that he thought this same thought every year at this time. *Funny, it doesn't seem that long ago,* he thought.

Now it was Dan he had to pluck from the fire. His mother had always wanted him and Dan to be close. At one time, Mother thought this might never happen. After all, they were so different; but as they matured and finally finished school, something magical happened. They were no longer competitors. *Did fate play a hand in this too? Dan's interest in medicine, and mine in the law? I wonder if we would have become such close brothers if we were in the same profession.* But it didn't matter why. He would go into the fire and out again for his brother and he knew Dan would do the same for him.

*But how to resolve this problem? Dan doesn't have the kind of resources needed to cover this case. If only it had been less catastrophic.*

*Then, anything was possible. He couldn't help thinking about the poor, helpless victim. He stopped himself. This could be very counterproductive. I just have to find those thieves who sold him the insurance.*

He still hadn't heard from Jake, but he hoped that when he got back there would be a call from him. Then he thought, *Gee, I wonder what Tildy knows.* When he thought of Tildy, he thought, *this one could be a keeper. Be careful. Go slow. Appearances are not always what they seem.*

After walking a couple of blocks, he felt refreshed. He resolved to call Jake again, if Jake hadn't yet called when he returned. He realized, too, that he couldn't wait for seven o'clock to come. Was it the girl, or the info? He knew in his heart that it was the girl. Barry smiled to himself. He hadn't felt this way since he was in high school. He laughed out loud, realizing that he had a crush. That's what it is, a crush. He was glad nobody was there to see him.

When Barry returned to the office, there were two messages. One was from Jake, which said he would only be in the office another thirty minutes. He noted that the call had come in at 2:00 p.m. and it was now 2:20. The other message was from a Dr. Sandler, who wanted him to call back. The telephone number was on the slip.

First things first, Barry thought. He dialed Jake's number and asked for him. In a minute, Jake picked up and Barry heard the familiar voice of an old friend.

"Jake?"

"Yeah, Barry? I don't hear from you much since I became Chief Prosecutor. Don't tell me that you've taken a criminal case. I thought you gave that up years ago."

Barry laughed. This had been the subject of a long discussion when Barry left the prosecutor's office and lost his daily contact with his old law school buddy. Jake accused him of going after the money instead of the bad guys. Barry agreed that the time had come to have a decent income and still go after the bad guys, only in this case it was the insurance companies. Jake never quite saw it his way but, though they seldom saw each other, they remained good friends.

"No Jake, not a criminal case, yet. But you never know."

"What's up, Barry?"

"Ever hear of the Adephia Security insurance company?"

Jake was noncommittal. "Mebbe."

"Well Jake, Dan's in trouble and I need to know if you have anything on these guys."

Jake knew Barry's older brother as the guy who took them to the Jets' games and occasionally bought them a steak in the old days, when Dan was starting to make some bucks and Barry and Jake were still hoping to pay the rent. He answered, "What kind of trouble?"

"He went and bought some cheap malpractice insurance and now that he needs it, the company's AWOL."

"Uh, oh. Yes, Barry, I can tell you in confidence that we have an investigation going on."

"I thought you might. Many doctors involved?"

"I can't tell you that. Besides, that wouldn't help you."

"I just thought—"

"Look Barry, I have to be in court in ten minutes. I can't discuss it with you, but I'm going to get a hold of Sandy Bishop, and set something up. Will you be in your office the rest of the afternoon?"

"Who's Sandy Bishop?"

"Our best investigator. He has the file and he has to clear with me anything he has. I'll see if there's anything we can share. Meanwhile, he or I will get back to you tomorrow."

"What's this crap, you'll see if you can share anything? For Christ's sake, Jake, this is Dan, my brother."

"I know, but I can't jeopardize an ongoing investigation, can I? You want us to get these guys, don't you? Look Barry, let me go now, I don't have much time. We can discuss the problem, later."

"Jake, think about this. The guy was good to us and, he's my brother."

"I am thinking. The thing is to do it the best way we can and help Dan—and us. Okay?"

Barry reluctantly agreed and said goodbye. He knew that Jake was one of the real "good guys" and would not make a promise he couldn't keep. He also knew that Jake would remember Dan's generosity and do all that he could. In the meantime, he couldn't tell anyone that there was an investigation in progress. All he could do was be patient until he heard from Jake or Bishop, tomorrow.

For now, he had to be content with seeing what Tildy had for him.

*Listen to me,* he thought. Under any other circumstances, he would be more than content at the thought of meeting Tildy for dinner, without thinking about what information she would have. In the meantime, he would attend to his other business.

Barry looked down and saw the curious message from Dr. Sandler. *Who the hell is Dr. Sandler and what does he want?* Barry dialed the number on the slip and was surprised to hear a voice answer, "Dr. Sandler."

"Oh, uh, this is Barry Chandron. I have a message that you called. How can I help you, Doctor?"

"Mr. Chandron, I'm your brother's physician. He's in the hospital. He suffered a serious heart attack and he's in emergency surgery. He was conscious before the surgery and gave me your number. I'm really glad you called back so soon."

Barry could feel his heart beat faster.

"Which hospital are you at?"

"Braverman Memorial; he was brought in by ambulance."

"You know he's a doctor."

"Yes, he has privileges here as well. Don't worry; he's in good hands and has an excellent chance of recovery. Uh, he didn't want me to call his wife."

"Really? I'll be right over."

"He'll be in surgery, and then in recovery for a couple of hours more. There isn't any need of you coming. You won't be able to see him until about five o'clock. And then you can only peek into the cardiac ICU."

"Well, okay, I'll come over about four-thirty."

"Have them page me when you get here."

"Thanks Doctor."

Barry hung up the phone and slumped in his chair. He couldn't believe that Dan, his big brother, had become so helpless overnight. *And where is Alex? Why doesn't Dan want the doctor to call Alex? Something must have happened between those two since yesterday. I guess Dan told her about the problem and she didn't deal with it well.*

He pondered whether to call Alex, and then he picked up the phone. *Whatever problems they are having, she is still his wife and, as Dan's brother, it's up to me to call her.* He dreaded having to call, but he picked up the phone.

"Alex?"

"Yes?"

"It's me, Barry."

"Yes, Barry." She sounded very cold and very distant.

"Uh, Alex. Dan's had a coronary."

"What!"

"Dan's at Braverman Memorial. He's having open-heart surgery. Emergency."

"Oh my God!"

"I thought you would want to know."

There was a pause, then, "Have you spoken to him since yesterday?"

"No, why? Is there something I should know?"

"I guess you're going to know sooner or later. I'm having him served with papers. I saw the lawyer yesterday. Uh, I don't know if he was served; it's a little soon."

Barry couldn't comprehend at first, what she was talking about.

"Papers? What kind of papers?"

"Uh, divorce papers."

"Divorce papers? You stupid bitch! Don't you know the strain he's been under?"

"What about the strain he put me under?"

"You? You goddam parasite. Dan's in this mess because of you. You probably caused his heart attack and—listen to me—if he doesn't make it, I'm going to hold you responsible, you stupid bitch." There was a pause.

"You already said that," she said icily.

"Said what?"

"You called me a stupid bitch—twice."

"Well, what should I call you, under the circumstances?"

"You know Barry; there are two sides to the story."

"Not as far as I'm concerned." With that, Barry hung up the phone. He got up from his desk and started to throw things. Hearing the noise, his secretary, Eleanor, came rushing in.

"What's going on?"

"Dan's had a coronary. He's in surgery now."

Eleanor looked at him, and said, "When?"

"Apparently, a few hours ago."

"Barry, he'll be okay."

"That bitch gave it to him."

"Who?"

"His goddam wife, my sister-in-law."

"Barry, you can't place that kind of blame on her. You know, in a marriage there's…"

"I didn't tell you, Dan's in another jam, and she just kicked him when he was down."

By this time, Barry recovered his composure and sat down in his chair. Eleanor could see that he was near tears and she offered him a cup of coffee. He slumped down in his chair. By the time she returned, he had recovered. She sat in the opposite chair and he told her the whole story.

Eleanor asked if she should cancel any appointments, social or otherwise. It was then that he thought of Tildy. He knew he wouldn't be very good company, but he also knew he couldn't see Dan for more than a few minutes. He decided to keep his date with her after he saw Dan. Besides, he thought she would be good for him and maybe this information she had might just be a lead in Dan's case. He told Eleanor just to cancel tomorrow's appointments. He decided he would see Tildy tonight.

Barry tried to look at some other papers that needed his attention. Eleanor told him which ones he had to sign and which could wait. Barry did only what he had to do and then left for the hospital.

He had been to Braverman Memorial many times to see friends, clients or treating physicians in his cases. He knew that his brother had staff privileges there, but that his main affiliation was with St. Margaret's. Nevertheless, Braverman was a good hospital and had a good cardiac unit. His brother might have been more comfortable at St. Margaret's, but he was in good hands where he was.

Barry had never heard of Dr. Sandler, but if he was a cardiologist there, he knew he had to be good. He sounded very competent and nice on the phone, and Barry was anxious to get a look at him. Besides, Dan was in the hands of the surgeons now anyway.

He took the elevator to the second floor and went to the nurses' station. When he inquired after his brother, the nurse told him he was still in surgery. He asked them to page Dr. Sandler, and went to the solarium to wait.

The solarium was large and was painted a pleasing peach color. It had dark plum drapes on the windows and comfortable furniture in a peach and plumb print. It was old furniture, but it had recently been refurbished, possibly when they redesigned this area of the hospital for the Cardiac Center. If it was designed to put the families of its patients at ease, it accomplished that. The room was almost cozy for a hospital waiting room. However, it did not alleviate Barry's fears.

Barry sat down for a long wait and he picked up a magazine. About five minutes later, Dr. Sandler appeared. The doctor was wearing a white coat and had a stethoscope around his neck. Barry looked at Dr. Sandler and estimated that he was about thirty years old. Barry thought, *How young he is*. He wondered about his experience. Dr. Sandler came right to him, stuck out his hand and shook Barry's with just the right pressure, not too hard, but with confidence. Barry set great store in a man's handshake and immediately took a liking to Dr. Sandler.

"I checked in and your brother's doing well. They're just now finishing up with him. He had three blocked arteries, and they were able to replace all three with veins from his leg, and all three grafts are looking good. He should be in the recovery room within the hour. You can see him then."

As he was talking, Alex appeared in the doorway. Barry's first instinct was to get up and shake her, but he held back as she introduced herself to the doctor. Dr. Sandler brought her up to date immediately and Barry relaxed. She appeared to have been crying. In fact, she was more upset than Barry would have thought and this caused Barry to reflect on the situation. Dr. Sandler left and he was alone in the solarium with Alex.

At first, they didn't speak. Then Alex spoke first.

"Look Barry, I had no idea that Dan had any heart trouble."

Barry, mellowed by then, answered, "I don't think he did, at least not that he was aware of."

"I mean, I would never have, you know, done what I did if I had any idea."

"I know, Alex," Barry heard himself say, in a sympathetic voice.

"You know, I never would have done anything to cause—uh—this."

Barry was torn. He could have gone in for the kill at this point, having all kinds of devastating answers ready, but he couldn't do it. Instead, he said, "I'm sorry; I was overcome with worry."

Alex answered, "I know how you feel about Dan. I understood. But it's important that you know how it all happened. Dan took me to dinner the other night and told me about the insurance problem."

"I gathered as much."

"I was so angry that he would do something so stupid, I just got up and left the restaurant. We haven't spoken to each other, since. The next day I went to see, Bob Brady, you know, the divorce lawyer."

"I know Bob."

"Well his advice was to sue right away, to try to keep some of the assets, which might otherwise go to pay for this blunder, you know—um—protected."

"You didn't even sit down and discuss it with Dan before you allowed that vulture to go after him. Alex, how many years are you married, now? Fifteen? Didn't you think you owed him that?"

Barry could feel the anger coming to the surface, but he brought it under control.

"I asked my lawyer's advice and this is what he told me. I figured that if it all worked out, with the insurance I mean, we could stop the divorce any time. At least that's what Bob said."

"I can't believe he just filed suit. The least he should have done was send a letter, although I think that might have had the same effect on Dan, anyway."

Alex looked helpless and vulnerable. Clearly, she hadn't thought of the consequences and was truly contrite about what she had done. *This is a time to hang together until Dan is out of the woods. Alex has nobody else, and obviously, she doesn't want Dan to die.* Barry really did think that Alex was stupid, so he shouldn't have been so surprised that she acted stupidly. *Maybe there is a way out of this whole mess, Alex would make nice, nice, to his brother and the whole nightmare would end. It was worth it to be conciliatory with her and not create any more stress for Dan.*

Alex started to cry. "Do you really hold me responsible?"

"I was upset. I'm sorry I called you a stupid bitch."

"Twice." Now Alex was smiling. "Truce?"

"Truce."

They hugged each other, each knowing that the other was sincere, at least for the time being.

Dr. Sandler returned and motioned to them to come to the door. "You can see him for a minute," he advised. As they followed him down the hall, he said, "He came through the surgery very well. We'll have to watch him closely to see if the heart sustained any damage but hopefully, we got to it in time and he'll have a good recovery. We won't know for a few days, anyway.

"I have to warn you that everyone looks terrible after this operation. He'll be asleep and hooked up to a respirator, so you won't be able to talk to him until tomorrow. When he wakes up the nurse will tell him you both were here."

In spite of the warning, when they entered the recovery area, Barry got weak in the knees when he saw his brother. He had to catch Alex as the nurse ran for smelling salts, but she soon recovered. Neither one was prepared to see Dan so helpless, hooked up to God knows what, white as the sheets upon which he lay. It was a sight that would haunt Barry for years to come.

They only stayed for a minute. As they left, both speechless, Barry broke the silence. "Can I take you home, Alex?"

"No, I have my car."

"Do you feel okay to drive? Why don't we grab a cup of coffee downstairs, and then we'll see if you perk up?"

Alex just nodded, as she held onto Barry for support. She was staring straight ahead, her eyes glazed over and walking like a person who was drugged, barely able to navigate. They stopped for a cup of coffee and Barry saw the color return to Alex's face. Neither felt like talking. They drank their coffee in silence, each lost in thought.

"Okay?"

She nodded. They left the coffee shop together and each walked to their respective cars. Barry looked at his watch. It was 6:30, but he felt so washed out, he almost wished he didn't have to meet Tildy. But as he thought of Tildy and her lovely green eyes, he knew he would feel better the moment he saw her. He smiled to himself. He had almost forgotten that she had some information for him. He just wanted to be near her. *Funny, three days ago, I didn't know she existed, and now I can't wait to be with her. What's going on, here?*

He eased the car out onto the thoroughfare, as a soft rain began to fall. As he heard the tharump tharump of his windshield wipers, he began to feel mellow again. He put on the radio and heard a familiar song. He couldn't quite place it, but it was a tune he liked. He was really in the mood for a relaxing dinner with a beautiful woman.

The next few months would see Dave busier than he ever dreamed, but he loved it. He traveled all over the Caribbean and even to Asia for his new associates. He bought racehorses in Argentina with cash they gave him and sold them to Middle Eastern sheiks for clean funds. He arranged, through old contacts in New Jersey, to purchase electronic goods in cash transactions to be sold in South America. He became the essential entrepreneur and continued to rake in profits, but for his purposes, losses would have been all right, because it would render the money usable again, and this was the main goal. For days on end, he sat at his computer making wire transfers in and out of the many accounts he had set up. He set up dummy corporations, and then deposited some of the illicit cash into them, ostensibly as legitimate business enterprises. He paid his "directors" handsomely, out of non-existent profits. He drew up phony life insurance policies which he "sold" to his associates (something he was well versed in) and, when they were cashed in, he paid them with their own money—only now it was reusable. He engaged in every known scheme and several hitherto unknown schemes which he developed. Never was he so challenged to be inventive, and never had he made so much money. Huge sums of money flew through his hands, making him feel like an alchemist, turning trash into gold.

It was the dream of a lifetime. In time, he became quite invaluable to his associates. And just who was watching all of this? ABSOLUTELY NO ONE! His activities were hidden behind walls of secrecy in "safe havens." He knew that there were global organizations threatening to break down these secrecy laws, but so far they weren't making too much headway. He was becoming richer than he ever dreamed possible. His friendship with Lindy grew stronger now that they were involved with the same people and Lindy flew him on most of his trips. But Dave wasn't stupid. Lindy and all of his new associates knew him only, as Steve

Graham.

Lindy liked to hang loose, picking up women wherever they landed, only to fly off without a care for them or about them. Dave, on the other hand, found one woman and attached himself to her. For him it was just easier. He never really liked the high-flying life that Lindy enjoyed. He was on top of the world. The only thing that made him sad was that his mother was very ill at home. She was dying slowly, little by little, and he knew the end was coming. He loved his mother but he also loved being the only son and heir. He knew that her property was worth a lot of money, but he didn't really need it now. Nevertheless, it would soon be his and he knew that here, in the Caribbean he could parlay the proceeds for a lot more than he could in New Jersey. If anyone had the know-how, it was he.

He and Lindy had landed in Nevis a couple of hours ago. They had a drink at the bar in the hotel, but afterward, he went home to Marianne. Marianne was a handsome native woman, who had been the realtor who sold him his house. Her skin was like onyx, very black and very silky. She was fine boned but soft where it mattered. Marianne was no floozy. On the contrary, she was an educated and elegant woman. He couldn't abide shallow and stupid women, even just for sex, and he needed more companionship than just his friendship with Lindy.

He knew Marianne would be waiting for him with all the comfort she could give him. She would have an elegant dinner prepared, a vintage wine, some Mozart playing, but the best thing about her was that she never asked him what he did, or where all the money came from. She had too much good sense for that. She was content with him and he with her, and he looked forward to the next three days with anticipation. He was happy with Marianne and he was always most relaxed with her.

He knew that Lindy would be out all night but would be up bright and early the next morning. He wondered where Lindy got his stamina. He, on the other hand, had it all worked out. Life was beautiful.

## Chapter Fourteen

As Barry entered the parking lot, he saw in the dim light, a figure cross the street. He thought it was Tildy. Better to get the car parked before trying to attract her attention. He pulled into the first space he saw, under the halo of yellow cast by one of the restaurant's tall neoclassic, halogen-topped lampposts. As he exited the car under the light, he heard, "Hey Barry, over here."

Tildy had spotted his car and knew he would emerge as she crossed the street. Despite the drizzle, she walked toward him, rather than toward the door of the restaurant. In fact, she carried no umbrella and seemed totally undisturbed by the rain. He felt a terrific desire to embrace her, as if they had been together for years, but thought better of it.

"Hi Tildy."

"Hi Barry. How are you?"

"Tildy, you wouldn't believe how I am."

As she looked at Barry, even in the dim light, she noticed a difference. He seemed to have lost his boyishness and seemed old and beaten. *What could have happened to this vibrant man, I just saw, yesterday?*

"What's happened?"

"It's a long story. Let's go in and have a drink. I may have just had the worst day of my life."

"You look like hell."

"Yeah, that compliment will get you nowhere."

"I just mean that I can tell you're not yourself. Can I help?"

"If I didn't think it would help me to see you tonight, I would have canceled."

"That bad?"

"No, worse."

As they entered the restaurant, Jerry the owner, who knew them both, appeared to be surprised to see them together. He seemed to sense that they wanted some privacy and gave them a table in a dark corner. Without hesitation, Barry ordered a Johnny Walker, double. Tildy raised her eyes and ordered a glass of white wine.

"What the hell happened?"

"My brother had a heart attack."

"Oh my God! Is he all right?"

"Yes, they got him into surgery and I just saw him. The doctor says he's going to be all right, but I felt that I was staring at the face of death when I saw him."

"No wonder you look so bad. You've had a rotten day."

"Dan and I are very close. That's not all."

Jerry returned with their drinks. He inquired and Barry said, "No, we'll wait a while to order." Jerry left.

"What do you mean that's not all?"

"Well, I had a big fight with my sister-in-law on the phone."

"Dan's wife?"

"Yes, I called her a stupid bitch."

Tildy's green eyes widened. Her irises had opened in the dark, so that Barry could not see much of the green, but only these two enormous black holes where her small pupils had been. He felt that if he looked deep enough into these dark wells, he would see her soul. He felt himself getting hard. Have to get this under control, he thought.

Embarrassed by his thoughts, he looked away.

"I told you about Dan's problems with the insurance company. Well, it seems that he told Alex, my sister-in-law—her name is Alex. Well, he told her about the problem and they had a big fight. The next day she consulted with Bob Brady—"

"That asshole."

"I guess you know Bob."

"Yes, he was on the other side of my friend's divorce."

"Well then, you know how he is. He told her to file for divorce right away to get her claim in first, so to speak. Jeez, he didn't even try to see if something could be mediated. He just went in like Rambo and filed."

"How do you know this?"

"She told me."

"Before or after you called her a stupid bitch?" Tildy was smiling.

Barry smiled sheepishly as he sipped his whiskey.

Tildy thought, *At least he didn't gulp it down and order another.*

"Before."

"So, you think that's what precipitated his heart attack?"

"I'm sure it triggered it. Some guy found him slumped over the wheel of his car and called 911. I'm really glad he did. Wish I knew who he was."

"So what about your sister-in-law; did you tell her about Dan?"

"Of course."

"And?"

"She came right down to the hospital, while I was there."

"Did she push him out of bed?"

Barry laughed. "No, she was very contrite. I even apologized for calling her a bitch."

"But is she?"

"Is she what?"

"Still a stupid bitch?"

"Of course she is. I don't lie."

"Never?"

"No, mostly never." With that they both laughed. Barry had never felt so comfortable with anyone, telling such personal things to a—to a total stranger. After all, he really didn't know this woman and here he was not just telling things, but telling her how he felt. *Man, this is not me.*

Barry asked if she was hungry. Tildy asked if there was a time limit on the evening.

"No, none."

"Then I'll have another glass of wine before we order."

He called the waiter over and ordered her wine. He said he was fine for the time being. He kept looking at her. Mostly he was wondering what was so special about this woman, but nothing in her looks gave him the answer. Barry had known many beautiful women and had even been involved with a few, but Tildy had something else. Something he couldn't define, something fascinating. *What was it?*

He realized that he had been appraising her and that Tildy had noticed. He caught her smoothing her hair as if he had seen something out of place and she was responding to his look. But there was nothing out of place. Not even from the rain. Not a hair. She was soft. Not soft looking. Not soft to the touch, for he had never touched her. No, she was just soft. Looking at her, he was feeling that she was comfortable and soft. Soft like flannel, soft like the clouds, not just comfortable, but comforting. She was warm and, yes, soft. He could feel the second scotch and he realized that something was happening, and that he was not in control. He was being seduced—not by Tildy—but by her genuine, kind nature. He could feel her empathy and he knew, no matter what else there might be, that he was safe with her.

What a funny word to come into his mind, but there it was. For the first time in a long time, he was utterly certain that he was safe with this woman. No need to be on his guard, no need to impress her with his wit. No, he was home. *Omigod! Better stop thinking. Better to get on with the conversation and not dwell on my feelings. It might not be so safe, after all.*

"You said you had some information on Adelphia Security."

Tildy sensed some of what Barry was thinking. He looked very tired, but that didn't hide the strength of this man. She could feel his power, no doubt the power he used at trial. He was a presence and she knew that not only she, but others in the restaurant had turned to watch him as they were seated. He had charisma, not just good looks, but the type of good looks that come from confidence, from power. Could this be the man she had been looking for for so many years? She thought he could be. *I'm a strong woman and I need a strong man. Here he is at his weakest, his most vulnerable, and I still see him as strong. Wow! This must mean something. But tonight, he needs me. I can sense it. If it weren't true, he wouldn't have met me. He's so tired. Visibly tired. I have this terrible desire to take him in my arms and tell him everything will be fine. If only I dared, I know he would respond. But this is one move he has to make, not me. Can he tell how very receptive I am to him? I hope so. I really hope so.*

Tildy answered, "Yes. I don't know if it'll be helpful, but Adelphia Security was once a client of ours."

"Your firm?"

"Yes. They had an insured, a podiatrist with a malpractice claim. Something about multiple operations, all unnecessary, on some poor

Hispanic woman who didn't understand English. She had no medical insurance, but was paying the doctor a hundred dollars a month or something like that to take care of her. Seems her husband got suspicious and went to see a lawyer."

"So they do exist and are in business."

"Well, let's just say they were. We started to defend the claim but found out that the case was indefensible. We had an expert look at the records and these doctors were real charlatans. They had messed her up beyond repair. We told the company to settle."

"And?"

"That's all there is. They just disappeared. Didn't pay our bill, didn't settle the claim, didn't answer the phone. In fact, the phone was disconnected. Seems they said they were chartered in Nevis/St. Kitts, or somewhere like that. Couldn't get any help from St. Kitts, either."

"Do you have any information on them at all?"

"Only the name of the people we dealt with. The house attorney was based in New York. His name is David Petersen."

"Petersen?"

"Yes. Petersen, with an 'e', you know, 'e, n.' We tried to find him, but he couldn't be found. Jason thinks he was one of the principals. Couldn't find him in any bar directory, either."

"You think he's the key."

"You never know. Maybe. I would say that absent any other lead, this is where we should start."

"We?"

"Yes, we."

"Since when are you involved in this?" Barry smiled at her. He really did want her help. He knew that she might be able to open some doors he could never get in, but he didn't know how that might work.

"I want to help."

"What would Jason say about that?"

"At first, we don't have to tell him, but after all our firm has an interest in collecting their money too. I think they feel they've reached a dead end."

"Let me think about this. But I'll keep you informed and up to date on anything that happens. Thanks, Tildy"

After a while, they ordered dinner and got around to talking about Tildy's grandfather, the good old days, the way the bar was changing, the inroads women had made, the way the future might look. It was nearly midnight when they finished. It had been a long evening. Tildy wondered how it might end. As they rose to leave the restaurant, Barry put his arm around her.

"Can I take you home?" he asked.

"Yes," she answered even though her car was in the parking lot behind her office. "Yes," she said again.

Barry eased her into the passenger seat, and got into his side of the car. She told him where she lived. He was familiar with the area; he didn't need directions. Tildy closed her eyes and they both knew that he wouldn't say goodnight at the door. Tildy wasn't worried about a ride to work in the morning.

The train had left the station with Tildy and Barry on board. Neither one knew the destination, just that the ride was comfortable.

Barry parked the car and helped Tildy out. They went into Tildy's apartment building and took the elevator to the fourth floor. The hall was dimly lit, but Barry could see that it had recently been redecorated. The carpet was gray with an all-over flower design in shades of pink and rose. The walls had been papered with a gray and pink striped paper. It looked very new for what Barry knew was an older building in a still good part of town.

They arrived at Tildy's door. She didn't ask if he wanted a cup of coffee. They were both grownups and she didn't have to be coy. She handed him her key and he opened the door. He looked at her very directly for a moment and she said, "Come in."

Barry held the door for her and followed her inside. He closed the door and she went over to it and locked it with the little knob above the lock, the one that throws the dead bolt. There was no mistaking that she intended for him to stay. She waved him toward the couch. He sat down.

"Drink?" she asked. He shook his head. She said, "I don't want one either." She went over and sat beside him. He looked at her and took her hand.

"Are you sure?"

Very quietly she said, "Yes, very." She stood up and led him to her bedroom. She pulled the spread off the bed and folded it, neatly. *No need to rush.* She excused herself and went to the bathroom. While there, she took her time, she took off her clothes, brushed her hair and brushed her teeth. After a few minutes, she appraised herself in the mirror. She looked pretty good for thirty. Satisfied with what she saw, she put on a robe.

When she came back into the bedroom, there he was, in the bed and under the covers, fast asleep. Tildy smiled. This had never happened to her before. She knew this was not a lost opportunity, that there would be plenty of time for them. She knew that what had happened between them so far was very special. *Poor darling, he's had a rough day.*

She went around to the other side of the bed, removed her robe and nightgown, and climbed in beside him. She reached for the lamp and turned it off. Then, in the dark, she leaned over and gently kissed him on the forehead, moving her naked body against his, barely touching him. Barry never stirred. She fell asleep, her foot touching his.

Barry awakened at about five. He couldn't believe that he had gone to sleep. She didn't wake him. What a doll she was. He needed that sleep. How many times before had he stayed up all night, or tried cases on just a few hours sleep, especially in a heavy trial where he had to do trial prep each night before court. But that was different. He was going on adrenaline because he loved the practice, the game, the battle of wits. He could try the most difficult case on just a few hours' sleep with no difficulty.

*Why had this happened? I guess you don't come close to losing your brother, tear your sister-in-law apart and then make up with her, and then have dinner with the most interesting woman you've ever met—all in one day. Either I'm getting old, or I'm so at ease with Tildy that I don't need to impress her. Whatever it is, I haven't even had sex with her and I think I'm in love with her. That's a new one. This has never happened to me before. Look at her. She's so goddam beautiful sleeping.*

She was sleeping with her back toward him, but he could see the sunlight on her skin, and make out the outline of her nose and mouth as he looked at her profile. He leaned over and brushed her hair aside and kissed her cheek. She stirred. She stretched, then yawned and turned toward him. Then she realized where she was and who he was, and remembering what happened, she grinned at him. He grinned back.

"Was it as good for you as it was for me, she asked?"

He laughed out loud. "If you had the best sleep ever, I guess it was." He looked at her intently. Her eyes were a soft gray. *My God, those eyes change color with the time of day.* He reached for her and drew her close. He whispered, "How did I ever live without you in my life?"

"Same way I did," she responded, "Empty."

As he rolled his body onto hers, she knew that she would always be there for him, no matter what happened in their lives. *This is the one I've been waiting for*, she thought. It was passionate, it was beautiful and it was tender. Everything she had known it would be. When she finally looked at the clock, it was nearly seven. Tildy got out of bed, showered and dressed. Barry said, "I'll drive you to work, and then I'll go home and shower. I want to see Dan. I told my secretary I might not be in this morning."

## Chapter Fifteen

Barry dropped her in the parking lot where she had left her car. He then went home to change. He sang in the shower—something he never did—and dressed in a pair of slacks and a sports jacket. He put on a tie; he thought he might just go into the office after he saw Dan. He left his house and drove right to the hospital.

It was 9:00 a.m. Dan was still in the Coronary Care Unit, so he knew that he could see him any time he wanted, even if just for a few minutes. When he arrived at the room, he was startled to see Alex there.

"Hi Alex. Have you seen him?"

"Yes, a few minutes ago. The doctor's in with him."

"How's he doing?"

"He looks like hell, but the doctor says he's doing well. We'll have to wait a few days to see if he's sustained any permanent damage, but Dr. Solomon, the surgeon, said he came through the surgery very well."

With that, Alex began to cry.

"Barry, if you think I wanted this to happen—" she sobbed. He put his arms around her and lied, "Alex, it might have happened anyway, next week, next month or next year. You didn't cause the plaque to build up in his arteries, did you?"

She took this seriously and answered, "No, I always tried to get him to watch his diet. He's put on entirely too much weight lately. And he's a doctor; he knows better. I didn't want to feel like a cop every time he took a bite of something rich."

With that, the tears came in a torrent and Barry gave her his handkerchief. When she gave it back to him, it was covered with mascara. Barry wondered if all that makeup had become a habit, or if she did it for Dan.

"Did you, uh, speak with him?"

"No, Barry, he's not able to talk, yet. Maybe tomorrow."

Barry didn't have the heart to ask her what she was going to say about the divorce. Still, he didn't want her to upset his brother again.

She volunteered, "I'm going to call my lawyer this morning and put everything on hold. To be perfectly honest, I don't know what I'll do when he gets over this. Barry, I just can't go back to being poor, again. I just can't."

Barry looked at her this time with pity and realized she was no longer young and probably was incapable of starting over. *Those rotten scam artists, they don't realize what havoc they wreak when they play their games*, he thought. He left her and went in to see Dan. He looked over and realized that Alex was right; Dan did look dreadful. He was still on a respirator, so he couldn't talk, but his eyes were open. He looked scared. Barry walked over to the bed and squeezed Dan's hand. Dan looked over at Barry with love and gratitude. He wanted to tell Barry something.

Barry smiled at Dan and said he had seen Alex, and that everything was going to be all right. He said he had a lead on the person who had sold him the insurance and that it would all work out. *It won't do anyone any good, if Dan doesn't make it,* he thought.

"After all," he grinned, "we're going to need you to testify to put the bastard away." *Jeez, what a liar I've become since this all happened,* he thought. Dan's eyes fluttered assent. Barry knew he had calmed his brother's fears. He also knew that he was no closer to helping him than he was when Dan first spoke to him about the problem.

Barry gave his sister-in-law a peck on the cheek. He reassured her that Dan would be all right and that they would solve this insurance problem. He also extracted a promise from her that she wouldn't do anything rash without talking to him. Satisfied that the fire had been put out, if not permanently, then for the time being, Barry left the hospital for his office.

When Barry walked in the door, everyone asked about Dan. Barry told them it was all under control.

Eleanor handed him two messages, which he didn't look at until he had sat down at his desk. One was from Sandy Bishop and one was from Tildy. Barry called Tildy first.

"Hi," he said, when she picked up the phone.

"Hi. You okay?"

"Of course I'm okay. Never been better. I saw Dan and he's going to make it, but we'll have to wait a few days to see if there's been any heart damage. Alex was there and I think I have her calmed down, too. At least, for the time being."

His tone changed and he said, "I've been thinking about you. Last night was wonderful."

Tildy laughed and said, "Last night was wonderful, but this morning was much better."

"Tildy, it was all very wonderful. From the time we met, until I left you this morning, something is different. I can't explain it, but I'm different. How about you?"

"Yes, Barry, something is definitely different. For me too. Why don't you come to my house later? I'll cook dinner."

"Sure you don't want to go out?"

"I'm very sure."

"What time?"

"I'll be home at 7:00. Any time after that."

"Oh, and Tildy. You know that name you gave me. David Petersen?"

"Yes?"

"Can I give that out?"

"Sure, it's no secret."

"Good, I'll see you later." Then without thinking anything about the implications, he said, "Love ya," very casually. Her response was unexpected.

"I hope you mean that."

"It slipped out, but it wouldn't have if I hadn't been thinking about you all morning."

"Oh Barry, I'm really so happy."

"Me too, Love. Till later. Bye."

"Bye, Barry."

Barry put down the phone and stared at it. *Did I just tell her I love her? This is going as fast as anything that ever happened to me, and I feel that I'm just floating along. There's no question that I love her, but how did it happen so fast. Should I be putting the brakes on it? No, not with this one. There's just nothing here to fear. She's genuine and as beautiful as she is real. Nothing to be afraid of here. I really think I've finally been blessed.*

He picked up the other message and dialed Sandy Bishop. Sandy answered his own phone. Evidently, Jake had given him Sandy's private line.

"Sandy, it's Barry Chandron. Thanks for calling me so soon."

"Jake said you're a friend."

"Yes, and a former prosecutor."

"Yeah, he told me that, too. He told me to share anything I had, and that you could be relied upon to keep it confidential. That true?"

"I just want to help my brother. I'm sure that he told you the three of us go back a long time."

"Yes."

"Did he tell you why I'm involved?"

"Yes, he said your brother bought some of that phony insurance."

"Yes. It was a dumb move, but sometimes the smartest people make the dumbest moves."

"Amen. I guess that's why we have jobs."

"I guess."

"Well Barry, it seems these guys have been operating in New Jersey for about a year and a half. Near as we can tell, they've sold about eight and a half million dollars in insurance to doctors, dentists and podiatrists. We believe that they intended to go legitimate when they started, but one of the principals got into a bad divorce, and started to use the company's funds. They tried to defend a few of the early claims, but when they were clobbered with a few big judgments, there just wasn't enough money to pay off all the claimants.

"They pulled this same scheme in Michigan, Illinois and now, here. The Feds are looking for them too for interstate mail and wire fraud, and I think when they find them, they'll institute a federal racketeering suit. In the meantime, we're trying to find them too so that we get first dibs on assets to pay restitution to the victims in New Jersey. They used an offshore address in Nevis/St. Kitts, but near as we can find, they aren't registered anywhere.

"It was a real shoestring operation, but as they sold more policies, it turned into a pyramid situation. They paid the first few claims by selling new policies, then couldn't keep it going after that." He paused, "Sorry they caught your brother. Jake says he's a good guy. It really hits home when someone you know, or know about, gets caught in one of these schemes."

"Thanks, Sandy, I appreciate that. By the way, does the name David Petersen mean anything to you?"

"Where'd you hear that name?" Now, suddenly cautious.

"I hear—through the grapevine—they got a couple of insurance defense firms. Didn't pay their bills."

"You have a good grapevine, there. Yes, that's true, but I'm not at liberty to say who got stung."

"That's not important to me. Who's this Petersen?"

"Petersen? Well, he's supposed to be the brains of the outfit. Seems he's a lawyer, admitted in Michigan, and he got caught with his hand in his clients' funds. Was disbarred in Michigan and then got a divorce. Looks like whatever he had left, after he paid the clients back, went to the wife. After he got into this scheme, and it went sour, he took off for the Caribbean. I think the Feds are looking for him, but can't find him. Probably changed his identity."

"Very interesting. Uh, how old a guy is he? Do you know?"

"Early forties, I think, why?"

"Uh, no reason, just curious. So he got his divorce in Michigan?"

"Um, Michigan or Illinois."

"When—do you know?"

"Yeah, about three years ago, but don't go looking there. We already looked and there's nothing there. Wife got a bundle and she's living in an expensive condo in Ann Arbor. I think she plays at being an interior designer or something. Most of the money made in the insurance scheme was after the divorce."

"Well, thanks, Sandy. If anything happens will you let me know?"

"Sure, you're a friend of Jake's; I'll keep you posted on anything that happens."

"I sure appreciate that. Thanks, Sandy."

Barry hung up the phone. He sat for a few minutes and rang for Eleanor. He asked if Ray Tobias was in the office. Ray was his senior associate. He had been with Barry for two years, ever since Barry decided not to remain a solo practitioner. He was quite impressed with how far

Ray had come. He judged him to be very smart and very persistent. He knew that if he gave Ray an assignment, not only would it be done, but it would be done quickly and thoroughly, and he would have the results ASAP. Ray was a comer, and he knew that every assignment that he gave him was regarded by Ray as another step to the top. He was a good kid and very ambitious. Barry was very quick to sense that kind of ambition and he admired it. *After all, if there were no high goal, why would anyone knock himself out? Hey, maybe he's my successor here.* He smiled at the thought.

Eleanor left to get Ray, and within a couple of minutes, an eager Ray was at his door. He asked Ray to come in and close the door. He motioned for Ray to sit down and told him he had a very important job for him. He told him to drop whatever he was doing and jump on this.

"Ray, I want you to check on a divorce within the last three years in Michigan or Illinois. Not only do I want the names and dates of all divorces between parties by the name of Petersen, but I want copies of all the judgments. I don't care if there are a thousand, I want them all. Get on the phone, get online, but get them. Use some charm if you have to, but get copies faxed here today, if you can. The husband's name is David Petersen, I don't have the wife's. I'm almost sure that the name is Petersen, with an 'e,' but maybe you ought to get all of them, the ones spelled 'o, n' too. Oh, and I might be leaving early so call my car phone if you get anything. Eleanor has it. And I'll leave another number with Eleanor in case you can't get me in the car."

"I'll get right on it, Barry." Ray smiled. He was glad that Barry asked him to do this job. *It sounds important*, Ray thought. He rose and left the office.

Barry thought about the phone conversation with Sandy. Evidently, the state guys had looked into the assets and the time line of the divorce. But what if there's a kid? The father probably has some kind of visitation arrangement. Does the wife get alimony? From where, might be interesting. *Got to get to the ex*, he thought. She might just be the key. Granted, it's cheap to live in Central America, so he has to have some big bucks left. Wonder what the amount of alimony or child support might be? It has to be based on his income, and if his income went downhill, then he might have come back in to get it reduced. Wonder if the guy ever risked it? *Lots of questions*, he mused. He's probably a deadbeat dad anyway.

Then his thoughts turned to Tildy. He looked at his watch. It was four o'clock. Wow, I have two overwhelming things on my mind, Dan's problem and Tildy. I can't do anything more here until I get those divorce judgments. He thought once more of Tildy and came to a decision. He picked up the phone and told Eleanor that he was leaving and she could reach him on his car phone. Then he said that Ray might want to call him later and to give him the car phone number. "Oh, and Eleanor, here's another number where I'll be later, if he can't reach me in the car." With that, he picked up his jacket and left the office.

## Chapter Sixteen

Barry's car was parked right outside the door. He didn't hesitate for an instant. He got in the car and headed for the mall, more specifically, to Rodman's Jewelers. He had represented Max Reinfeld when he was negotiating with old man Rodman for the store. Max was not just a client; he was an old friend.

Barry had also represented him in buying his other two stores. He remembered Rodman as being a shrewd old guy, and how badly Max wanted the store, his first in North Jersey.

He had to hold Max back more than once, so that he didn't let Rodman know how eager he was. Max almost caved in on the deal several times, but Barry had sized up the old man correctly. He knew that Rodman was just as eager to sell, but was a better poker player than his client. Not only did Barry get the store for Max, but he negotiated a price that Max marveled at.

Max was extremely grateful, and had let Barry handle two subsequent negotiations, without his even being present. But Barry had never called upon Max before. He didn't doubt for a minute that Max would treat him extremely well.

Max was just putting some items in the case when Barry walked in. Max looked up at the sound of someone approaching, but immediately broke out in a grin when he saw Barry.

"Well, well, if it isn't my old friend. How are you, Counselor?"

"Great," Barry answered.

"I can see that, you look great." Max smiled a benevolent smile.

"So, my friend, what brings you here? Is there something I can help you with?"

"As a matter of fact, there is. I need a present for a lady."

# INTENT TO DEFRAUD

"Someone special?" Max asked a little slyly.

"Could be." Barry answered, just a little cagey.

"Is there something you want to tell me?"

"No Max, not yet. I want something special for someone I just met, but yes, she is special."

"Barry, do you want something in a ring, a watch, a necklace, a pin? Tell me does the young lady go to work?"

"Yes, Max, she's a lawyer."

"A lawyer? Well you don't want anything too flashy. Something professional, say to wear on a lapel?"

"That sounds good."

"I have a beautiful gold pin; just came in from an estate. I think it's very pretty. Want to see it?"

"Sounds interesting, let's have a look."

Max went in the back and returned a minute later. He was holding a velvet box, which obviously had some age on it. He opened the box. In it was an exquisite pin in the shape of a bird, with its head down so that it formed a circle. The body was made of a large black pearl set in gold, and the eye was a small ruby. Barry knew immediately that this was the perfect gift.

"You like?" asked Max.

"It's perfect."

"I just got it in yesterday. It came from the estate of a very wealthy woman in South Jersey. When you said special, I knew this was the perfect thing. Barry, I paid nine hundred for it; I would normally get eighteen hundred in the store."

"So, how much for me?"

"Barry, wait a minute, I want to show you something." Max went again into the back of the store. He walked out with a piece of paper and showed it to Barry. It was a list with numbers marked next to each one. Barry looked at it and saw "Bird Pin———$900.00."

"Max, you don't have to show me that. I know you wouldn't lie to me."

"Barry, I always wanted to do something for you, but you always said you didn't need anything. So, now you need something, right?"

"Yes, so how much?"

"So, Barry, you think it's worth nine hundred?"

"Yes, of course, but how much retail?"

"Barry, I'm telling you. Nine hundred."

"But that's what you paid for it."

"So the pin is a present from you to the girl, and from me to you—the present is my profit."

"Oh, Max, I can't let you do that."

"Don't worry, I'll make it up on the engagement ring, okay?" Max smiled and started to polish the pin with a cloth. He then got a new box, placed the pin in the box and then wrapped the box in beautiful silver paper. Barry watched as he worked. He thought to himself, *I really know this girl well enough to know that she'll love this.*

He took the package and with a big smile and several thank yous, left the store, but not before promising Max he would bring Tildy around to meet him. He was very pleased with himself.

It was now half past five. Barry decided that he had just enough time to go home, shower, shave, and change his clothes. Promptly at 7:00, he was parking the car on Tildy's street. He went upstairs and rang her bell. Tildy had obviously just walked in. She appeared to be rushed and her hair was still tied up in the back, with little wisps escaping, forming coppery ringlets all around her face.

As Barry entered, he spotted supermarket bags on the kitchen counter, filled with the groceries she had just bought to make the dinner. He asked, "Are you sure you want to cook? We could go out, do this another time."

She answered, "How hungry are you? It'll take about forty minutes, think you can wait?"

"Sure, if that's what you want to do." She nodded, told Barry to fix himself a drink, and walked into the bedroom to change. He fixed a scotch and soda, and fixed one for her too. He called into the bedroom and asked her if she was ready for a drink. She told him just to leave it on her dresser. He walked into her bedroom and—for the first time—he noticed the room. Tildy was in the bathroom, washing up.

The room was neatly furnished, but with some very old pieces of furniture that he took to be family pieces. She had a solid color navy blue spread on the bed, with some plaid and flowered throw pillows. There was a bed skirt in a matching plaid. The walls were covered with navy wallpaper with a textured fleur de lis pattern. Very stark, but very straightforward. *Just like Tildy,* he thought. No frilly patterns for her, just fine old quality furniture. He thought that if he had to imagine how her room would look, he would have figured it something like this. He saw a white afghan folded neatly at the foot of her bed, and a cherry red armchair in the corner with a matching ottoman. There was a floor lamp next to the chair, and he could imagine her taking work home and reading it in this chair. *Very comfortable looking,* he thought.

He left the drink on the dresser, left the room, and closed the door behind him. He then looked over the living room. The living room sofa was upholstered in a very abstract white print on a red background. It was also very comfortable, but with very straight, clean lines. The print was perfect. She had two matching chairs upholstered in white. They looked like old chairs that had been reupholstered recently.

He liked them, but sensed that this furniture, like the pieces in the bedroom, had been in Tildy's family. He wondered if any of them had come out of Roger's home, a place he had visited once or twice, so many years ago. He tried to search his memory, but couldn't quite remember. He guessed he had been too young in those days to notice those things. But he did remember that the Jennings had a beautiful home.

He picked up a magazine, while he sipped his drink. He was reading an article about starvation in Africa when Tildy came out in a pair of jeans and a very large white shirt. Her hair was loose and fell softly to her shoulders. She was lovely, even in old jeans. Barry quickly took another drink before he said something stupid. He just kept appraising her as he sipped. She took a sip of her drink, and took it with her into the kitchen.

She said, "Just make yourself comfortable while I fix dinner."

"Can I help?" he asked.

"Yes, if you stay out of my way. Otherwise it'll take twice as long."

"Okay, you're the boss."

She set the table with navy blue place mats and put simple white plates on them. She put a very small arrangement of flowers in the center and lit two candles on either side. She set out wine glasses and left the bottle of chilled white wine on a coaster at Barry's place, with a corkscrew next to it.

Barry watched her out of the corner of his eye. She moved with grace and authority. He smiled and asked himself if these two words went together. When he decided they did, but only in describing Tildy, he was very pleased with himself.

After about forty minutes she called him to the table. She had prepared a tasty dish of Neapolitan shrimp over pasta and served a beautiful fresh salad with it. It was delicious and Barry said so. He ate as if he hadn't had lunch, but he had. Then she cleared the table and set out small demitasse cups, into which she poured espresso putting a twist of lemon on the saucer. As she put a small cake plate down with a few pastries on it, Tildy's phone rang.

"Hello? Just a minute. It's for you."

Tildy handed the phone to Barry.

He picked it up and said, "Ray? Yes, yes, okay, what's the date? Excellent! Yes, yes, thanks a million, just what I wanted. Yeah, yes, okay, see you tomorrow, and Ray—thanks."

Tildy asked, "What was that all about?"

"Guess what? You know that name you gave me. David Petersen. Well, I found out through other sources that he was a disbarred lawyer from Michigan. Seems he was married and then when things went bad, got a divorce in Michigan, three years ago."

"How does that help us?"

Barry noticed the "us."

"By itself, it isn't much. I had Ray Tobias, from my office, check the divorce records. I was hoping there was a child, you know, support, visitation, but there were no kids. Wife lives in Ann Arbor. Husband seems to have disappeared to somewhere in the Caribbean. The Feds don't know where he is; neither does New Jersey. It might lead up a blind alley, but I think I'll take a trip to Ann Arbor."

"When are we going?" Again the "we."

"What do you mean we?"

"I want to go with you. She might talk to a woman more easily."

"Can you get away?"

"I'll find a way. So, when?"

"I want to make sure Dan is out of the woods, and then I'll find out how soon I can book a couple of tickets."

"Great."

"Tildy?"

"Yes?"

"I have something for you." As he said this, he pulled the box from his pocket. He handed it across the table.

She looked at him, quizzically. "What's this?"

"A little gift."

"What for?"

"I saw it and I thought of you. I hope you like it."

Tildy opened the package and saw the pin. Her eyes misted over. "Oh, Barry, I've never seen anything more lovely. Wherever did you find such a pin?"

"A client of mine is in the jewelry business. He got it in yesterday in an estate. It's very old."

"Yes, I can see that. They just don't make things like this anymore." With that, she got up and went to him. She put her arms around his neck and kissed him, first tenderly, then with passion. The espresso and uneaten cake stayed on the table as she gently led Barry into the bedroom.

## Chapter Seventeen

The next morning, Barry left early. He wanted to stop at the hospital before going to the office, so he arose, kissed Tildy and told her he was going home to dress and that he would call her later. She turned over, kissed him back and mumbled something. She promptly went back to sleep.

Barry left quietly, not wanting to disturb her, went downstairs and drove home. He found himself whistling as he drove. *Gee,* he thought, *I haven't whistled like this in years. Is it the good news about finding the wife, or is it Tildy? Damn it, Barry. Leave it alone*, he thought. *Who cares why I'm happy, I'm just happy. Oh, that Tildy. I must be the luckiest guy in the world. And to think she's Roger's granddaughter. Who would have thought it? My God, I must have met her when she was a little girl. Surely she came to the office once or twice. Wish I could remember.* But try as he did, he had no memory of seeing a little redheaded girl during the years he was with Roger. Fate is really strange.

Barry arrived at the hospital around nine. He went up to the CCU and was glad to see that Alex wasn't there. He found his brother in a private room, lying in bed with his eyes closed. He no longer was hooked up to the respirator. He approached the bed, and Dan, seeming to sense that someone was approaching, opened his eyes and smiled. Barry noticed that he was beginning to get some color back in his face. He smiled at Dan and said, "Hi, brother. You sure gave me a fright. What do you mean scaring me like that?"

"Hi Barry." Barry noted that, though he had color and was smiling, his voice was still a little shaky. Barry made a mental note not to stay too long.

"So, how goes it?" Barry said, cheerfully.

"I guess I should be asking you that."

"No, first I want to tell you that I know everything that happened. The divorce papers, etc. I had a talk with Alex. She agreed to withdraw the complaint for divorce."

"Yes, she and I had a good talk, yesterday. She feels guilty, you know, that she's responsible for what happened."

"Dan, you should know better than any of us that what happened was predictable a long time ago. Did you ever try to do anything about your cholesterol?"

Dan smiled and said, "Doctors, you know. We never take care of ourselves. I guess we all think we're invincible, till it happens."

"Well, now it happened, and you'd better be glad that you got the warning. Besides, you know what Mom always said. 'Only the good die young.' I guess we'll both live forever."

With that Dan and Barry both grinned at each other knowing that—more than anything else—the bond they had would always be strong. It was strong when they were kids, when Dan could be called on to intimidate any bully who picked on Barry. It was strong when Barry was in law school and Dan would take him to a game or treat him to dinner. And even though Barry disapproved of Dan's choice in marriage, he never let Dan know it. Even now, he wanted Dan to know that he would always be there for him, and that they shared a common bond—their great love for their parents. Barry thanked God every day that he and his brother were close.

Then, for a moment, he shifted his thoughts to Tildy and wondered if he should tell Dan about her. He had never discussed any woman with Dan before, but this was different. He knew he was in love with her and Dan needed some cheering up. He also knew that Dan had been hoping for a long time that he would meet the right girl and settle down.

"Hey, Dan, you really put a crimp in my plans."

"Oh? How's that?"

"You had to go and have this lousy heart attack just when I met a terrific woman."

"Woman? You, Barry? Really?"

"Yes, really."

"I don't believe it."

"Remember Roger Jennings?"

Dan looked at him, quizzically.

"You know, the lawyer I had my first job with after law school. Remember, he became a judge."

"Oh yes, I remember. Old money, very dignified. Yes, I think I met him once or twice."

"Yes, you did."

"So?"

"Well, it seems he had a granddaughter."

"Now don't tell me you're going after children."

"No, she was a child then, but she's all grown up. She's a lawyer."

"The old man died, didn't he?"

"Yes, a long time ago, but I met her at a bar dinner and—this time, well—I might have some news for you very soon."

"You're kidding!"

"No, but don't say anything to Alex. I want to keep this under wraps for a while."

"When can I meet her?"

"When you're up and around, we'll have dinner together, or something. Okay?"

"Sure, sure it's okay. Wow, this is great news."

"Now Dan, I have something else to tell you. I have some leads on that son of a bitch who sold you the insurance. Tildy and I are flying to Detroit as soon as I can get a couple of tickets."

"Who the hell is Tildy? Oh—that's her name."

"Tilden Jennings. Roger's granddaughter.

"We have a line on that crook through an ex-wife. That's all I have at the moment, but I want you to know I'm working on it. Oh yeah, the Feds are after him too. Seems he pulled this shit in Michigan, Illinois, and New Jersey. Serious mail and wire fraud. We're all after him, and we're going to get him. He's down in the Caribbean, somewhere. Dan, I don't want you to worry. We will find him and get you out of this mess. I promise. In the meantime, the kid, your patient, hasn't surfaced yet, so that gives us time to find the bastard. Okay? So don't worry about this; it will turn out all right. I promise you."

Dan gave Barry a half smile. He was getting a little weary. He knew that Barry was just giving him some bullshit to make him feel better.

There was no way Barry could promise to get him out of this mess. He smiled again, thinking, *I almost got myself out of this mess by dying. Now I have to deal with it all.*

"What's so funny, Dan?"

"Oh nothing. I always knew you were a feisty bastard. Go get 'em tiger. And Barry, I want to meet this Tildy. I'd like to see the girl who would get your attention. She has to be something pretty out of the ordinary to have you talk this way."

Barry leaned over and kissed his brother on the forehead.

"Dan?"

"Yes?"

"Get yourself well and get the hell out of that bed. We all need you. Don't forget that."

"Yeah Barry, okay." When Barry left the room, Dan was smiling. Barry knew that Dan wasn't out of the woods yet, but today he seemed a little better. He wondered if it was all right to leave town. *Maybe I'll wait a few more days. The wife's not going anywhere.*

Barry left the hospital and went to the office. He was feeling better too. In fact, he had never felt this well at all. *Uh oh,* he thought. *This must be what it's like to be in love. No wonder everyone writes songs about it.* He laughed to himself as he entered his office. *Better not look too good, or everyone will start asking questions. Only Eleanor suspects something, but she's too smart to ask. Best to leave it that way.*

Eleanor got up and followed him into his office. She was holding a stack of messages in her hand. Barry made a face when he saw them. Eleanor handed them to him and said, "How's Dan?"

"He looks lousy, but he'll make it. I caught the doctor as I was leaving the hospital and he said that Dan was doing pretty well, under the circumstances. He thinks that Dan's had minimal permanent damage, but even that might be better when all the test results come back. He said that Dan was lucky that man found him and called 911. I wish I knew who that guy is. I would like to thank him. Eleanor, what are all these messages?"

"I thought you would want to see them, but Ray or someone can handle most of them. There is one or two I thought you might want to take care of yourself."

Barry leafed through the messages fast. He made two piles. He put most of them in a pile for Ray and the others he kept. There were a few clients who would want to hear from him personally and these he was ready to call. Pointing to the larger pile he said, "Give these to Ray, he'll know what to do with them, and when I finish making these calls send Ray in. I need to speak with him."

Barry looked at his calendar and said, "Oh Eleanor, call the travel agent and book two flights to Detroit on Friday. The other person's name is Tilden Jennings. Uh, keep that under your hat, okay?"

"When do you want to return?" Eleanor said, as unflappable as ever. She had learned a long time ago not to ask Barry anything personal. She knew that that was why she kept her job, despite the many times she had to leave early when the kids were sick or something came up. Barry depended on that relationship and he trusted her entirely. She also knew that if the chips were down and she had to have his personal advice, he would always be generous and—more important—helpful. It was a good feeling to know there was someone you could depend on if you needed to. She also knew to use this relationship sparingly. She only sought his advice when it really mattered, so that when she did have to speak to him about something, he would understand it was really important.

They never socialized with each other. Their relationship was strictly professional, but down deep in her heart, she felt that Barry was her closest friend. She had talked to him that time when Ralph lost his job, and then again when they needed a surgeon for Melanie. But that was a long time ago. She would never bother him with something trivial, and he knew that.

Barry made his few calls and then he called Tildy.

"How is Dan?" she asked.

"I think he's on the mend."

Barry didn't mention that he had told Dan about her. *Too soon, too soon. I don't want to slow this down, but I don't need to make it go any faster either,* he thought.

"Can you go with me to Detroit on Friday? I have Eleanor booking a couple of flights."

"Yes, Barry. I'll make it my business to get away. Uh, when will we come back?"

"I thought Monday, is that okay?"

"Yes, Barry, it's okay. Will I see you tonight?"

"Sure, why do you ask?"

"I thought maybe you might want to slow it down a little."

"Do you?" Now Barry thought she was reading his mind.

"No," she said. "But I'm willing to be a little cautious, if you are. I mean, things are happening a bit fast."

"Tildy, don't try to read my mind, but be honest with me. Is it too fast for you?"

"No, but I thought—"

"Don't think. I'm a very direct guy. If I thought it was too fast, I would have said so. Okay?"

"Okay."

"But, tonight, how about a movie? I'm so relieved that Dan is okay, I thought maybe just a night out, nothing too big. We could grab a bite after work, and then the movie. Okay?"

"Anything, any time, anywhere. Okay, Barry?"

"I do love you; you know that, don't you?"

"Yes, Barry, I do. And I feel the same. You know that, too, don't you? It's quite remarkable, isn't it? Does it always happen like this? I only met you a few days ago."

"I wouldn't know, Love. It's never happened to me before."

"Same here, but I feel as if I just joined a very exclusive group of people and now I understand what they're talking about."

"You, too? Yeah, I always thought they were all full of shit. I guess love, real love, is different. Whadda you know?"

"See you later."

"I can't wait."

Barry hung up the phone. He was glad nobody was in the office. He knew that he had a stupid smile on his face, but he couldn't help it. Yeah, what *do* you know? He rang for Eleanor, who told him she had gotten two seats on a 4:00 p.m. flight to Detroit on Friday, returning Monday at 8:00 a.m. He told her that was fine.

He then asked her to send Ray in. He met with Ray for an hour going over all the cases he wanted Ray to handle in the next few weeks, and which associates he wanted to assist Ray on the various cases. He didn't want to have to worry about anything for a few days, and certainly not over the weekend. He wanted to concentrate on Dan's problem. He really didn't have to think much about Tildy. That was happening all by itself.

## Chapter Eighteen

Friday afternoon, Barry picked up Tildy at her office. He had driven her to work and already had her suitcase and his in the trunk of his car. After a short ride to the airport, they found themselves together, bound for Detroit.

Tildy was wearing a soft beige suit with a dark brown blouse. She was wearing her new pin and it looked great. *She looks fantastic*, Barry thought. They settled in and relaxed. It was a direct flight, which would take about two hours. Tildy was glancing at a magazine; Barry was looking at the "in flight" catalogue of overpriced, useless gadgets. He took the time to relax. He had seen Dan that morning. Dan was recovering very well. He was out of the Coronary Care Unit and in a private room. The doctor had told him that he was a very lucky man. There had been no permanent damage to the heart, and with proper diet and exercise he could live to be an old man. When he left Dan, it seemed that he and Alex were going to try to work things out. In his heart, though, Barry knew he was the one who had to work things out to make their reconciliation a success.

Two hours later, he and Tildy were in the rental agency picking up a car. The drive to Ann Arbor was short. They had reservations at the Hilton. They figured on settling in, getting a bite to eat and taking it easy. In the morning, they would try to contact the ex Mrs. Petersen. Barry figured he and Tildy would talk about how they would approach her. When they reached the hotel room, however, it was Tildy who made a dive for the phone book.

"Oh Barry, there are ten Petersons in Ann Arbor."

Barry said, "Tildy, it's spelled 'e-n,' Petersen ending in 'e-n.'"

"Right, I forgot. Um, there are only two. One is a Dr. Ronald Petersen, the other Mrs. Helen Petersen." Now she was smiling, "Which one do you think it is?"

"Honey, for a beautiful woman, you sure ain't too smart," he quipped. "Let's try Dr. Ronald first, okay? Seriously, hon, let's put it away until tomorrow. Okay? C'mere."

She put the book away and walked over to him.

"Somehow being in a hotel room with you makes it seem so—uh—so illicit," she said. "It really turns me on." He took her in his arms, and looked at her, very deliberately.

"No, honey, powerful, exciting maybe. Illicit, no. Nothing with you could ever be wrong. Do you have any idea how happy you make me?"

He kissed her.

She said, "Can we skip dinner?"

"Exactly what I had in mind," he answered.

The next morning, they awakened early. They showered, dressed and, after writing down Helen Petersen's address and phone number, they went out for breakfast. There was a restaurant across the street and Barry was surprised to see how much Tildy ate. He had coffee and a muffin. She ate bacon, eggs, hash browns, toast, coffee and juice. He watched her, lovingly, but he smiled when she finished.

"Are you sure you don't want anything else?" he asked. She laughed, and said, "Did you forget, we didn't have dinner last night?"

He said he had had everything he wanted.

Tildy smiled back at him, and said, "Good sex gives me a good appetite. You'd better get used to it."

He answered, "We'd better take it easy, then, or the plane won't be able to take off." They both laughed. Barry paid the check and they left the restaurant.

They went back to the hotel to call Mrs. Petersen. It was nine o'clock. After quite a bit of discussion they decided that the best approach might be just to tell the truth. They also decided that perhaps it would be more reassuring if Tildy called, so she took a deep breath and dialed the number.

"Mrs. Petersen? Helen Petersen? Were you married to a David Petersen? Um—Mrs. Petersen, you don't know me, but I'm trying to locate your ex-husband. I wonder if I could take a few minutes of your time some time today. Yes, I would also prefer it be in person. Yes, he is. No, I'm not with law enforcement. Great. Where?" She wrote down an address. "At 2:00 p.m. That would be great. No, it's a business matter. No. I'll discuss it with you when we meet. Thank you. Yes, later. Goodbye."

Tildy got off the phone and gave Barry a thumbs up. "She owns a store. She was on the way out. She said she would see me today at two. She asked if he was in any trouble. I said, 'Yes.' She said, 'I knew it.' Something like, it was just a question of time. She didn't hesitate. We are meeting at 2:00 p.m. Should I go alone?"

Barry thought for a moment and then said, "Yes. That's a good idea. You seem to have gotten off on the right foot with her."

"Sometimes the truth is the best way, but we really took a chance, didn't we?" Barry and Tildy decided to spend the rest of the morning driving around Ann Arbor. It was a college town with nice homes and big trees. They found a park and stopped the car.

It was a beautiful day, brisk and sunny, a good day for a walk. They walked into the park which, it being a Saturday, had quite a few people. There were young people jogging, and older people walking. There were several people riding bicycles and a few mothers watching their children playing on the lawn.

Barry and Tildy found a bench just opposite a young mother throwing a ball to a little boy. He was about four and was having trouble catching the ball. He was an especially beautiful child with light blond, almost white hair.

The mother was very pretty, with sandy colored hair. There was no doubt the she was the child's mother. Not only did the little boy look like her, but also the way she looked at him with such love in her eyes gave it away; it was obvious that she adored him. She threw the ball several times and each time the child missed it, or caught it and then dropped it.

She looked over at them and laughed. She said, "Do you think he's ready for the Tigers?"

Barry and Tildy laughed. Barry said, "Maybe just a little more practice."

The mother answered, "Practice? I don't know who'll give up, first. I don't think I have that much staying power."

Barry could see Tildy in a few years, looking at a child the way this lovely young mother looked at her's. Yes, Tildy, all businesslike and efficient, but yes, she would be a wonderful mother. I can't believe I'm thinking this, but—yes. I think she's a very good person to be the mother of my son and heir. But I don't want to scare her with that, just yet.

With that, a jogger stopped by, and picked up the ball. The little boy ran to him saying, "Daddy, Daddy, I catched the ball. Watch me." The man picked up the child, hugging him. Then he put him down and threw the ball. Miraculously, the child caught it. Both parents ran over to the child, who was saying "I catched the ball, I catched the ball, I catched the ball."

Tildy was thinking, *How happy they seem, especially the mother. I wonder if she gave up a profession to become this child's mother. I wish I could ask her how it is to be a mother. She's a stranger; I wouldn't have to worry about what she would read into it.* Tildy was smiling. Barry asked her why. She said, "Oh, I don't know. They seem so happy. He's really darling isn't he?"

"Who, the father?"

"No, you know who I mean."

"Oh, I thought you were getting ready to ditch me."

"Ditch you? I wouldn't dream of it." She kissed him on the cheek and held his hand. When she looked up the woman was smiling at her. Tildy wondered if the woman saw herself when she looked at Tildy. Tildy hoped that this lovely woman had been as happy when she first met her husband as Tildy was now.

Tildy smiled back. *Of course, she was—and still is.*

Barry broke the spell. "After that breakfast you ate, you don't want lunch, do you?"

"Sure I do. What time is it?"

Barry looked at his watch. "It's 11:30. I looked at the map and that address where you have to meet her is on the other side of town. Why don't we drive over that way? We'll scout out the place, and then find a nice place to eat near there, okay?"

"Sounds like a plan."

They got up to leave and Tildy turned to look at the family, who had resumed the game with the child. The father was throwing the ball. She saw the woman, still smiling at her, and Tildy waved goodbye. The woman waved back.

Barry consulted a map in the car and then started out. He said it would take about fifteen minutes to get to the right neighborhood. They found the street and then the address. The shop appeared to be an upscale decorator and accessories shop, in an area with small restaurants and shops. Barry figured he could kill an hour in this neighborhood easily.

They found a charming French style bistro with French posters decorating the walls. Tildy ordered a salad with onion soup and Barry had an open steak sandwich. They had a leisurely lunch but Tildy had one eye on the clock. Barry had briefed her on all the things she should try to find out. *Too bad there's no child,* he thought. *That would have been too easy.*

Barry, with more than a little trepidation, watched Tildy leave. He hoped she would find out as much as he needed to know. He was sure she understood, but what if she forgot something? He wondered if he should have insisted on going with her, or on meeting Helen Petersen himself. *No*, he reassured himself. *Tildy will do fine. She can handle it.* He ordered another coffee, drank it slowly, and then left the restaurant.

He looked at Mrs. Petersen's shop with curiosity but walked in the other direction. Barry wandered up and down the street, looking in the shop windows. There was a pricey men's store. He looked in the window and marveled at the expensive, but casual clothes. He thought about the change in attire that had occurred in the last few years. *Suits are becoming obsolete; first it's dress down Friday, and in the tech industry, it's dress down every day.*

Barry always tried to keep up with the most current fashion trends but he knew that the courts would be the very last place to give up the formality of a business suit. *I'll bet the banks will capitulate before the courts,* he mused. *I wonder if, in years to come, I'll have difficulty even finding a suit.* He laughed. *Don't I have enough to worry about without worrying about that?*

Nevertheless, he entered the shop and saw a beautiful blue cashmere sweater. He gasped when he saw the price. He had never let price stop him, but this was ridiculous. Besides, he almost never wore a sweater and had a closet full of them. *Oh well, when the time comes that I can wear it to court, maybe I'll indulge myself; right now, no. But maybe I'll show it to Tildy to see if she likes it.* He smiled again when he thought about how important she had become to him in such a short time.

He quickly left the shop. Next, he passed an art gallery. Barry was—by no means—a collector, yet he loved and appreciated good art. He saw some really fine paintings in the window, by an artist he had never heard of. The gallery was on a corner and he walked around the corner to see the rest of the window exhibit. Then he entered the gallery. He was under its spell immediately. He could hear it only faintly, but there was a beautiful Mozart trio playing in the background. *Not so intrusive that a customer would be annoyed by it—as if anyone could be annoyed by Mozart—but so soothing for an art gallery. How very clever.*

A young man approached him. "Please, just look around; if you have any questions, feel free."

"Thanks," said Barry. "Uh, who is the artist who painted the window exhibit? Is he local?"

"Oh yes, he lives right here in Ann Arbor. Isn't his work great? I have a few smaller pieces around this corner," said the man, slowly walking toward the back where there was a moveable wall. As Barry followed him and turned the corner, he saw a wall of smaller paintings. *Yes*, he thought. *These are very good.*

The salesman handed him a price list and explained that the prices referred to the small numbers above each painting.

"I'll just leave you to look at these. I'm trying to finish up some paperwork, but I'll be right at my desk in the front, should you need anything."

Barry nodded in assent. He was really struck by the sensitivity and quality of the paintings. They were no more than eight by ten at the smallest and sixteen by twenty at the largest. Even the smaller ones had the deft stroke of a painter who knew exactly what he was doing.

They were confident, fresh, and vibrant. This was an artist who knew what it was all about. *He could have been a trial lawyer. Nothing hesitant or tentative about this work.* He looked at the prices. *Not too bad. He must be a beginning artist. His work is fantastic and the price is still reasonable.*

Barry called to the salesman. "Excuse me. Can you tell me something about the artist?"

"Why, yes," said the man, obviously pleased. "He teaches art at the University. He moved here about two years ago from New York. He's been turning out more work here than he ever thought he could. He says the atmosphere here is much more conducive to his working.

"He's in his early thirties. See those blue stickers next to the number of the painting? Those have already sold. I predict in a few years, you won't be able to touch his work for three times the current prices. This has been a very successful show for him."

Barry looked closely. He found a painting of horses in a pasture. The horses were depicted from various angles, some eating, some standing, some facing out and some facing another field in the distance. The thing that appealed to Barry was the impressionistic style in which it was rendered, giving only the suggestion of horses, but in colors that were electric. *Yes,* he thought. *I really have to have this one, and it isn't too much more than the cost of that sweater. The sweater will stay in the closet, but this, this I'll hang in my office to inspire me.*

He was about to buy it, when he stopped and rather impulsively said, "I, um, I would like my fiancée to see it. She's just down the street. I'll be back in a few minutes." Barry left the store and couldn't believe what he had said. *Fiancée? Now where did that come from?* Tildy wasn't his fiancée. What will he say if the clerk mentions it? He certainly wanted Tildy's stamp of approval on the painting, but he didn't need to consult with her. After all, for the past twenty years, he didn't have to ask anyone about anything he did. *Is this where my feelings have taken me?*

Barry decided to reenter the store. He told the clerk that he wanted the painting, and that his fiancée appeared to be tied up looking at clothing. The clerk asked him if he could wait to have it until the exhibition ended next week. Barry told the clerk that he was from out of town and that he was leaving in the morning. The clerk offered to ship it to him at no cost, if he would leave it.

"A small deposit will hold it." But not wanting to lose the sale, he said, "Well, it's small, I guess we could rearrange the wall if you really want to take it with you."

Barry replied, "If you could, I would really love to take it. It's less complicated."

The clerk hurried to the back and found some packing materials. He deftly wrapped the painting, and cautioned Barry to be careful while traveling with it. Barry glanced at his watch. Tildy wouldn't be back for about fifteen more minutes, so he relaxed. He thanked the salesman and walked out into the bright afternoon sunlight.

Barry walked by a mineral shop. He was beginning to feel a little guilty about not waiting to show Tildy the painting. *Why did I go back and buy it? I guess commitment is still a problem. Well, no harm done. She'll see it back in my office when I hang it. Hmm, I wonder when she'll ever come to my office.*

While he was admiring a pen set on a red quartz base, he felt a tap on his shoulder. Tildy was behind him and smiling the happiest smile he had seen in a long time.

"What do you have there?" she asked.

Barry couldn't believe how beautiful she looked with the sunlight shining on her hair. All he could see were shining strands of color, mostly copper and gold, where the sun reflected the strongest.

"I should have gone with you," he said. "I bought a painting."

"A painting?"

"Horses."

"A painting of horses?"

Barry nodded his head, sheepishly. "I couldn't resist it. I'm going to put it in my office."

"It's a good thing I didn't leave you alone, longer. You might have bought a whole farm," she laughed.

"Now, quick, let's go have a cup of coffee, I have an earful for you." Barry realized that the smile was not just for him. She had good news.

Barry and Tildy found a little café on a side street and entered. They each ordered a latté. When the waitress left, Barry looked at Tildy and said, "Okay, shoot."

"Well, she's mad as hell at the guy. He ditched her for a woman half his age and ran off with the other woman to New York. I guess that's when he went into the insurance business. It seems the other woman isn't in the picture anymore. He's moved to somewhere in the Caribbean, has been out of the country for about two years, and has taken on a new identity. She doesn't know what it is. She has information that he comes back, clandestinely, once in a while. She says he turned out to be a real crook, not the guy she thought she married. She couldn't believe it the first time he got in trouble and got himself disbarred. She stuck by him, but couldn't stand the things he was getting into. Finally, when he began doing cocaine, she left him."

"Cocaine? How does that help us?"

"Oh, that's just an aside. It seems he has an old, sick mother in New Jersey. Richmond County, to be exact. Mrs. Petersen and the lovely Mr. used to live there when they were young. Near his mother. She keeps in touch with the old lady, who still has her marbles, but is not in good physical condition. She's ninety three years old."

"So, this is all interesting, but that's not why you're smiling. I know you; you have something good for us, right?"

"Okay, you win, there's a lot more. Old Mrs. Petersen owns a large piece of property in Richmond; an old horse farm. By the way, it's interesting you should buy a painting of horses, while I was getting news of the horse farm."

"Yeah, okay, but so what? She has a horse farm. How much could a horse farm bring, if it was sold?"

"What would you say if I told you that young Petersen is an only child?"

"Okay, so he'll get a horse farm, and I can send my young painter there to paint some more horses."

"Don't be so quick. I was saving the best for last. The farm is located at the intersection of two major roads. She's had an offer of five million for the land for a new shopping center."

"An offer?"

"Mrs. Petersen, the younger, still has friends in Richmond. They told her that her mother-in-law, Mrs. Petersen, doesn't want to sell and plans to leave it to her son."

"Wow! Five million! We have to get home, Tildy, and act on this. My God! Five million. That should be enough to settle Dan's case. I couldn't be happier if I won the lottery. This could make the difference. Now, you know that you have to keep silent on this."

"Of course; I'm not stupid."

"Oh, Tildy, of course you're not stupid. I wasn't thinking. Wow! I'm just so excited with this news. You said the old lady's health is bad?"

"Yes. She's had a stroke, and the doctors say another one might kill her. It seems she has other ailments too. Mrs. Petersen thinks it's just a question of time."

"Did she say if the old woman was the sole owner of the property?"

"Yes. Says the woman doesn't trust her son but since there are no grandchildren and she's been a widow forever, Mrs. Petersen, the daughter-in-law, says it—undoubtedly—will go to her ex-husband. She was very sure of that. But she also said she had no regrets. The guy is a bum from the word go and she doesn't want any part of him, or his money.

"When I pressed her, she said she thought the old lady might leave her a little something, but nothing too big. She calls her regularly but doesn't talk about anything but her health. She said if she's left anything it would be great, but she's not counting on it. She likes her work and is happy with her little store and says she has made a whole new life. She told me she doesn't need anything more. I really liked her."

"Well done, Tildy."

"Is that all you bought?"

"Yes. Oh, I did see a nice sweater, but it was really pricey and I decided I didn't need it."

"Oh, we have time. Let's go look at it."

"Okay."

Their flight home had been booked for early Monday. Barry decided that it would be good to celebrate the first good news that they had had. He made a reservation at one of Ann Arbor's finest restaurants and he and Tildy went out for a very special meal. He ordered champagne, and when they had had a couple of drinks, Barry was glad that they left the car at the hotel and had taken a taxi.

He couldn't take his eyes off Tildy. She was wearing a simple light green dress that was cut elegantly. In the soft candlelight, her eyes had turned a soft green, matching the dress exactly. Her tawny skin became a mellow cream color in the glow of the candle, which only served to set off her copper hair.

*I can't believe I have this girl. She's beautiful, and smart. What more could I ask for? I never get tired of her company. She has a great sense of humor, and a presence which seems to dominate any room she's in. I know I'm in love with her, but who knows how long it will last. I don't even know if that's the test. Could I live without her in my life? I don't think so.*

*Not now, after knowing how happy I am with her. Is that the test? I never thought that I could feel so strongly about someone. I saw other men fall like this, but I was always skeptical. They all seemed so sappy to me. Now I'm the one who's sappy. I don't even know when it happened. It was just so easy.*

"You seem far away," Tildy said, as she took his hand across the table.

"Tildy, I'm never far away from you, even when I'm not with you. I always have you on my mind. Does that seem foolish?"

"Not foolish."

"If not foolish, then what?"

"I don't know, but I always sense that there's a kind or war going on inside of you."

"War?" But he was surprised at how perceptive she was.

"Yes. Like you can't decide what to do about your feelings for me."

*Jesus, she's right on target.*

"So, what should I do about you?"

"Love me. Don't question it too much. Let it happen. I just want you to know that I'm not going to pressure you into anything. I'm enjoying the moment, moment by moment. You're making it far more complicated than it is."

"Maybe that's because I'm forty two, and you're only thirty. I can't afford to make too many mistakes."

"You won't. I won't let you. I may be thirty, but I've already made my share of mistakes."

"What mistakes?"

"I was married, once."

"Married? You never told me. Why did you keep it a secret?"

"I didn't think it was relevant to our relationship."

"Not relevant? How could you think it wasn't relevant? I want to know everything about you—how it felt when you fell and skinned your knee, how you felt the first time you went to the dentist. You know—everything. Tildy there shouldn't be any secrets."

"There aren't any secrets. At least, not about anything important, I mean. We were only married for six months. I knew, immediately, it was a mistake. He was the nicest guy in the world, but I never loved him."

"Then why in heaven did you marry him?"

"I was alone. Mother died when I was fifteen, and three years after that Daddy died. I couldn't believe it. They were both so young. I was alone. Of course, Grandfather was still going strong, and he was a big influence on my life, but he was an old man. Barry, believe me when I say I didn't know what love was until I met you, but I don't want to make a mistake either. This has been going very fast. I would almost say too fast, and that's why we're both so scared, but darling, I do think it's the real thing, or I wouldn't have invested so much of myself in it so soon. Let's both give it a chance. If it's right, all the doubts will go away by themselves. If it's wrong, we'll know it sooner or later. I think we're both being a little self-protective."

Barry just looked at her. *Yes, she was entirely correct. She had analyzed their situation as if it were a case she was working on, and she had hit the nail on the head. Of course, they were both scared. That's what it was. But she never said she was married before. I wonder why she didn't tell me.* They had a wonderful dinner, but neither had his mind on the meal. They had been very candid with one another and this had somehow heightened their intimacy. Barry yearned for her more than he ever had. Neither one had eaten much, but they managed to kill the bottle of champagne. The waiter came over and asked if they wanted dessert. Barry looked at Tildy. Tildy shook her head. *Good.* He didn't want anything but Tildy. They left the restaurant, and Barry realized Tildy was a little tipsy.

He was feeling especially good. *What a great day*, he thought. *Can it ever get better than this?* He hailed a cab and they went straight back to the hotel. When they got to the room, Barry got the ice bucket and left to get some ice. He had thought to bring a bottle of vodka, and had managed to buy a big bottle of tonic for the room. When Barry returned to the room, Tildy had already changed into a soft gray nightgown and was sitting in a chair, waiting for him.

*Just when I think I can't love her any more, she becomes even more desirable than the last time. Is this an elevator that only goes one way? Always escalating? Better every time? Oh God how much I love this woman.* He slowly poured them both a drink. Barry sat in the other chair and sipped his drink. He just wanted to look at her. It was going to be a long and beautiful night.

Tildy took the drink and looked at him intently. Yes, she did mean every word. She had never loved any man like this. He was so handsome, so tender. He was such a man and yet, such a boy. He loved her, of that she was very sure. She meant it when she said she wouldn't pressure him. *It's too fast. Maybe real love is always too fast. How would I know? I've never had it before.* She smiled; he asked her why.

She said, "I think you got me drunk."

He answered, "I certainly hope so."

They both laughed, drained their glasses quickly. Tildy got up and sat in Barry's lap. They kissed, slowly and tenderly. They kissed again but this time with more urgency. Barry lifted her to her feet, and then they kissed again, this time with complete abandon. He gently pushed her onto the bed and fell down beside her. She undid his shirt as he pulled down his zipper.

They made love, as they never had before, slowly finding each other, slowly exploring each other's body and finding each other's soul. They made love far into the night. Barry was glad that he wasn't that young anymore. He had been able to keep it going until Tildy came several times. When she fell asleep, satisfied and completely exhausted, he cradled her in his arms long afterward, praying that the Gods would not abandon him. He wanted this to last forever. Finally, sleep came and he fell asleep with Tildy still in his arms. His Goddess, his little girl. Funny how she could be both.

They awoke late and had a leisurely brunch. Having accomplished all they set out to do, they had a whole day free. They decided to ride around the streets of Ann Arbor and tour the University. The weather was quite warm for October. They parked the car and strolled around the campus. Afterward, they stopped at a little café and had a light supper. Tildy noticed a movie theater and they decided to take in a movie and get to bed early. They had a 7:30 flight the next morning.

On Monday, they rose early; it was still dark. They left without breakfast. They decided breakfast on the plane would be sufficient. Barry always flew first class, and while the food would not be excellent, it would suffice. Neither said much. They boarded the plane without incident and stowed the baggage in the overhead compartment. Barry was careful with his painting, laying it gently on top of his luggage.

They had their breakfast in silence. Both were still overcome with the emotion of the night before. Each had a lot to think about. They were on the threshold and didn't know what the next step would be. Barry looked over at her when the trays were cleared away and, acting on sheer impulse said, "Tildy, move in with me."

Tildy looked back lovingly, with tears in her eyes, and said, "No way."

Barry just stared at her. He couldn't believe what she was saying.

"No way?"

"You heard me."

"But why? I thought you would be pleased."

"I am pleased that you asked. It's just too soon."

"Too soon? After last night, I know it's not too soon. I love you Tildy, and I want to spend the rest of my life with you, but this would be just a first step."

He thought she wanted marriage and that asking her to move in was an insult. *Gee, an old-fashioned girl, I would never have believed this,* he thought.

"I'm not joking, Barry. I'm a real grump until I have my morning coffee."

"So I'll get up early and bring you your coffee in bed."

"And I squeeze the toothpaste tube from the top."

"Oh, then it probably won't work. Okay what else?" He laughed.

"And sometimes I snore"

"I already know that."

"You do?"

"Yep, last night, you almost roused the hotel detective, you snored so loud."

"Well you do, too."

"So that's not an issue."

"Do you promise you'll put the toilet seat down?"

"Yes, I swear on my life."

"Well, sometimes I like to gab with my friends on the phone."

"Great, do it when I watch football."

"Yes, that would work."

"But what are we going to do about the toothpaste? That could be a deal breaker."

"We'll each have our own tube, how's that?"

"Solves that problem. So, what do you say?"

"Promise you'll tell me if I get on your nerves? You know I've been living alone for a long time. I'm not sure I can do this. I do love to be in control."

"Ah yes, I figured that would be a problem. Well, you'll just have to let me be in control. I want to baby you and take care of you and do everything for you. You just can't be in control."

"I never had anyone say that to me before. Promise me, you'll take care of me. I look tough, but I'm really very fragile."

"Is that a yes?"

"Are you sure?"

"You know me well enough by now. You know that I hesitate, that I'm careful, that I think everything through a dozen times, but Tildy, I love you and I don't want to be without you. Not for a moment."

"Yes; then it's yes. I've been hoping you would ask and that you would be sure. Yes, yes, of course, yes." He took her in his arms and kissed her softly, ignoring all the glances and smiles of the people around them. He was in love and he didn't care who knew it.

## Chapter Nineteen

Life had been going very well for Dave for the last six months. He was now getting very comfortable in his new life as front man for his employers. He enjoyed his relationship with Marianne. He was making more money than he had ever made in his life, with not too much effort and not that much risk. He had been making regular deposits into his accounts in Nevis and he and Marianne had settled into the easy life. Did he love Marianne? No, of course not. He just enjoyed the easy life she provided and this was enough for him. She never asked about marriage, never seemed to care. He provided everything she needed, and she still did some real estate, she said to keep her hand in. They were both happy.

Dave began to feel that it was all too easy. He had brought something valuable to the equation with his new employers. He was smart and canny. Soon, he knew more about the many ways to launder money than they did, and he was proving himself invaluable to them. He had been given larger and larger sums to sanitize as time went on and as he gained their trust. He worried that something might happen to change it all.

Dave was in touch with his old boyhood friend, Ron Dykstra. Ron was now president of the Old Farmer's Bank in Benson, near his hometown of Vreeland Corners. Besides his mother, Ron was the only person stateside with whom he kept in contact. Ron knew that he had had trouble with the authorities and that it wasn't easy for Dave to return to Richmond County.

Ron had come to him with a deal. Some developers wanted to buy Dave's mother's horse farm and turn it into a shopping center. He had been very instrumental in putting a deal together, including the financing. The Farmer's Bank that Dave remembered as a boy had grown with the development of Richmond County and now had ten branches, all over North Jersey.

Ron, whose father founded the bank, had become a very important man. He had been approached by the developers to contact the owner of the Petersen farm with an offer, on the recommendation of one of the town planners. Ron said he was interested in financing the project, which would be a big one for the bank to handle, but very profitable, if he could make the sale happen and the developers agreed. In this growing county, there were a lot of people who were connected, and their paths were quite interwoven. The planner knew the developers and told them just whom to contact.

Ron had tried to talk to Mildred Petersen, Dave's mother, but she was not inclined to sell. He knew that Dave was his mother's only heir, so when Mildred finally went into the nursing home, he found out from old Mr. Donahue, the caretaker, how to contact Dave. It seems that Dave was using a mail forwarding service in Toronto to receive mail, and this address only was given to his mother and to Jim Donahue. In the event of an emergency, this service could also reach him by phone.

This land deal had not been an easy one to put together, so Ron just bided his time, trying to keep the developers on the hook until his old friend, Davey, came into his inheritance. He knew that Davey was interested in selling. Davey had told him so, but his hands were tied until Mildred died. Well, it wouldn't be long now, she had had several strokes, but the old lady seemed to always hang on, as if deliberately preventing them all from participating and benefiting from this transaction. Patience, patience, he often cautioned. After a few letters back and forth, Ron became Davey's pipeline to what was happening in the county.

Dave called his mother on occasion, but the last stroke had so debilitated her that she could only speak with great difficulty and often unintelligibly. For this reason, he had stopped calling her. He wished he could go and visit with her, if only to stay in her good graces, but the risk was too great. He figured that all of his business could be done long distance—if necessary—and then a great idea occurred to him.

His employers had large sums of money that were difficult to move out of the States. Once freed from the prying eyes of the government, he could pass it through several corporate ownerships he had set up, therefore decontaminating it to allow its reuse in the drug business. The banks had to report any transaction over ten thousand dollars to the government, necessitating too many transfers of smaller amounts. His employers had been somewhat hamstrung by the increasing unwillingness of small check cashing operations to convert the cash for them. The government was starting to crack down on these operations.

Old Ron might be of some use in this matter. He figured this would be a real coup, if he could get the banker involved in handling larger sums for him. It was too delicate a matter to handle by phone or even email. Ron had indicated a willingness to talk to him, when he mentioned some "real" dollars might be a possibility. Ron always was a greedy son of a bitch. Davey smiled.

He had been thinking that when his mother died, he would come in for the funeral, using his alter ego, Stephen Graham. He found out through sources that the Feds were no longer that hot on his trail anyway, having diverted their interest to the laundering of drug money. They had no time to devote to a small time operation, such as his was. Wouldn't the FBI have been surprised if they knew that now that they had stopped looking for him, he was engaged in money laundering? *Ironic,* he thought and laughed to himself. How very convenient that he was no longer a high priority. If he ever thought that he was compromised in some way, though, he could easily get a passport with still another identity. Lindy could do that in a heartbeat. But he really didn't think it necessary. The law would probably not be watching his mother, since he was no longer of interest to the authorities. After all, he had always been "small potatoes" to them. And getting Farmer's Bank set up would be a real coup for his employers. They could funnel a great deal of money through the bank, and Ron would welcome the chance. Ron, as he, had always been a real risk taker.

Barry dropped Tildy at home. Before going home, he stopped at the hospital to see Dan. Dan's room was filled with flowers from well-wishers. Dan grinned when Barry walked in the door.

"I missed you," said Dan. "Why the mysterious quick trip?"

"I had to go to Michigan on business."

Dan grinned again, and asked, "Did you go alone?"

Barry grinned back and said, "Not exactly."

"I noticed something different about you. Anything you want to tell me?"

"Well," Barry started cautiously. "Remember that girl I told you about?"

Dan nodded, expectantly.

"Well, things are getting sort of serious."

"What do you mean, sort of?" demanded Dan.

"Well, very serious, then. Tildy's going to move in with me."

"I guess it's 'sort of' serious," laughed Dan. "You didn't even ask how I feel."

"Sorry about that. How do you feel?"

"The doctor says there was no permanent damage to the heart, and if I follow orders and take care of myself, I could live into a ripe old age."

"Wow, that is great news. I'm so relieved. Uh, anything new with Alex?" he asked, cautiously.

"Yes, she's agreed to wait until things are more settled and to try to work things out. I told her you said that there might be a way out."

Barry had an immediate unkind thought. *Sure, if this thing could be fixed, then Alex could go on being Mrs. Doctor, as before, so why act precipitously?*

But his reply to his brother was, "That's great, Dan."

He couldn't help but think that his brother would have been better off if the bitch had walked, but he would never let his brother know his true feelings on that score.

"So, when am I going to meet this clever creature who was able to hook my brother, the elusive Barry Chandron?"

"Hey, I was just waiting for *Wonder Woman* to come along, and she has, Dan," Barry said quite seriously. His brother looked at him, approvingly. This was the real thing, finally. He had never heard Barry talk like this before.

"When can I bring her over?"

"As soon as possible. Unless you don't want her to see your broken down older brother."

Barry looked at his brother carefully. Actually, Dan was looking better. He didn't know if the good news about his condition and the lifting of stress about a possible divorce had rejuvenated him, or if he was really past the acute phase of the attack.

"Actually, Dan, you look so good, I'm not sure if I want to bring her around. You're liable to steal her away."

Dan smiled, but it was then that Barry saw the fatigue in his eyes. His heart may not have been damaged, but he definitely did look older. Barry wondered if it had been coming slowly—this aging—and if he wasn't just more conscious now because he was scrutinizing his brother. After all, Dan was ten years older than he was and Barry himself wasn't getting any younger either. No, stress can take years off your life and he guessed his brother had had more than his share the past few weeks.

"I'm very anxious to meet this Tildy, when can you bring her?"

"Tonight, okay?"

"Great!" With that, Alex came into the room. Barry noticed that his brother visibly brightened when she came in and pecked him on the cheek. Barry dutifully offered his cheek, when Alex came over to him and kissed him. So things were all back in place. Now, all that remained was for him to pull the rabbit out of the hat. Better not let Dan know the progress he made. After all, all he had so far was a good lead, nothing more definite. Why should I let him get his hopes up?

Barry looked at his watch. It was noon.

"Dan, I haven't been to the office, yet. I came straight here from the airport. I'd better go."

"Okay, will I see you tonight?"

"I'll try."

Barry was anxious to get to the office and make some phone calls. He left it to Dan to tell Alex about Tildy. He really didn't want to have to go through that insincere hugging business again. He was glad that Dan waited until he left. Barry went directly home, showered, changed into a suit and went straight to the office. Things were definitely looking up.

Tildy unpacked her clothes. She undressed and got into the shower. She laughed when she caught herself singing, "I'm in love with a wonderful guy." She should have been having doubts—right about this time—but for reasons she couldn't explain, she was as sure of what she was doing as if she were accepting a check for winning the lottery. There was just nothing else to do. It was right. Somehow, she knew it was right the first time she met him. It was only a week ago, but it felt as if she had known him forever. Moreover, she did already know, even before she met him, that he was a well-respected member of the bar and that everyone, even Jason, who had had many trials with him, knew to be decent and honorable. If he was a friend of Grandfather's, she knew it was so. Grandfather had no patience for stupid people, nor for those who walked a little too close to the edge. For him to be Grandfather's friend and protégé, she knew that Barry was as straight as a die. Grandfather would have demanded no less.

Of course, there was another large problem. She couldn't continue in her job at Wright, Landwehr, and Cummings. She would be no great loss to them. There were dozens of grunts out there, just out of law school, eager to fill her job. She only got the job because of her name and some of Grandfather's old contacts she remembered and whom she had called upon. But now, she was "sleeping with the enemy." *Funny how your life can turn on a dime,* she mused. Last week she was wondering how to meet him for a job, she told herself. This made her laugh. She really did want to work for Barry, but the first time she spoke with him, she knew that he interested her in other ways; but it had moved very fast. She never would have believed that it could happen this way. Now she wondered how much to tell Jason, when she should tell him and what she would do once she was finished at Wright, Landwehr, and Cummings.

She thought, the big question is what Barry will do, once she's unemployed. Oh well, she could help him with his brother's case. There's always that. Actually, she liked playing detective, but that's not what she went to law school for. She knew that Barry had contacts in the prosecutor's office and thought that maybe he could set something up. Well, she wasn't worried, in any case. Barry and she would figure something out.

She had told Jason she wouldn't be in until tomorrow. She decided to take the rest of the day off. This was not like the ambitious Tilden Jennings, but she was so happy. Why spoil it with mundane matters, like working? Oh yes, there was one thing she had to do. She fished in her purse for the card she had picked up in the men's store in Ann Arbor while Barry was looking at a shirt. She called the store and ordered the cashmere sweater that Barry admired. Tildy thought, *he's been so good to me. Surely, I can do this.*

Barry sat down at his desk. Eleanor filled him in on the phone messages that had come in while he was gone. For the most part, Ray had handled all of them and he had yet to speak with Ray. There was a call from Sandy Bishop. He called Sandy back before sending for Ray. He knew where his priorities were.

"Hi, Sandy, Barry Chandron, here. What's happening?"

"Oh, hello Barry. Just get back?"

"Yes." Barry wondered what, if anything, Sandy knew.

"Vacation?"

Barry heaved a sigh of relief. He wasn't sure what he was going to do with the information he received, but he sure as hell didn't want any partners in it, at least, not for the time being. He needed some space and didn't want anyone breathing down his neck.

"Just had some family business, you know. Out of town wedding."

"Those can be a pain in the butt."

"Well, you gotta do what you gotta do."

"Yeah, well, just wanted to tell you there's good news and bad news."

Now, Barry was interested. "Okay, what've you got?"

"We found our guy. That's the good news."

"And the bad news?"

"He's in Nevis/St. Kitts."

"How is that bad?"

"We can't touch him."

"Why not?" But Barry already knew the answer.

"He's down there living the life and keeping his money company. No extradition. It's a great place to hide money. We can't get our hands on it, no way. Neither can the Feds. I think they're going to drop the case."

"What do you mean, drop the case?"

"Well, they'll keep it open, but it's a dead end for them. They have bigger fish to fry, mostly drug cases. He was always small potatoes to them, and they just don't have the resources. Of course, if he returns to the States, then they might nab him, but they won't actively try to lure him back. It's a low priority. You know, as good as dead."

"At least they won't be getting in your face." There was dead silence on the other end. "Sandy? You still there?"

"Yeah, sure they won't get in our face, but we don't have anything either. I'm sorry, but it's going on a back burner here too. We just don't have the money or the personnel to pursue it too actively either, especially now. We'll probably pull the plug. Not definite yet, and don't repeat it, but, well, Jake said to tell you everything, and I thought you would like to know. I'm very sorry. Bastards like him shouldn't get away with defrauding innocent people, but it happens every day."

"Sandy, thanks anyway for keeping me in the loop. I owe you one, okay?"

"Anyway, we tried. Thought we had something, but this guy's smart. If you need anything else, just holler."

"Yeah, thanks. Bye."

"Bye."

Barry had a lot to think about, but first, he had to see Ray and find out what was happening in his practice. After all, Dan was not his only client.

He rang for Eleanor and told her to send Ray in. Two minutes later, Ray arrived with a stack of files. They spent the rest of the morning going over cases, and talking about strategy. Barry looked at his watch. Ten to twelve. It was time for his lunch, but more important, it was time for a walk. He had a lot to think about, and Tildy, for the first time, was not on his list of worries. He knew that the answer to Dan's problems lay somewhere in the information that Tildy had gotten from the good Mrs. Petersen, but where, how?

He still had to develop a strategy. He thought of getting Ray involved, but then decided that Ray was pretty much handling everything else. No, this wasn't the time. There was, however, a young kid in the office who knew something about debtor creditor law. He had come to Barry from a firm which specialized in this field. Barry had met him through another colleague and the friend told him that he was more interested in personal injury. It just so happened that his timing was good. Barry was looking for someone. Barry hadn't come in contact with that stuff since he took the bar exam twenty years ago. He studied it for the bar and then, like most personal injury litigators, he promptly forgot it. No need to clutter up your mind with something you'll never use. Yes, he would sit down with the new kid—Jeff? Jim? John? No problem, he would ask Eleanor. Seemed like a good kid, but damn it, he couldn't remember his name. *I must be losing my mind,* he thought. Well, he's new. Whatever was happening with Tildy, he knew it would just happen. She would handle it. What a girl! He knew he was free, finally, to concentrate on strategy.

Barry left the office. It occurred to him that he hadn't called Tildy, but there was time this afternoon. She had said she wouldn't go into the office today, so he could call her later. It was also a foregone conclusion that they would have dinner together, so he could wait. With this settled in his mind, he ran to a local luncheonette and had a tuna sandwich. Funny, why did this tuna taste so good today? He asked the owner if they had a new recipe? The owner seemed bewildered and shook his head.

"Same old, same old," he said, looking at Barry in a peculiar way.

Barry knew the guy was thinking, this guy's nuts. Barry looked at the people in the restaurant. These were the same people he saw, day in and day out in the courthouse. Most he recognized on sight, but realized he didn't know anyone's name. He knew that most of them knew who he was, but didn't know him well enough to do more than just nod. They were the oil that kept the courthouse humming; the clerks, the sheriff's officers, the secretaries. Barry had found this a great place to stop in for a quick bite when he was in trial and didn't have to take his client to lunch. A quick lunch here left him time for his strategy-planning walk, a habit he had gotten used to when he was clerking for Tildy's grandfather.

The old man would pose a new wrinkle to him on a case he was researching, and Barry liked to ponder the various outcomes, by playing the "what if" game—what if I do this, what if I do that. This immediately brought Tildy back to his mind but, with his usual discipline, he forced her and everything else from his mind. He was determined to reserve today for developing a plan on how to approach the problems in Dan's case. The information about the horse farm was good, but how to use it to keep the largest part of the pie for Dan, and yet not mislead the state officials or the Feds? He didn't really care about the Feds, but Jake had been fair with him and he hoped that he wouldn't have to keep him in the dark too long. He had some ideas, but they needed to be developed.

Barry ate quickly and paid the bill before he got the check. He needed time. He left the restaurant, and prodigiously avoiding the courthouse, where he was likely to meet someone who wanted to chat, he turned the corner and started his walk. He had a well-worn path through the residential side streets surrounding the courthouse, where he did his best thinking. He had taken this route during his most important cases and had been doing so for twenty years. Oh, the changes he would have seen had he been looking all these years, but it was his route for the greatest concentration. Folks who lived in these houses would be at work and the kids would be in school at this time of day.

It was a beautiful day and Barry knew that he would come up with something. He had to. It was critical. He figured that he had to rely on the information. There was this old woman, not in good health. For all he knew the son probably already had a power of attorney over his mother's affairs. If this were so, he either had an agent, or sneaked back into the country to see to her needs. *Or,* he thought, *maybe it was all done by mail. Well, let's hope that's not the case.* He thought that Tildy said she had extracted a promise from Petersen's wife to call her if anything significant happened. Of course, Tildy would do that, but he'd better check with her tonight.

*Okay, what if Mama dies? Before the sale of the property? After the sale of the property? Okay, if she dies before the sale, Petersen stands in her shoes, and the deal goes through. Easy enough. After the sale. Well, if he has a power of attorney, he gets the money, he takes it to Nevis/ St. Kitts. Finito!*

*Wonder who the attorney is who's handling the purchase. He won't tell me anything, except maybe the date of closing, an important date. Can't put a lien on the funds without a judgment. Better start suit right away.*

*Okay, missing defendant, no problem. Service? Well that's another matter. Unless the property is transferred to Petersen prior to the sale, can't start an action against the property. How to get a judgment? Do I have to have him in the country? No, I could do it by publication. How would that affect the judgment, if he doesn't show. Would that alert him to his tenuous hold on the dough? Wow, this is more complicated than I thought.*

*Okay, what if mother dies and he comes in to the funeral. I could get him then. Don't like to serve a man at his mother's funeral, but he's such a sleaze and my brother almost died because of him. Can't let that bother me. How could I find out exactly when mother dies? Don't want to have*

*Petersen get the money and wire it to Nevis. Wait a minute. Before the transfer, the purchaser wants to be sure he has the right zoning. Need to see if the land is zoned for farming or commercial.*

*I also need to find out if an application has been made, by whom, and who the lawyer is. But they can't make an application if Mama still owns the land. Unless the whole area's been rezoned. Okay, that's my first order of business. I guess I'll have to go up to the courthouse in Benson, and find out what the status is. I should probably take Tildy with me, but she has a job. When to go? Okay, okay, I have a plan.*

*Now what's the next step? Right! While I'm there, Tildy and I get married.* Barry laughed at himself. Right in the middle of a knotty problem he was fantasizing about Tildy. He broke out in a grin, but got right back to the job.

*Find the purchaser's lawyer. Approach him or not? What else can I do? Okay, have to get to the purchaser's lawyer. No confidentiality there, and they have no obligation to tip my hand. The first thing we would want to do is to sell it, if we get a judgment, and of course, they're the likely buyers. That's good.*

*Okay, we'll start suit against him and Adelphia Security for coverage, serve him by publication. If the bastard appears, so much the better, but he won't. I'll publish in the local papers, someone will send it to him, probably his lawyer. What will that do? Will that suggest that we know about the impending windfall? Not necessarily, and if so, so what? A guy who comes into a doctor's office and sells him phony insurance has to be cocky. Even if he suspects, he'll figure he'll beat it. Maybe. Don't underestimate this guy. He's on the beach with Dan's money while Dan's in the hospital. And, if we get a judgment before Mom dies, he'll figure out some way to protect it.*

*Okay. We move quickly for the information. Take a reading when we know more and then we can decide. Jumping the gun right now is the worst thing we can do. Got to get to Benson and check the status of the land.*

Barry now had the problems firmly in mind. He found himself walking toward the office, even before he realized it. He had accomplished something, but Barry knew it wasn't that much.

Tildy wondered how busy Barry would be today. She didn't know whether to make dinner, or if they would go out. She knew that he was planning to see Dan first thing and then on to the office. She wanted desperately to call him, but she hated to interrupt him. She picked up a book she was reading and had just settled back in a chair when the phone rang. It was Barry.

"Hello?"

"Hi, sweetheart."

"Hi, I was just wondering if I should call you?"

"You can call me anytime."

"Well, I thought you might be busy and I didn't want to interrupt you."

"Actually, Ray did a good job of fending off clients or dealing with them. What are you doing?"

"I went back to sleep this morning after my coffee. Then I got up and had lunch. Have you had your lunch yet?"

"Yes, I just grabbed a bite at Joey's and then I went for a walk. Just got back."

"Did you see Dan?"

"Yes, he's doing much better. They've moved him out of intensive care, but he looks—well—much older."

"He's been through a lot. He'll probably look better once he gets home."

"I guess. Oh, Tildy, I told him about us. He wants to meet you."

"What did he say?"

"He said you must be someone really special if you've hit me this hard."

"Really?"

"Well, I never told him about anyone else, all these years."

"Wow, when do I get to meet him?"

"How about four o'clock? We'll go to the hospital, then we'll grab some dinner out."

"Are you going to stay here tonight?"

"What a hussy you've become," he said laughing.

"I just wanted to know how much to straighten up."

"Don't worry about that. I already know you have a beautiful home. We'll probably stay at your place, but I have to stop home to get some more clothes. I'll pick you up at 4:00."

"Sounds like a plan."

"And Tildy?"

"Yes?"

"I love you very much."

"I already knew that. I love you, too." Tildy hung up the phone and just sat there for a few minutes. She wished, for the first time in a long time, that she had a mother with whom she could share this moment. A mother, or a sister, or even a brother. *Dan and his brother are so close. How I've been cheated,* she thought. Poor Barry, he doesn't know he's going to have to be mother, father, brother, confidante, all wrapped up in one. I've never been needy, but now, it would be so great to even have a best friend.

She realized that she had literally put an end to most of her friendships when she made the decision to go to law school. Too little time to do the social niceties required. True she had made a few acquaintances, there, but no one really that she could call a real friend, a confidante. She did keep up with them and called them occasionally, but that was all. She decided to abandon these thoughts; she didn't want to break the euphoric feelings she had earlier and these thoughts were a downer. She heaved a sigh and walked into the bedroom to make up the bed. She would read later.

By the time Barry finished talking to Ray, it was three o'clock. He told Ray to call him if he needed him. It was a little early, but Tildy was the kind of girl who wouldn't care if he found her just getting out of the shower, or whatever. He left the office and went to the garage. In a few minutes, he found himself driving toward Tildy's house.

He was happy that he was going to introduce her to Dan. He knew Dan would like her and, after all, Dan was the only family he had. Besides, Dan had been after him for years to settle down. He thought of all those shallow women Alex had tried to fix him up with. He prided himself on having enough insight to know they weren't for him. *Wonder how Tildy will get along with Alex. That should be interesting,* he mused.

When Barry arrived, Tildy was ready. She was dressed in a tailored soft pink dress with a dark green jacket. The pink set off her red hair and the green brought out the olive tint of her skin. She had spent most of the day reading and relaxing. She was happy that she was going to meet Dan, but just a little anxious. *What if he doesn't like me?* she thought. She laughed then, realizing that he would like her. Most men did. It was women she had to strain to get along with. They often resented her looks and now, her achievements. She had to bend over backwards not to appear to be too smart with most women she met. Boy, what a burden that was! On the other hand, if she were careful, she could win over most women, with a little more effort.

## Chapter Twenty

When they arrived at the hospital, Alex was already there; no doubt Dan had alerted her. Dan greeted Tildy warmly and, with a look toward Barry, which did not escape Tildy, he nodded his approval. Alex was equally warm, but her curiosity came through and Tildy knew she would have a little work to do to win over this woman.

"So Barry tells me you two just met last week. Is that right?" asked Dan.

"Yes, we met at the county bar dinner. I don't usually go to those dinners, but something compelled me to go."

Barry chimed in with, "Something compelled me to go, but it had to do with trying to find out some information. Little did I think I would meet this wonderful girl," he said, beaming at Tildy.

Alex asked, "Do you come from around here?"

Before Tildy could answer, Dan said, "Oh, didn't I tell you, Tildy is Judge Jennings' granddaughter." Alex shot him a puzzled look. "You know that big lawyer who Barry clerked for years ago, remember, when we were first married, and then he became a judge, and Barry went out on his own."

It suddenly registered. "Right, Judge Jennings. Yes, I remember. The Jennings were a very prominent family." Alex brightened at the thought of that one. "Didn't they belong to the West Wind Country Club?"

Tildy knew that her grandparents shunned country club life. Her grandmother was engaged in volunteer work for the hospital and her grandfather avoided conflicts of interest by not getting to know too many people socially. Nevertheless, Barry had coached her, and she was careful not to be too dismissive.

"No, I don't believe so. Grandmother was very shy, and well,

Grandfather was a total workaholic." Alex broke out in a smile indicating an immediate bonding with Tildy.

"So is Dan," she exclaimed. "I just can't get him to join in the activities at the club. Don't you think that a man his age has earned the right to break down and have a good time?"

Tildy responded with a warm smile. "I certainly think that Dan should reward himself with a good time after this scare. Maybe you two should go on a trip or something, when his doctor says it's okay."

Alex was conquered. Tildy knew that she had said all the right things. She also knew that Barry would be pleased. There were enough problems in the family without her contributing to them. On the other hand, if things were patched up between Dan and Alex, she would have to work very hard to be nice to Alex and to still keep her at a distance. Alex just wasn't her type. Nevertheless, she knew she would always care for Dan. For one thing, he had the same smile as Barry and, for the other, she could feel his sincerity. He's a very real person, like Barry. How nice that he and Barry are so close.

Fleetingly, she hoped that she and Barry would have at least two children. Yes, she wanted what she never had, a family. The greatest gift she could give her child was a brother or sister. How often did she wish she had a sibling to confide in?

Barry and Tildy left the hospital and went to dinner. They talked of many things, not the least of which was Barry's plans to go to Benson and nose around. Tildy said she wished she could go with him, but that she had to go into the office tomorrow.

"You do know that I'll have to resign," she said. "I'm working on a case right now that you're involved in."

Barry looked startled. "Oh Tildy, I didn't think. Of course, I often have cases with your firm. I was so full of Dan's problem, I just didn't think. When are you going to tell them?"

"If we're going to move in together, I guess I have to tell them tomorrow and, of course, I have to offer to leave right away, if they want."

"There's really no problem, you could come to work for me."

"Barry, that's so sweet, but that would produce problems in your own firm. I wouldn't want to be in a position in competition with some of your associates. It just wouldn't work."

"Yes, that's true. There could be real problems."

"Would you like to work for the prosecutor's office? I have lots of friends. Then there are others I could call. Don't worry, we'll find you something. Wait a minute. How about working with me on Dan's case, until it's resolved? You could help me and, when it's over we could find you the right spot. I really need you on it. I know I sound selfish, wanting you with me all the time, but that isn't the only reason. You've already been such a help."

Just then, Barry had a wonderful idea. "Say, do you know anything about debtor creditor law?"

"Sure, I had the course in law school, and I just had to review it for the bar. What do you need to know?"

"I'm going to put off my trip to Benson for another day. You go in tomorrow and do what you have to do. Then you go on my payroll, but only on a *per diem* basis. You won't become an associate of the firm, but you'll work on Dan's case, maybe help on others, if there's time. Then after it's over, we'll decide what to do about your career. How's that?"

"That sounds wonderful. I would really like to continue to be involved in the case. In fact, I was dreading having to go back to my firm for that very reason."

Barry suddenly frowned. "By the way, how much are you making? I'm not sure I can afford you."

Tildy told him.

" Hmmm, don't know," said Barry. "Would you come for double that amount?" He broke out in a big smile.

"No," said Tildy. "I would come for the same amount, even less if you asked me."

He said that if she insisted he would pay her the same amount. They both grinned. She agreed to tell Jason tomorrow. They decided that it would be better if they didn't tell anyone else, just yet. They thought that Jason would keep it secret. He just wasn't the kind of person to be that interested or to tell anyone else, either.

It was settled then. Tildy would stay with Jason if he needed her to finish up a few things, but if he wanted her to leave right away, that would be even better. They then talked about the logistics of moving in together. Tildy would have to sublet her apartment. Barry owned a condominium in a new complex, which was big enough to give Tildy a study of her own. Barry had a spare bedroom he wasn't using and this could be the perfect place for Tildy, and for her computer, and it had a nice corner in which to read. He was all excited at the prospect of helping her fix it up. She could move in next week and start working on furnishing it. She could bring her furniture, if she wanted. Barry had never gotten around to fixing his place up and she could feel free to throw out anything he had. He was sick of his "bachelor" furniture anyway. They both laughed.

He said, quite earnestly, that he wanted her to make a home for them. She said she would sleep at home tonight, because she had a big day tomorrow. She told Barry that he could sleep there tonight, if he promised to leave later tonight, or early in the morning. He opted for the morning. They left the restaurant and went home to Tildy's. Things were beginning to fall in place.

The next morning, Tildy was in the office bright and early. Jason was also in early, and she knocked on his door.

"Hi Tildy, how was the trip?"

"Fine."

"Good, what can I do for you?"

"Jason, I have something to tell you. I hope you understand that life sometimes changes very quickly."

Jason frowned as he looked at her expectantly. He could see she was nervous, but he didn't want to interrupt her. *This is important*, he thought.

"Jason, remember last week when you couldn't go to the bar dinner, and I went alone?"

"Yes?"

"Well, I met someone there."

"Uh oh, don't tell me someone offered you a job."

"Well, not exactly. It's more than that. I met Barry Chandron."

"Barry Chandron? Uh, you're going over to the enemy?" he said, smiling.

"Well, it's not exactly that. I'm not going to work for him. We—uh—something happened—of a personal nature. I guess what I'm trying to say is that I've fallen in love with him."

"What? Tildy, Barry's a great guy, and well, a charmer I guess, but you only just met him last week." Jason thought this might be too strong a remark. He softened it with, "How do you know it's not just a sudden infatuation? I mean it's very fast. He's been a bachelor for a long time."

"He says he loves me too. We're going to move in together."

"My God, this IS fast. Are you sure?"

"Yes, I'm very sure."

"Well, Barry's a good guy. Quite a catch, but then, so are you, Tildy."

Tildy smiled. Jason had never said anything so personal to her before, but she always sensed that he liked her and had no doubt he would wish her well. She appreciated this unexpected fatherly interest in her.

"I know this is sudden," she said. "I realize the implications, and I'm prepared to leave as early as it's convenient for you. On the other hand, I'll stay as long as you want. You've been very nice to me and I don't want to leave you in the lurch. I want to do the ethical thing."

"I would never doubt that. It's not that I think you would do anything wrong, but you'll have to leave right away, anyway. I mean you're working on one of his cases, aren't you?"

"Well, just last week, I started to look at one, but I didn't get very far. There was only that one. Nevertheless, I realize that there is the appearance of impropriety if I stay."

"There are others that can take over for you on most, if not all the cases you're working on. What are you going to do, professionally? Are you going to work in his firm?"

"I think that would be awkward, given the circumstances, but I will work with him on a special case involving his brother." Tildy then told him about the case.

Jason said, "Yes, I remember those bastards. We took them on, then got stuck for the fee. I'm glad Barry's going after them. I hope he gets something for his trouble. Then what, after that? What will you do?"

"Barry says he has lots of contacts and that he'll find me something."

"Well that's true enough. He came out of the prosecutor's office. And he knows just about everyone. He could get you placed with no trouble. Okay, Tildy. Bring me all your files after lunch. I'll go over each of them with you. If you want to leave right away, I think we can finish this afternoon. You're sure you know what you're doing?"

"Yes, I'm sure. Jason, I know I can count on you not to tell anyone, at least not right away. I think it would be better that way."

"Tildy, I don't need to tell anyone. You know you can count on that. And Tildy, when you do look for another job, call me. I'll be glad to tell anyone how much I valued your work. You're a very good lawyer and very ethical. You would be an asset to any firm."

"Thanks, Jason. I'll remember that."

## Chapter Twenty-One

Barry looked at his messages. There was one from Ted Jernow, a fellow plaintiff's lawyer, whom Barry respected very much. He picked up the phone and called Ted. After a brief moment, Ted got on the phone.

"Hello Barry."

"Hi Ted. How can I help you?"

"Barry, remember our conversation at the last bar meeting?"

"Yes?"

"I have the case, Barry."

"What case?"

"The case against your brother. The family came to see me, Friday. The boy's paralyzed."

"Oh. Well, if anyone had to have it, I'm glad it's you. You know there's a problem with his insurance."

"So you said. Any news on that front?"

"Well, I'm surprised you took the case without a deep pocket to go after."

"Barry, if it wasn't your brother, I might not have, but I know you. If it's possible to find another pocket, you will. I also know that if you find anything, you'll be on the up and up about it. I wouldn't want to go after your brother, personally, but we have a boy in trouble, and I'm going to do what I have to do. I was hoping you found the S.O.B. who sold him the policy."

"To tell the truth, I have a couple of leads, but not much yet. I'm working on it. By the way, Dan's had a heart attack and had to have bypass surgery. He's still in the hospital. If you have to start suit right away, I'll accept service on his behalf."

"I have time to start suit. Do you need some more time?"

"Yes, I may be on to something, but nothing definite."

"How long do you need?"

"Can you wait a week? I've given all my cases over to Ray Tobias, and I'm working exclusively on this. I'll probably know in a couple of days if we have anything or not."

"No problem, I hope you find what you're looking for. Oh, by the way, you're lucky to have Ray. I've seen him in court. He's a good kid, and very competent."

"Yes, I think he's a big asset. Just to have someone you can rely on. And Ted, I'm sorry there's a case but since it was inevitable, I'm awfully glad you have it."

"Thanks Barry. I'm not so sure that I'm happy about it. They seem to be good people."

"So's my brother. I'll call you as soon as I can."

"I know that, Barry. Thanks."

"Bye." Barry hung up the phone and pondered this new wrinkle. He was glad that Ted had the case, but he knew Ted was a good lawyer and would do anything he could to get a big award for this boy. He would be a relentless adversary, and would have no problem going after Dan's assets, if he had to. But one thing Barry knew. He would be truthful, no matter what. No sneaky tricks, especially with him, because they both knew each other a long time, and he would know that Barry would always level with him, no matter what. No need trying to transfer any of Dan's assets, now. It was too late for that.

Barry also thought that if and when Ted filed suit, he would be able to file a third party claim against Adelphia Security and Petersen, personally. This would put the case in court, and allow him to do something against the only asset he knew of, the farm in Richmond County. He just had to go to Benson, tomorrow, hopefully with Tildy.

Barry looked at his other messages and decided nothing needed his immediate attention. He would let Ray make the calls. They were mostly from clients wanting to know the status of their cases. Nothing was coming to trial in the next few weeks, which was a lucky break. What would he have done, if suddenly one of his cases were called for trial?

Eleanor buzzed him. "While you were on the phone, Miss Jennings called. Shall I get her back for you?"

"No thanks, I'll ring her back."

After a short wait, Tildy picked up her phone.

"Hi, did you talk to Jason?"

"Yes."

"And?"

"He's really a prince."

"What'd he say?"

"He said he would miss me. That I was a good lawyer and very ethical."

"I'm glad he appreciates you."

"He also said I could finish up today so I'm free to go with you tomorrow."

"What did he say when you told him about us?"

"He said you're a great guy, but that you've been a bachelor a long time. He thinks it's too fast. He also thinks you're a catch."

"He thinks I'm a catch because I took a million dollars from his carrier the last time out," he said, laughing. "Been a bachelor too long. He might be right. As far as too fast. Maybe he's right."

"Are you going to renege on me?"

"I mean for you, Tildy. Maybe it's too fast for you."

"I wasn't as sure that I wanted to be a lawyer, as I'm sure about you. Barry, I knew a lot about you before I met you. You know, all the good things. You've far exceeded my expectations. It's right for me, there isn't any question."

"Did you feel this way about your husband?"

Tildy was taken aback. This was the first time he had mentioned Jack.

"I can't talk about that now. I have to get back to work, so I can finish today. Barry, are you having second thoughts?"

"No sweetheart, absolutely not. Let's talk later, okay?"

Tildy went back to work. She really wasn't in the mood, so much was happening so quickly. It was fast. Too fast? Not really. But she had no time to dwell on it. At six o'clock she was just putting the finishing touches on the last memo. Jason came by her office. Tildy saw him coming down the hall.

"Oh Jason, what timing. I'm just finishing."

"Great Tildy." Jason scanned the memo, briefly. He looked up and said, "I'll miss you."

Tildy couldn't believe this was the same businesslike man she had been working for for the last six months.

"I've learned a lot from you in the short time that I've been here. Thanks for the opportunity."

"Tildy, I never knew your grandfather; they said he was a great judge and a great person. If he were here today, he would be proud of your accomplishments and your character. I've never gotten too close to my associates; they come and go. But I've had my eye on you. I had high hopes for you to work your way up in this firm. I was never much in favor of all these women coming out of law schools, but you've changed my mind. But I realize that you're young; you need to have a life. The law would be little comfort in your old age if you made a great success at the sacrifice of your personal life.

"I want you to know that I'm disappointed that you won't make your career with us. But, you've made the right decision. I've been happily married for fifteen years, and I couldn't imagine how my life would have been without Sarah. I wish you and Barry much happiness. I just want you to know, I'm not really a cold fish. Oh, I know what people say about me, but I'm your friend; if you ever need a favor, or someone to talk to, you can call me any time."

Tildy was so touched, she broke down in tears. "No one has ever said that to me. I lost both my parents when I was young. After Grandfather died, there was never anyone else that I could feel close to. I don't really have any other friends. I'm deeply touched by what you've just said. You've been very kind, in your own way. I've never thought of you as a cold fish, just professionally aloof. I understood that and understood that it was also because I'm a woman. If my leaving makes us better friends, then I'm happy for it. You're a lucky man to have it so all together. Sarah's a lucky woman. I only hope that I'll be able to say that in fifteen years."

"There's no reason that can't happen. You're both good people, and you deserve each other."

Surprisingly, Jason walked over to her and gave her a big hug. He left quickly. Tildy got her coat, took one last look around the office put her things from her desk in a bag she had brought for that purpose and turned out the light.

Wonder what people will say when they realize I'm gone. Jason will cover it all right. I have no doubt. Then without another backward look, she left the office. She was thinking, this is the first moment of the rest of my life. She smiled. She was very happy.

## Chapter Twenty-Two

Barry stayed the night. The next morning he and Tildy awoke early and set out for Richmond County. It was fun having her along, especially on this long ride to a distant county. His was the kind of practice where he had to appear quite often in distant courthouses. Usually he traveled alone, often rehearsing in his mind the way he wanted the proceedings to go, trying to anticipate what arguments his opponents would make and how the judge was likely to rule.

Today was different, though. He was not on his way to a trial, or a pretrial motion; he was on an investigative mission, something he seldom undertook. He usually sent one of his investigators or a young associate. In this case, however, it was something that he had to do himself. He wasn't sure what he would turn up; he wasn't sure what the next move would be and he needed to accomplish as much as possible in one day. The fact that Tildy was here with him only served to heighten his anticipation and hope of finding something worthwhile.

It was approximately half past nine when they got to the courthouse in Benson. Richmond, being a rural county, parking was available on the street near the courthouse. He and Tildy went directly to the office of the tax assessor. They sought out the alphabetical listing of property holders in the county.

After about ten minutes of looking, Bingo! They found one Mildred Petersen, owning twenty-five acres of land fronting county road 581. They asked the clerk to see the maps of the lots and blocks defining the property. When they looked at the map, they found that there was about one thousand feet of frontage on the county road, which was bisected by another county road. So far, it was very promising. While Barry was examining the map, Tildy got chatty with the clerk.

"Can you tell me about Vreeland Corners?" Tildy asked the clerk.

The clerk, a woman about fifty, looked at Tildy and responded to her warm smile. "Used to be pretty up there. I grew up in Vreeland Corners. It's a damn shame, though, what's going on there, now."

"What do you mean?"

"They're getting ready to ruin it, that's what."

"How come?"

"Now, they're planning to build a big shopping mall up there."

Tildy didn't want to appear too obvious. "Do they have the population to support a mall?"

"Have you been there, lately?"

"No. Not lately." Tildy had never been there in her life.

"Then you haven't seen what's going on. Townhouses springing up all over the place. Don't say you heard it here," she said, looking over her shoulder. "The whole area's up for grabs, and if you ask me a whole lot of money's changing hands. But if you repeat that, I'll deny I said it."

Tildy said, "My fiancé and I are looking to buy a piece of land. Maybe raise some horses. I love horses."

"It used to be so great there, when I was kid. We had a small farm and we boarded horses, racehorses. My father was a breeder. I grew up practically glued to a horse."

"What happened to your farm?"

"My folks got too old, my brother became a doctor, and well, it just became too much for me to run, alone. I'm not married. So I sold it about ten years ago."

"Oh, well you must have gotten a lot of money for it, anyway."

She laughed a bitter laugh.

"No, on the contrary, things were very depressed here ten years ago. I guess the price was fair for the time, but the people who bought it from me, turned around and sold it for five times what I got. Today it would be worth twice that again. I guess if there's anything in my life I suffer from, it's bad timing." Again, that bitter laugh.

Out of the corner of his eye, Barry could see that Tildy was getting on well with the clerk, so he pretended to study the map, even though he had gotten all the information he needed, long since.

"Well, you know that map my fiancé's studying? Actually, a friend of ours told us about that farm, and that's why we came here. Uh, do you know the owner? Mrs. Petersen."

"Sure I know her. I know most of the old timers up in Vreeland. Like I said, I grew up there. Yeah, poor Mrs. Petersen. I grew up with her son, David."

"Why poor?"

"Well, there she is lying up in Mason's. Gee, she must be up in her nineties. Only has the one son, and I doubt he ever comes to see her."

"Mason's?"

"Yeah, it's an old nursing home in Vreeland. Very clean, well run, you know, but still—"

"Oh, do you get to see her?"

"Actually I do. My Aunt Tess is up there, and I try to run up whenever I can. It's a small place and I often see Mrs. Petersen, but she's very frail. She had a stroke a while back and her face is all paralyzed. I think her son must have a power of attorney, or somethin' 'cause she really can't take care of her affairs, but she's still pretty alert. Problem is she doesn't speak too clearly and you have to listen carefully. She still remembers me, though and always asks how my brother, Phil, is doing."

"What's happened to her property?"

"They're renting it, I think."

"Oh, do you know if it's for sale?"

"No, I'm the last to hear. I don't live up there anymore, so I don't know what's happening on a day to day basis, but that property is worth a lot of money now. You're probably too late. The price of land has just gone through the roof. You have to be a millionaire or better to buy land up there, and if you could afford it, you probably wouldn't want to invest in land that had all those townhouses nearby. Most of it's still zoned for farming, but developers are gobbling it all up.

"Like I said, there's a rumor they're looking to buy land for a mall, and it wouldn't surprise me if those developers don't just pick up Mrs. Petersen's farm. If her son were here, he probably would've sold it by now. He's a real sharp guy."

"What do you mean, sharp?"

"Oh, I don't mean his looks or his dress. Just his way. He's smart but—well you know, if there's a straight way to do something and a crooked way, well, you know the type. I still see some of his old friends. They say he's in the Bahamas or somewhere, on the lam. I don't think any of them really knows. It's just gossip, you know, but I wouldn't really doubt it, knowing him as a boy."

"How would I go about finding out more about this property?" Tildy sensed that the clerk felt she had already talked too much, and seemed to be getting a little suspicious. She was sorry she asked the last question.

"Well, Vreeland is just five miles out of Benson. There's a real estate broker there. Palmer. Palmer's Real Estate. Think they're a Better Homes and Gardens agency. They could probably tell you if anyone's interested in it. But you should look at it first. Like I said, it might not be what you're looking for. Sue Palmer's a friend of mine. I'm sure she could find something else for you, if you really want a farm. I don't think Vreeland's what you want. Not anymore, anyway. Twenty years ago, maybe, but not anymore."

Tildy thanked her and Barry, not missing the cue, gave her back the map. They left with one piece of the puzzle and decided to ride to Vreeland, past the property and maybe even talk to the tenant.

Barry was amazed, even after listening to what the clerk had said. He hadn't been to this area for many years and could not believe the changes. As they drove into town, they saw rows and rows of townhouses. No wonder the clerk had said that we wouldn't want a farm in this area. They passed Mason's nursing home and found their way to Mrs. Petersen's property.

It had seen better days, they were sure. The grassy pastures were overgrown, and the barns were falling down. One could only imagine what it looked like in its prime.

There was a large Federal style home on the property, which was different from most of the old houses in the area. The others were either large Victorian, on the main street, or small farmhouses, but this house bespoke of money and successful farming.

The house, at least, appeared to be in good shape, although it was difficult to know if this was because of its intrinsic construction, or because it, alone, had been maintained. Mrs. Petersen had lived there, albeit alone, until about a year ago, so it was probably due to her loving care of the place that it was still in good repair. On the other hand, the barns were all in need of painting and it was obvious that the siding on them had just been left to weather and rot away. They decided to drive in and look around.

A man, apparently in his late sixties, was leading a large brown horse by its halter, back toward the barn. They drove up toward him. As they approached, he looked up, shaded his eyes, and peered at them. They stopped the car.

"Hello," Barry called. "Are you the owner, here?"

"Just a minute," called the man. He led the horse into the barn, and did not reappear for a full five minutes. Tildy and Barry got out of the car and waited patiently. Suddenly the man appeared and approached them.

"How can I help you?" he said, not unfriendly.

Barry introduced himself and Tildy. The man wiped his hand on what looked like a clean handkerchief, and extended it to shake Barry's hand. "My name's Jim Donahue," he said.

Barry told him the same cover story, that they were looking to buy a farm, maybe raise some horses and did he know if the farm might be for sale. The man chuckled softly.

"Well, I don't own the place, but Mrs. Petersen does. She's in a nursing home, but she still has her wits about her. Poor thing, suffered a stroke last year. She's up in her nineties. I used to work for her, but she lets me use the place and I keep it up for her, as best I can.

"Heard she's not doing too well, since the stroke. After her husband died, she ran the place by herself. She was one tough lady. But to answer your question, I just don't know. Can't see what she's holdin' on to it for. The horse farms are all sellin' out. Can't make any money anymore with horses, and the developers have been gobblin' up the land like crazy. Are you interested in developin' this land?"

"No, I was looking for a farm. You know, a place to go weekends, and have someone run it for me."

"Not too good an idea. Not too many around who would want to run a farm, anymore. I've been in this business for thirty years, and I'm goin' to retire next year. Getting' too old for it.

"I heard tell Mrs. Petersen turned down five million for this land last year. I guess she knew somethin' 'cause the same people came back again this year, probably upped the offer. Land up here is like gold. I think they want to put a shoppin' center on this farm. A big mall's goin' up about a quarter mile from here, and this here land is settin' on two main roads. Wish I'd a bought me a farm when I was young, but back then, a good paycheck was all I wanted. Didn't want the responsibility. Lottsa folks got rich with their land 'round here."

Barry and Tildy remained silent for a few moments, thinking Mr. Donahue would say more. They weren't wrong.

"Mrs. Petersen's got a son. He lives in Mexico or somewhere down in the islands. Not too sure. Seems he had some trouble with the government and had to leave the country. But sometimes he shows up. He goes up to see his Mom, but I hear he comes in on the QT. You know kinda sneaks in and then goes back right away. No, he don't stick around too long.

"I guess he'll sell the land when his mother dies. He don't have any use for it, and the way I hear it, he don't need the money neither. Folks say he stole plenty and then went down there in South America and livin' like a king."

"I'd sure like to talk to him about this farm."

The man took stock of Barry, gave him the once over, and seeing his well-tailored clothes, decided he might just have the money to buy this place. Hesitating, the man said, "I don't really know how to get in touch with him, but I have orders, you know, to contact him in case his mother passes. Or, maybe when he comes in. Sometimes he comes to see me, and if he does, I could talk to him. I still do my business with Mrs. Petersen. Mainly, I go see her just to report on the place. See, I don't pay nothin' for the use of it, but I have to make repairs to the house if somethin's needed. So far, no major expenses, and the small stuff I just pay for out of my own pocket. It's the least I can do for the use of the place. I still keep a coupla horses here.

"Of course I could ask Mrs. Petersen. I know she don't want to sell to no developers, but she really don't know what's goin' on here. Place ain't no good for farmin,' serious farmin,' that is."

"Well, I would really prefer to speak to Mr. Petersen himself. Um, if you could just let me know when you think he may be coming in to see his mother, maybe I could get in touch with him. I would prefer not to give him too much time to think about it. You know, just kind of catch him when he comes in, and then bring the matter up."

"Well, that might be better. Mrs. Petersen isn't going to last too much longer. I see her failing more every time I go up there. I don't think Mr. Davey will do anythin' until after his mom passes. Like I said he don't need the money and she don't wanna sell. So I guess he'll just wait it out. No, last time I seen her she din't look like she was goin' to last much longer. Darn shame. She was such a strong woman."

Barry reached in his pocket, careful not to give Mr. Donahue his card. He found a scrap of paper and wrote his home phone number down.

"Mr. Donahue, I would appreciate it if you could let me know when Mr. Petersen comes in the next time. I would sure like to talk to him. I'm giving you my home phone number; you can call me in the evening, if you wish, or leave a message. I'll call you back. I guess Mr. Petersen can't sell the land until his mother passes on, right?"

"Yes, that's right. When he got in all that trouble, she was afraid to put the farm in his name, so she just kep' ownership till she dies. I guess she figured that what happens after that wouldn't hurt her any." He smiled ruefully. It was clear he cared what happened to this woman.

Barry realized that this man also cared about what happened to the land, so he made one more point in his favor. "You know, I'm interested in preserving these places. This place is big enough to keep the house away from all the hullabaloo. I could plant some trees around the property as a buffer. I only want to use it weekends. I would probably need someone to look after it, you know, like a caretaker. Someone to hire people to do any of the heavy work and to supervise any construction."

"Well, like I said, I was thinkin' of retiring next year, but who knows? I might just be innerested if I din't have to do no heavy work, myself, you know, like a caretaker. I might just be innerested in that."

Barry had hooked him. He knew that Mr. Donahue would be sure to call him if something happened to Mrs. Petersen. That's all he wanted. Barry shook the man's hand and he and Tildy got in the car and drove away.

Barry took one more swing down the main street of Vreeland. He could see what had happened. Many of the stores on Van Dam Street, the main street, were boarded up. Those that were still open looked shabby, not kept up.

This was a town that once had charm but was now in a decline. On the other hand, there was new construction everywhere, outside of the main area. He had noticed a big Walmart on the way into town, earlier, and realized that this is what had happened to the downtown; discount stores all over America had ruined the mom and pop stores that had been there for generations.

It was an old Dutch town, as so many in New Jersey were, mostly inhabited by dairy farmers and shop keepers. Here and there, some of the old dairy farmers had turned their farms into nurseries to satisfy the demands of the growing suburban population, but lately, with the growth of townhouses in the area, even that business was drying up.

Some, he realized had "Wholesale Only" signs on the property and even more signs that said "Closed Sundays." He passed several Dutch Reformed churches, still looking well kept and he surmised that these were still well attended. To these old Dutch farmers, their religion was only second to their making a living and providing for their families.

There was no evidence of the dairy farms that had dominated this landscape, years earlier. One thing would never change, though. The land was hilly and there were the foothills of the Catskill Mountains in the distance. These were the Ramapo Hills, which still made up some of the most picturesque land in New Jersey. Even though the landscape was marred by the overgrowth of townhouses, the development was not sufficient to spoil the beautiful view, especially on this sunny fall day. The air was crisp and people were already wearing warm jackets, although in the sunshine the air was quite warm. The leaves on the hillsides were changing color and there was a smell of apples in the air. Tildy wondered if God had made this day especially for her.

She was more familiar with tragedy than Barry was, and she wondered if there would ever be another day as perfect as this one. She looked at Barry and could not believe the overwhelming feeling she had for him at that moment. She hoped there would always be days like this for them.

On the road, they found a rustic but attractive looking place for lunch. It was shingled and stained red. It had a windmill on top and was made to look like a Dutch windmill. Perhaps it was, in an earlier incarnation, but Barry thought it was an imitation. Attached to it was an outdoor vegetable stand. Tildy said that she would like to stop and buy some fresh produce and cook dinner that evening. Barry liked the idea. She had only cooked for him once, but he knew she was a good cook and he looked forward to a quiet evening with her.

First, they had a lot to talk about, especially the ramifications of what they had learned. Second, they had to decide how they were going to manage the move of her things over to his place.

He liked the idea of having Tildy to talk to. Not just the romantic or the sexual side of their relationship, either. He was eager to have her "take" on the events of the day, and what she thought should be the next move. As a lawyer, he had never liked to talk strategy with his associates. This was a big failing of his, he knew. But Tildy, well, she had such native intelligence that he knew she wouldn't just spit back at him the legal issues, trying to impress him. He knew he could count on her instincts too. He was really looking forward to this evening.

He told her that he would like to think about the day, before they talked about it, so during lunch she went into more detail about her leaving the firm, and her conversation with Jason. Barry smiled. So old Jason Kraus has a heart, after all. Interesting.

They arrived back at Tildy's apartment about half past two and Tildy started on the dinner early. She had explained to Barry that she was just getting it all ready to cook and then the actual cooking could be done later and more easily.

Barry called Ray Tobias and went over the events of the day. Ray told him that one of his cases, a slip and fall case, was called for trial in four weeks. Tildy heard Barry say, "You start outlining the proofs and we'll go over it tomorrow. Maybe you'll try this one."

Tildy finished in the kitchen just as Barry hung up the phone. She asked if he wanted a drink, but he said, "Later." She sat down beside him as he dialed the hospital.

"Just checking up on Dan," he said.

Dan answered on the first ring. Tildy heard Barry say, "That's great. Wonderful. What time? Do you want me to pick you up? Oh, Okay. Well, I guess then we'll see you at home tomorrow. Yes, I'll tell her. Yes. Great news! Yes, Goodbye."

To Tildy he said, "Dan's going home tomorrow. He said don't bother to come tonight. He's fine. We'll visit him at home. Alex is coming to get him. I offered, but he doesn't need me to come. Oh, and he said to tell you,

I don't deserve you. Imagine, my own brother."

"Oh Barry, I'm so glad he's done so well. I know you were very concerned. It looks like things are okay, now, between him and Alex, right?"

"For the time being," he said, somewhat skeptically.

Tildy had the good sense not to discuss it any further.

"Okay, you took the bar exam very recently. What do you know about debtor creditor law?"

"Well, you said that Ted Jernow was ready to start suit. I guess one thing you could do is third party in the insurance company and David Petersen, personally."

"How can I sue him, personally?"

"Well, you certainly can allege that the insurance company was operating fraudulently and that it was all David Petersen."

"Yes, but we would have to wait until he appears to serve him in New Jersey. That means we have to be tipped off that he's here."

"Yes, that's true. Or you could hope that someone will alert us if the mother dies."

"And, if the mother dies, then what?"

"Well, if it passes to Davey boy, you could attach the property and have a lien."

"Before judgment? What about the other possible creditors?"

"With a writ of attachment, the first in time would be the one to get the lien on the property, for the whole ball of wax. What's dicey, of course, is that it can't be attached, until his mother dies. After all, she doesn't owe the money."

"So, it's vital that we get the word on the mother."

"Or, if she transfers it before death, then we can move. It has to be in Davey's name."

Barry looked at her with curiosity and much admiration. He knew that he had forgotten all this years ago and was happy to have her up to date knowledge to guide him.

"You really got that farmer interested, when you said we might need someone to oversee the place in the event we buy it. I could see his eyes light up as if he thought of it."

"Yes, I thought that was a nice touch. It might make him call us if something happens to the mother. He knows that Davey boy will sell the property in a heartbeat and he would be out on his rear. This gives him an opportunity to still be involved with the land and have some work. I think he'll call us. It's a shame. He seems like such a decent person. I hated to misrepresent our intentions, but it's still my brother on the line."

"I think he'll call us, too, but we just can't leave that to chance. I think I'll give Mrs. Petersen a call in Ann Arbor. We hit it off quite well and I have to think of a reason for her to call me if the mother dies. In the meantime, if she does, there's a good chance old Davey will come to the funeral, don't you think?"

"No, I don't think so. He knows the government is likely to watch for that to happen, so they can nab him. I would like to find another way to grab him, and not wait for his mother to die."

"Don't forget, if mother dies and he doesn't show, we can then put a writ of attachment against the property, without service on him. You know, you could feel out Ted Jernow for what it would take to settle the case. That way you would know if they would take what the property will bring."

"There's a lot to think about here. What if he comes in and the government arrests him? It would complicate everything. Dan might get a small share, not enough to satisfy the claim. On the other hand, the government's case is on a back burner. They're probably not even looking for him anymore. The best way to approach the matter is probably just to go against the property. Question, do you need to have a judgment or just a debt? If we can go forward on the debt we will have to have a number from Jernow. I think we also have to find out just how much the property is worth. Of course, now that there's a claim against the policy, there's more owed than just to have the premiums returned."

"But that's the only amount we're sure of. Also, there could be attorney fees involved, since the insurance company, aka Petersen, is obligated to defend the claim. Boy my head is swimming. I think I'll take that drink now. Time to relax and think about this some more."

Tildy got up and went into the kitchen. She returned with a large glass of scotch on the rocks. She handed it to him, and he watched her return, take a glass for herself, pour in some scotch and add a splash of soda before she returned to sit beside him. Barry took a sip. Boy that felt good.

He felt the warmth as he swallowed.

"Too much to think about. Let's finish our drinks and make love. I'm so horny for you, I just can't think anymore."

Tildy smiled.

"At least you said let's finish our drinks. You can't be too horny."

"No," Barry laughed, "I know what a drink does to you, too. Why would I rush you, when the effects of the drink make it so much better? No, patience has its own rewards, and I'm a very patient man."

Tildy laughed out loud as she snuggled close to Barry. He just continued to sip his drink, as he stroked her hair. He didn't know he could love her any more, but it seemed each day he did. More and more. *She sure captivated Dan*, he thought. *There was approval written all over Dan's face. Even Alex liked her. Alex isn't smart enough to put on an act, but Alex was really warm to her.*

He had finished half his drink when he took hers away from her and set it on the coffee table. He lifted her gently in his arms and carried her to the bedroom. As he lay her across the bed, he could see her face in the fading light. Her eyes were closed, but there was a smile of expectancy on her face. God she was beautiful. Dan was right. He really didn't deserve her. He kissed her closed eyes, her lips, her chin. Slowly, but gently, he unbuttoned her blouse and removed her bra. He kissed her neck, her shoulders and her breasts. As he took her nipple in his mouth, she moaned with pleasure. She stroked his hair. He continued undressing her and, in the dim light, he saw her. It was as if he saw her body for the first time. He drew her into his being with his eyes. Her skin was warm, soft and unblemished. He tried to imagine what she would look like when she got older, but the strength of her youth and beauty were too much. He knew one thing, though. It was not just her beauty he loved. He would love this woman with all of his being, no matter what, until he died. Nothing this powerful had ever touched him and he left her lying there while he removed his clothes.

He lay down on the bed, not wanting to spoil anything by rushing. They had the whole evening. He stroked her gently and she opened her eyes and looked at him. Yes, he could see she loved him, too. God, I'm one lucky bastard, he thought, as he rolled over on top of her. As he entered her, she moaned again. Again, he cautioned himself to go slow. All he wanted was to give this woman so much pleasure that she could never leave him.

When they climaxed it was about as good as it ever was for him. She clung to him as no woman had before. Her urgency was as great as his. Please God, let this last forever. He let her come before he did. He looked at her afterward, still in a semi trance. He lay beside her and stroked her back.

She turned and whispered, "I love you Barry Chandron. I love you so much."

He answered, also in a whisper, "I'll love you till I die." They both fell asleep.

When they awoke, the room was pitch dark. Tildy was the first to open her eyes. She looked at the clock and saw it was nine o'clock. For a minute she thought it was morning, that she had overslept and was late for work, but the darkness had her confused. Slowly she realized where she was and that they still hadn't had dinner. She got out of bed and slipped into the bathroom. She took a quick shower. She hoped the noise would rouse him a little. She was glad that she had everything ready to cook. *Damn it, I'm hungry*, she thought. But she was not sorry that dinner was delayed. No, not at all sorry.

She stepped out of the shower and into her robe and slippers. She saw that Barry was still asleep so she started to open the bedroom door quietly when she heard him,

"Where're you going?"

"I'm just going to start dinner."

"Good," he said, "I'm famished."

She told him to rest awhile, that dinner would take about twenty minutes. He grunted but as she went into the kitchen, she heard him turn on the shower.

They ate a wonderful veal dish, which she prepared with the veal she had bought the day before, and the fresh vegetables they had bought earlier. They just kept glancing at each other, neither of them feeling very talkative. He praised her cooking, and finished his meal with a zest he hadn't felt for a long time. Wow, all this and a good cook, too. Someone should have snatched this girl up a long time ago. Then he thought of her first marriage and he frowned.

"What's the matter, don't you like it?"

"No, no, I love it. No, it's great." Tildy didn't want to break the spell, but she wondered what that little frown meant. This was not the time to break the magic of this wonderful day. No, she would wait to see if it appeared again. In the meantime, she was content. They finished dinner and Barry helped Tildy clean up. They watched a little television and went to bed. It had been a wonderful day, but all good days end.

The next morning, Barry got up early and left. Tildy was still asleep. He knew that she would call him at the office when she awakened. He went home and changed his clothes. He looked at his watch; it was only eight o'clock. He decided to stop at Dan's on the way to the office. He rang the bell and Dan answered the door. He was fully clothed and some of the color had come back to his face.

Actually, Barry hadn't seen Dan look this good for a long time. Except for a few more lines around his eyes, Dan was looking like his old self.

"You look great!"

"You don't look too bad yourself, for an old man."

"No Dan, seriously, you're beginning to look like your old self."

"Actually, I feel a lot better. Come in, Alex is out playing tennis." He said this as if he was telling Barry that it was okay to come in. Barry never missed anything, and he wondered about it. Had Alex told him of their argument? *Wouldn't put it past her,* he thought.

To Dan he said, "I'm just on my way to the office. Uh—there's been a few new developments since we last spoke. Tildy and I might be on to something."

"Tildy?"

"Oh yes, she's helping me with your case."

"I thought she had a job."

"Well, that's a long story. She had to leave it because of me."

"Because of you? Why?"

"She was with a defense firm and I have a lot of cases with them. She had to tell them about her involvement with me."

"Oh, I didn't realize it would matter, but I suppose it does. By the way, just what is your involvement with her? Should I be taking my tux to the tailor?"

Barry laughed. "Actually, not just yet, but she's going to move in with me. I'm not quite ready to say it, but I think she's the one. Neither of us want to rush into anything more at the moment."

"Well, it has gone rather fast, already, hasn't it?"

"Yes, but I am forty-two. I don't want to wait much longer, and I never met anyone quite like her. She's so beautiful and smart. And guess what."

"What?"

"She's a good cook too!" Now, Barry was really grinning.

"Well then it's settled," said Dan, smiling back at him. "You know what I think?"

"What?"

"I think my kid brother's a goner. I don't think there's any saving you."

"Not sure I want to be saved."

"Now, seriously," Dan said, "Barry, if it's worth anything, she's the greatest girl I've ever seen you with. What the hell are you waiting for?"

"I don't think she's in such a hurry. Don't want to make a mistake."

"Alex likes her too. Maybe it would be good for Alex to have a sister-in-law with a head on her shoulders. Maybe she'd be a good influence on her."

"Well, let's not jump ahead of ourselves, okay? Now Dan, as I said, I have some new information. First of all, a very good friend of mine is representing the boy."

"Is he any good?"

"After me, he's the best," Barry said honestly. "But that's actually better. He'll be relentless against me, but there won't be any tricks. The guy doesn't operate that way. He strictly WYSIWYG."

"What's WYSIWYG?"

"I was just showing off. It's a computer term that means, 'What you see is what you get, W.Y.S.I.W.Y.G.' He's one of the good guys, but he won't go easy just because you're my brother. Anyway, he's agreed to hold off suit for a week or so. I told him I may be on to a way of getting some money for his client without taking any of your assets."

"Is that true?"

"Yes, Tildy and I have found out that the guy who sold you the insurance has a mother up in Richmond County. She's sitting on top of a farm that's a gold mine. He's her only heir. What's even more significant, is that she's very old and very ill. She's presently in a nursing home up there. She's had a stroke and is failing. I think it's just a question of a short time."

"How do you know you can get hold of this money?"

"Well, it's very complicated, but there's a chance. That's all I want to say, right now. Okay?"

"Sure it's okay. Barry, I always said you were a good kid."

"Not always."

"What do you mean?"

"I mean you didn't think I was such a good kid when I took your catcher's mitt and lost it."

"Damn it Barry, why did you have to remind me? I had almost gotten over that." The brothers laughed and Barry was happy to see his brother so light-hearted again. He hoped he could fix this thing for Dan. Dan deserved it. He's the best brother anyone could have.

## Chapter Twenty-Three

Eleanor had come in early to do some filing. She never liked to get behind in her work. As long as she kept up, everything was fine, but backlog created pressure, and Eleanor did not need pressure. For this reason, she often was in the office before anyone else came in.

She had been there for about two hours when Barry came in. He looked younger and better looking than he had in a long time. Eleanor took a very maternal interest in Barry. She had no sons of her own, and had sort of adopted Barry, shortly after starting to work for him. She had been with him fourteen years. If he was overworked and looked haggard, she often fretted over him, and when things went well, like when he won the Bellows case, she basked in his glory.

Eleanor tried in every way to take the pressure off her boss, and consequently herself, by staying on top of things. She knew he relied on her for everything and, instead of feeling overburdened, as many secretaries did, this made her feel needed. She knew that she worked for the best lawyer in the county if not in the state.

Eleanor was very quick to take note of any changes in her boss and today she saw a livelier spring to his step. Besides, he was whistling as he walked in. *Now what was that about?*

Eleanor didn't miss much and she was sure that that Tilden Jennings had something to do with it, but she decided to wait until he said something to her. The last thing a man needs is a nosy secretary. She also knew that Barry would tell her everything, in his own time.

She did say, however, "You seem happy."

"I am."

"Anything you want to tell me?" That was as far as she had ever gone, and nearly took it back, but it was already out of her mouth before she caught it.

"Maybe. I think we're making some headway on Dan's case. Give me a minute, Eleanor, and come in, I want to talk to you about something."

"Yes, okay, oh by the way, there was a call here for Miss Jennings. From a Mrs. Petersen."

"This could be important. Give it to me and I'll call Tildy and tell her. Did Mrs. Petersen say what she wanted?"

"No but she seemed to want to talk to Miss Jennings, in a hurry. I didn't know where to reach her."

"Come in when I finish my call." Barry went into the office, took off his jacket and sat down. He called Tildy right away.

"Hi."

"Oh hi, Barry. What time did you leave; I didn't even hear you go?"

"You looked so peaceful; I didn't want to disturb you."

"I got up around nine o'clock. It really feels funny not having to go to the office."

"I know. Don't worry, we'll find something for you. By the way, Helen Petersen called you. I have her number. I think you'd better get back to her right away. Then call me back. If you're going to get calls here, I think you'd better come here for the time being. I can work that out; I have an empty office in the back. That way you can work with me, whenever I need some help and you can manage some of the details of Dan's case. What do you think?"

"If you're sure it's okay, I mean you'll have to talk to Ray and Eleanor and the others so I'm not a threat to them. Sure, sure I'd like to have something to do. Let's talk about it later, okay. I'll get to Mrs. Petersen right away. Oh, and Barry?"

"Yes?"

"I love you."

"Love you too, babe." As soon as Barry hung up, Eleanor came in. She looked at Barry expectantly. Barry looked a little uncomfortable. Well, he always did when he talked to her about anything personal, so she thought she knew what might be coming. She sat opposite him.

"Eleanor, I have some news."

"Yes?" She was a patient woman.

"You know Miss Jennings? Well, I know you don't know her, but you will, soon enough."

"Okay," she said expectantly.

"Eleanor, Tildy's moving in with me." Barry waited expectantly for Eleanor to say something. As hesitant as she was to ask him anything, she was never hesitant to voice her opinion once he opened the door. Of course, Eleanor also knew that Barry would never open the door unless he wanted her to be candid with him.

"Boy that was sudden, wasn't it?"

"Yes, I guess it was but you know we've been together a lot since I met her, and she's been a big help to me on Dan's case."

"Isn't she working for Jason Kraus?"

"Not anymore. She had to tell Jason about us, since she was working on some of the cases I have with him. So, she's kind of 'at liberty.'"

"Oh." Eleanor looked worried, as if afraid of what else was coming.

"Of course, I can't have her come in here. I mean there are just too many people in line for partner, and I wouldn't want anyone to get nervous."

Eleanor was relieved to hear this. She immediately realized what problems that could have caused.

"I will have to have her come in here for the time being." Eleanor sensed that he wanted her approval, so she immediately said, "Well, we have that back office that Richard used to be in. She could use that."

Barry was happy that she so willingly accepted the idea.

"Yes, that's what I was thinking."

"Have you told Dan about her?"

"He's met her and he said I'd better tie her up, quickly, or I could lose her." He smiled sheepishly as he said this. Eleanor smiled back.

"Well maybe you should take your big brother's advice."

"I am, don't worry."

"No you're not."

"What do you mean, no, I'm not?"

"What kind of commitment is moving in together? Give the girl a ring and set the date. That's how you close the deal. You're no spring chicken anymore," she said, grinning.

"Wow, you really know how to lay it on a guy, don't you?"

For a minute, Eleanor thought maybe she went too far, but he was laughing good-naturedly. He became serious, suddenly.

"You really think I should, right away? I mean it's only been two weeks."

"Barry, you've been around with dozens of women. I could always read you. I know you fourteen years and, Barry, you've never acted so happy. She must be quite a woman."

"Yes, Eleanor, she is. Maybe I should go and pay Max Reinfeld a visit."

"Not a bad idea."

"And Eleanor, don't say anything till I've had a chance to talk to Ray and the others, okay?"

With that, he got up and walked around the desk. Eleanor got up and Barry gave her a big hug. He had never done that before. Eleanor got tears in her eyes. She knew that he would never take a step like this without telling her, but there was still a little of the boss secretary reserve between them. She was touched. She stepped back and said, "I'm very happy for you Barry. This is a good thing." Barry knew that she was sincere.

He knew that they had a special relationship, even if they didn't always show it, that it had existed ever since he gave her her first raise. He had said, "Eleanor, it's time for a raise. Take an increase with your next paycheck." She had said, "Great, how much?" He answered, "Whatever you think is fair." He knew she wouldn't take advantage, and it cemented their friendship for all time. It was the best investment he had ever made.

As she got up to leave, the phone rang. Eleanor answered and said, "It's Miss Jennings." With that, she left and closed the door.

"Hi, honey. What'd she want?"

"She said her mother-in-law's had another stroke. This one is pretty bad. She's flying in. I offered to pick her up at the airport but she said her friend, the one she's staying with, is going to get her. She'll be here late this afternoon. She said she would call with the details once she finds out what's going on. I gave her my home phone number. I really like that woman. How could a nice down to earth person like her have been married to such a crook?"

"Well done, Tildy. Yes, I agree with you. What are you going to do in the meantime?"

"I've decided to start packing. I was in the middle of packing my good china when you called. We don't have much time, you know."

"I've been thinking, Tildy. I have an empty office, here, for you to use on an *ad hoc* basis, until we get something else for you. I can tell everyone it's only temporary, so there shouldn't be a problem. What do you say?"

"It might be a good idea. Let's talk about it later. I have a lot of packing to do."

"Okay, I already told Eleanor about us. Of course, good old Eleanor already knew. I sometime think that woman is psychic. I'm going to have a talk with Ray and then the others. I wouldn't want them to hear it from anyone else, okay?"

"Sure Barry, if that's how you want to handle it. Sure." He thought he heard a little hesitancy in her reply, but it was a fleeting thought. *Not to worry. It'll all work out.* Barry hung up the phone and looked at his messages. There was a call from Jake. He called the prosecutor's office and asked for Jake.

"Hi, Barry. Haven't got much time, got to get to court, but I wanted you to know something. The Feds are completely out of the case in New Jersey. It seems there are no other suits in New Jersey except your brother's. The others were minor and they all settled and the docs paid from their own funds. So anything we find by way of assets will go to your brother's case, as restitution."

Barry was elated. One of his problems was how to get hold of the money without telling Jake what he was doing. He had felt a little guilty about it.

"Gee, Jake, that's great news. I might be onto something, but I really can't talk about it yet. Does that mean if I find a pot of gold, it could all go for Dan? I mean, do I have your assurance of that?"

"Yes, Barry, as much as is needed to settle his case. That's why I called you. We know you were in contact with the ex Mrs. Petersen. I thought you might have found something, and I really don't mind letting you do the legwork. Save the state some money. But I didn't want you to feel guilty for too long."

"You goddam shrewd S.O.B.! How'd you know?"

"I know everything. That's all you have to know. I won't ask any more of you. Just so you help us catch the guy. That's all we want. I want to catch that bastard so he doesn't screw anyone else. I want you to promise me that if there's some way to lay our hands on him, you'll give me a heads up. Okay?"

"Yes, of course. I guess we just made a contract, a promise for a promise."

"That's right, and Barry?"

"Yes?"

"Give my regards to Judge Jennings' granddaughter."

"My God, do you know everything?"

"Yes, just about. Go get 'em, tiger. And call me when you do. I'll tell my secretary any call from you is high priority."

"Jake?"

"Yes?"

"I don't know how to thank you."

"I'm glad there was something I could do for Dan. He doesn't deserve to get crucified by this no good bastard. No one does, but certainly not Dan. By the way, how's he doing?"

"You heard about his heart attack?"

"Yes."

"He's doing very well. He's home and if there's any good news, it'll do him a world of good."

"Glad to hear it. Gotta run. Bye."

"Bye, Jake."

Tildy hummed to herself as she wrapped her grandmother's plates. She loved these plates almost as much as she loved her grandmother. She wrapped each one carefully in newspaper, knowing that she would have to wash each one by hand when she unwrapped them. They were not dishwasher proof, but that made her love them all the more. They were delicate, like Grandmother, and had a soft, classic beauty. They were ivory with salmon pink roses around the rim of each plate and cup. Someone else might think them old fashioned, but Tildy would not have traded them for anything.

She wondered what her grandparents would say about this hasty romance and decision to move in so soon after she met Barry. Grandfather would certainly have approved, because he knew Barry and knew that he would always take care of her. He was old fashioned in that regard. But

Grandmother? *I wonder what she would think.* Yes, she knew Barry, too, but Grandmother was a little more protective of her. *Wonder what advice she would have given me, especially after Jack. She would probably have cautioned me to go slowly. Well, too late for that. But at least he didn't propose marriage. Now, that would have put a different wrinkle on things. No, I rushed into marriage once before, and that's not a good idea. I think we should be together for at least a year before we go any further. Barry's careful. He won't pressure me, I'm sure. If it doesn't work out, well, I have all my furniture. I could always find another place and be comfortable. It's not as if I'm getting rid of all my things.*

*I want to be with him. Even when I'm separated from him for a few hours, I can't wait to see him. No, I made the right decision to move in with him, but marriage. Well, let's try it out and see. If nothing changes in a year, well there's plenty of time for that.*

Tildy's thought switched to Mrs. Petersen. *She must have loved her husband once. She seemed like a pretty sharp woman. How could she have been so fooled by him?* Tildy wondered if she knew all there was to know about Barry Chandron? He seemed so perfect, but Tildy knew that no one is that perfect. *When will I get to see the faults? I guess when we live together. I guess I have to go back on the pill. No need, now, to have any complications in our lives, at least until I'm sure. God, imagine having his child. No, don't go there,* she thought. *This could lead to a problem.*

As she mused, the phone rang, again. It was Barry.

"Honey?"

"Yes?"

"Thought you might like to know, I got a call from Jake." Barry proceeded to tell her about their conversation. Boy, everything was falling into place. "Hopefully, we can get past this problem with Dan and get on with our own plans."

"That's great news. Makes our job a little easier. If his mother dies and he comes to town, you can keep your side of the bargain."

"Just what I was thinking. Oh, hon, don't bother with dinner tonight. Let's go out and eat. I might be a little late."

"Any problem?"

"No, just something came up I have to take care of and I don't know how long it will take me. I should be home by half past seven or eight."

"Okay, love. See you later."

"Bye." Barry called Ray Tobias in and they went over certain matters that Ray was handling. He told Ray that he was seeing a woman lawyer, named Tilden Jennings. He told Ray that because of their relationship Tildy had to resign from Wright, Landwehr and Cummings. He told him that Tildy would be working with him on Dan's case and that she might be able to help Ray on some of the other things that he was working on. He also reassured Ray that her position with the firm was very temporary and that he was hoping to help her get established somewhere else, quite possibly the prosecutor's office.

He then told Ray that she was going to move in with him. Ray thanked him for leveling with him and said that he thought he had met her with Jason Kraus, once or twice. He said that it was important for Barry to speak to all of the associates, since this kind of thing sparks rumors and that most associates were insecure about their future with the firm. Ray thought that his talking to them would go a long way toward allaying any fears they might have. Barry said that that was what he had in mind, and that since Ray was his senior associate, he felt that he should tell him first.

Barry then spoke to each of his associates and thus cleared the way for Tildy to come there to work. Barry was truly elated at what Jake had told him. He began to feel that there might be an end to Dan's problems regarding this lawsuit. He didn't want to speak to Ted Jernow, just yet. He wanted to have something more concrete. He knew that if there was a substantial enough sum coming to Petersen, and if he could get his hands on it, Jernow would probably convince his clients to settle for that amount. The stakes were high, though, because the boy needed a lot of rehabilitation and training, on top of the pain and suffering award. The former, of course, would have to be calculated to present value. He hoped the amount that Petersen would get would be enough for everyone to leave happy.

This was a tall order, but if he pulled it off, it would be a real coup. He had gone out for a quick lunch but had skipped his usual walk. Things were falling into place very nicely. After speaking to everyone in the office, and making the few phone calls to clients that Ray suggested he make, he looked at his watch. It was nearly four o'clock. He picked up the phone and called his old friend Max Reinfeld.

"Max? It's Barry Chandron."

"What can I do for you, Barry?"

"Will you be in for a while? I need your help with something."

"Sure, Barry. Any time for you."

"Great, I'll be there in about half an hour."

Barry left the office, got into his car and drove to the mall. By the time he arrived, cars were leaving the parking lot and he had no trouble finding a space near Rodman's. He got out of the car, whistling, and walked briskly to the jewelry store.

Max was waiting on a customer, but waved to Barry as he entered. In a few minutes, he came over to Barry and gave him a big smile as he shook hands with him. While he was waiting, Barry had been looking at engagement rings in the case.

"So, my friend, what's on your mind?" said Max, knowing full well why Barry was there. "Did your friend like the pin?"

"Yes, Max, she loved the pin. It was exactly the right thing for her and she's been wearing it ever since."

"Can I help you with something else, young man?"

"Come on Max, you know why I'm here. I can see by your face you know what I need."

"You have something to tell me?"

"I guess I'm going to dive off the big board, Max. I found this marvelous woman and if I don't tie the deal up soon, and nicely, I'm afraid she'll get away." Barry was grinning from ear to ear.

"So, some smart lady finally caught the great Barry Chandron."

"Yes, Max, it sure looks that way."

"Don't waste your time looking in the case. For my special customers, I keep the stones in the safe." Max nodded to his clerk and took Barry into the back of the store. He motioned for Barry to sit down and went to the safe.

"Aren't you going to ask how much I want to spend?"

"No, my friend. I'm going to look to see if I have something special enough for this special woman. Then we will talk price."

Max opened the safe, and took out a tray and put it on his desk. He turned to Barry.

"If she loved that pin, I know what she would like. Something not too small, but not too big. But only the best quality stone. It must be perfect, right?" Barry nodded. Max took out his loupe from his pocket, and taking one stone at a time from the tray, examined each with the loupe. He rejected several before he found one he liked. He then took it out and put the tray back.

"This is the stone." It was a three and a half carat solitaire. Barry picked it up and studied it. He knew absolutely nothing about diamonds, but it looked very nice. He turned it back and forth, so that the light caught it and he saw the flashes of blue and red and yellow, as it twisted and turned. He knew he could trust Max to give him something good. It was beautiful, but as to value, he would have to rely on Max. He said, "It looks nice, how much is it?"

"If you like it, you will have it. If the price is too high, you will pay me when you win your next case. For this person, only the best from Barry Chandron. So, my friend, this is the one, the only one. It's a perfect stone. So, what do you think?"

Barry looked at Max and said, "I'm at a total loss. I don't know one stone from another, I'll have to rely on you completely, that's why I'm here."

"Okay Barry, this is by far the best diamond I have."

Max went over to a small filing cabinet and looked for a piece of paper. He thumbed through the file and found what he was looking for. He then looked at the diamond through the loupe one more time. Then he took out a pencil and started writing numbers on a piece of paper. He was figuring the price. When he was done, he showed Barry the paper. Barry said, "Max, are you sure it's good enough, I'm prepared to spend a lot more than that."

Max said, "I could charge you more, if you want, but this is the right stone. I'm giving it to you for a very special price. If you double it, that's what I would charge anyone else, pointing to the paper. Barry looked at the stone, again. It's beautiful, Max. I know she'll love it."

"Look, Barry, I could sell you a stone twice the size and it wouldn't cost you a dime more. But this is a perfect stone, and if that's what you want, this is the one." Barry thanked Max.

"When do you want it?"

"How soon can I have it?"

Max smiled and said if Barry would okay a setting, he could have it in an hour. Would that be soon enough? Barry needed a pair of shoes, so he told Max he would take it and would be back in an hour. After they picked the setting, Barry left the store.

In an hour, the ring was ready and Barry could see for the first time that it was gorgeous. He thanked Max, wrote a check, and left with the ring in his pocket.

It was six o'clock. Alex had arrived home and found Dan sleeping. She tried not to disturb him, but he heard her footsteps and awakened instantly.

She walked over to him and asked, "How are you feeling?" Dan said he was feeling quite well. She sat down to talk.

"How was your tennis game?"

"Oh fine," she said. "I played with Joan. She asked how you were doing and said she and Rob would like to come over, when you're up to it." Dan nodded. *How can she just pick up as if nothing had ever happened?* He couldn't believe her ability to change so completely. *Maybe I should have had a heart attack years ago,* he thought and a smile came to his face.

"What's so amusing?" she challenged.

"Oh nothing. I was just thinking of Barry," he lied.

"What about Barry?"

"Well, he and Tildy are moving in together."

"That was fast."

"I would have thought the same thing, but he's forty-two years old and it's time he settled down. I've seen him with a lot of women, but this one is different, and I think he realizes he may never find someone else like her. I have faith in his judgment. If he thinks she's the one, he probably knows. God knows he's known enough women to have a basis for comparison."

"I suppose," she answered, noncommittally. She wondered if this would change things. She liked the girl pretty much. It might be good to have a sister-in-law. *I never had a sister to be close to. But, of course, she's a lawyer. I don't know what I would have to talk to her about.* Dan read her face as disapproving.

"I really liked her, didn't you?"

"Oh, yes, I did like her. Yes, it's time he settled down. But moving in together? Is this like a trial marriage or something?"

"Oh, Alex, you know that that's what people do these days. I guess too many of them got stung in bad marriages."

"I guess," she said without expression. "I guess it's like a first step." Then she thought of her own marriage to Dan and wondered if it would have been any different if they had lived together before marrying? She suddenly started to cry.

"What's the matter?"

"I've really messed everything up. Where did I go wrong? Everything seemed to be so perfect. Finally, we were able to afford all the things we always wanted. Now it's all in jeopardy."

"Alex, I wanted to wait a little while before we had this conversation. The problem is that we had the life you wanted. The big house, the country club, all the shallow trappings. I never wanted any of those things. I just went along because I thought that that was what you needed to be happy."

"I didn't know."

"Yes, Alex, I hate the big house and the pressure of this big mortgage. I hate the club. I don't like those stupid friends of yours. They don't give a crap about you or what happens to me. They're only interested in the best clothes, the best cars, and their goddam golf game. I never wanted this life. All I ever wanted was for us to be together. I thought that was enough for you, too. When did that all change?"

"It changed when you became a workaholic. When you never came home, and when the kids grew up and didn't need me anymore. It changed when I decided that one of us should enjoy the fruits of all your labors. You certainly didn't."

"Workaholic? I'm not a workaholic. I had to work all the time to give you all these things that you seem to need. Even if we come out of this legal thing, I'm not going to go back to work at the same pace I was working. I'll have to take in a young partner and take it a lot easier. Alex, we're going to have to give up the club and maybe the house, too. That's even if Barry can, by some miracle, fix this thing."

"Does that mean you won't work so hard? You'll come home at a reasonable hour. Does it mean we can take trips together and get to know each other again?"

"Would you like that?"

"Dan, it's all I ever wanted. If I thought we could spend more time doing fun things, you know, enjoy each other as we once did, I wouldn't miss this life at all. Or the people. You're dead on about them. Oh, they mouth the right words, but it doesn't take much to see how very insincere they are. I found that out when you got sick. They all asked about you, but did anyone ask if they could do anything? Not one. Not one."

"There was more to Barry's visit. He didn't want to get my hopes up, but he thinks the crook who put me in this fix might be coming into a lot of money and that, somehow, he might be able to get it and settle the case with the boy.

"You know Alex, that's how it happened. I didn't want to worry you, but I've been having chest pains for some time. I guess I was in denial. You know, sometimes doctors know too much and this keeps us from getting help. When I had that boy on the operating table, I was having severe pain. I didn't want anyone to know, so I just kept on going. How stupid I was. I almost died, and I ruined that boy's life. I don't know why God spared me, but maybe he has a use for me, after all.

"I've been thinking, if we get out of this, I might just want to change my life, altogether, you know, like open a clinic where we could do some good. What do you think?"

"If I thought you would be happy and would spend more time with me, I would be happy. How did we ever get on that merry-go-round, anyway?"

"I have to do some good. If I don't give back something from this gift of life I was given, then I don't think I could live with myself. Maybe we'll find something abroad. Would you like that?"

"I might. You look into it, and we'll see. Let's get out from under this legal thing, reassess our situation, and then make a decision. Maybe we've been given a second chance. Let's be careful how we handle it. Oh, Dan, why didn't we have this conversation years ago? You know I always loved you. Somewhere our train got off the track."

"Yes, Alex. I guess we're both to blame for that." She went over to him and they embraced. Dan thought, *I think the worst is over.*

## Chapter Twenty-Four

Barry quickly got into his car and felt for the ring in his pocket. He was very excited at the thought of seeing Tildy when he gave it to her. She couldn't help but be happy. Yes, Max was right. It was a beautiful ring. In about twenty minutes, Barry was at the door to Tildy's building. He got to her apartment and rang the bell. She opened the door. She was wearing a royal blue pants suit with a pale yellow blouse. Funny, he thought. Other women in suits always look so mannish and severe to me, but when this woman puts on a suit, she's so feminine. I don't know what it is, but she looks great. Even in a suit. She kissed him lightly on the cheek.

"Just a minute, I'll get my coat. Where are we going?"

"I thought maybe we would go to Le Veau."

"Great, I love that place. Best veal in town." Tildy locked her door and walked ahead of Barry. The dim hall light played on her hair and the lights danced as she passed under each of them in turn. Barry thought to himself, *I must be smitten. I never watched whether a girl's hair shone or not. But this is positively hypnotizing.* He laughed softly to himself. Tildy didn't notice.

They took the elevator down. A couple got on at the third floor. Barry couldn't help noticing the man's quick appraisal of Tildy. It seemed that just looking at her brought a smile to most men's faces. Luckily the guy's wife didn't notice, or he'd have been in trouble. Barry smiled a knowing look at the man and the man gave him a slight nod. Nice.

They got in the car and drove the short distance to Le Veau. Barry helped Tildy out of the car and she took his arm as they entered the restaurant. As they made the way to his table, Barry saw a few of his colleagues and one client who nodded to him and he to them. Barry had asked for a table in a far corner and they were seated. He had wanted as much privacy as possible when he gave Tildy the ring.

He didn't ask Tildy what she wanted. He ordered a bottle of champagne.

"Don't you think we're celebrating victory a bit early?" she asked. "After all, we haven't won yet. It's looking up, but I don't want to jinx anything."

Barry smiled.

"Can't we just have champagne when we feel like it? It's not a victory celebration. It's just being out with you. I feel like celebrating." He smiled a little enigmatically, and made Tildy wonder if something was up. She decided against saying anything else. The waiter brought the champagne and poured them each a glass. He discreetly did not ask them to order. Barry held up his glass.

"To the most wonderful woman in the world."

Tildy smiled at him. "When did you decide this?"

"The night I met you."

"Oh, okay."

"To the most wonderful man in the world," she said smiling coyly at him. She was still wondering what was up. Barry looked serious, all of a sudden. Fear came over Tildy. *Oh my God*, she thought. *Oh no, I think he's going to propose. No, Barry, don't.*

Barry was quick to notice a change come over Tildy. He couldn't read her, but felt in his pocket for the ring. He took it out and handed it to her.

Tildy looked back at him, evenly. Slowly she said, "What's this?"

"Open it and see."

Tildy took the package and unwrapped it with a feeling of dread. She knew what was in it. No, she wasn't ready for this. Why hadn't he asked her first? *Oh, God, what am I going to say?* She unwrapped it very slowly, trying to figure out how to tell him she wasn't ready for this without hurting his feelings. The last thing she wanted was to hurt him, but it was too soon. She just wasn't ready for this. Tildy opened the box and saw the ring.

It was truly the most beautiful thing she had ever seen. The dim lights of the restaurant caught each facet and sent out sparks in every direction. She knew it was an expensive stone.

"Barry," she said, gently. "Barry, dear."

"You know that I love you and I've decided that I can't live without you. I want you to be my wife, Tildy."

"Oh Barry." Tears welled up in her eyes and for the first time ever, she didn't know what to say. "I don't know what to—"

"Shh, sweetheart. Don't say anything but yes."

"But Barry, I love you so much." She saw a smile light up on Barry's face. He thought she was saying, yes, but she didn't know how to answer.

"I do love you, and I hope you love me enough to understand what I'm going to say. Barry, I can't accept. Not yet. It's way too soon for me. I just can't rush into this, again. I did this once before and it was a disaster. I can't, I just can't."

Barry was visibly crushed and Tildy knew it. She had put a stop to his fantasy and this was not easy for him. Besides, she knew that Barry had a lot of pride, and she hoped that she had not said anything to wound him. He took the ring from her and, without another word, he put it in his pocket. The waiter came back and Barry said they were ready to order.

After the waiter took their order, Barry told Tildy about the conversations he had had with Eleanor and the rest of his staff. He told her the office would be ready as soon as she wanted to come in. He never said another word to her about the ring all through dinner. Tildy didn't know how to react to his complete denial that they had ever had this conversation. If he had been angry, she could have dealt with it. But this. It was as if he had rewound and erased the tape and went on with the story, as if it hadn't happened.

In a way, she was glad not to have had a confrontation, but in another way, this was scary. He gave her no hint of what he was feeling, and so she didn't know if she should explain what she meant or let it go. Every mouthful she took went down her throat as if she were swallowing a golf ball.

She bravely finished her dinner, but a kind of thorny hedge had grown between them to ruin the mood. She worried about how he was feeling and what he was thinking. She fretted over the consequences of his silence. She remembered her grandfather once saying, "Beware of the anger of a patient man." She didn't want to lose him, but she couldn't make another mistake. A chill went through her, and he noticed.

He pulled her jacket from the back of the chair where she had placed it and put it on her shoulders. She smiled a grateful smile at him, but the one he returned was forced. Yes, she thought, his pride was wounded. That was the last thing she wanted ever to do to him. But there it was. Now what to do about it? They went back to Tildy's apartment and Barry saw her to the door. As she waited for him to enter, he said, "I think I'll go home tonight and sleep in my own bed, for a change." Now, she was crushed. As she turned to him, she saw the blinking message light on her answering machine.

"Barry, I think Mrs. Petersen may have called. There's a message." Barry came in and sat down as Tildy picked up her phone. She motioned to him that it was, indeed, Mrs. Petersen. She was looking downward as she heard the message. She nodded her head as she replaced the phone.

"Barry, it was Mrs. Petersen. Her mother-in-law died. She never made it in time. The woman died an hour before she arrived. She said the caretaker of the farm would call her ex-husband and that she wasn't sure if he was coming in for the funeral, but she would try to find out. She said the funeral would be next Friday. She said she'd call me back with the arrangements. I knew we could count on her."

"Yes, I figured you were right."

"What do we do now?" she asked, glad that they didn't have to talk about themselves.

"I guess I'll call Jake to have some people there on Friday to arrest Mr. David Petersen. Then we have to hope that his mother did leave him the estate and that Jake will follow through on his promise, which I'm sure he will. He'd have had no reason to call me and tell me he would. I guess I have to trust him. Of course, we'll have to go, too. At least, I will."

"What do you mean, at least you will? Of course, I'll go. Besides, I think Mrs. Petersen will expect to see me there. Uh, she left a number where we can reach her. I'll call her first thing in the morning. She sounded a little upset. You know, I think she really cared for the old woman. Barry?"

"Yes?"

"We need to talk about us. I don't want you to leave with this thing unsettled between us."

"What's unsettled? I asked you to marry me, and you said no."

"Barry, I didn't say, 'no.' I said it was too soon. That's not no."

"I thought you would be so happy. Did I misread you all this time? Are you still in love with your ex-husband?"

Tildy could not believe this. She remembered Jack with a certain fondness, but he was like a brother. He was a good boy, but there was no passion, ever. She couldn't imagine having grown old with this nice, affable, but totally boring person. Finally, she had talked to her grandfather who had assured her there was no shame in having made a mistake. He said it wasn't too late, especially since they hadn't had children. He told her there was nothing to lose.

She still remembered the relief on Jack's face when she told him she wanted a divorce. They had stayed up half the night saying how they should never have rushed into marriage. Jack made Tildy promise she would never rush into marriage again. They both said they had learned a valuable lesson. She thought of how shocked she was, when she heard that Jack had found someone else, a man. After the initial disbelief, she realized the signs were there, all along.

"Oh my God, Barry! Is that what you think? Oh, no, that couldn't be further from the truth. No, you didn't misread me. I love you more than I ever loved any man, and I couldn't care less about my ex. In fact, there's something I should have told you."

She told him about her relationship with Jack, her grandfather's advice and what she eventually learned.

"I wondered how I could have been so wrong about him. How I could have even thought I loved him. I knew as soon as I met you that I never loved him or any other man for that matter. You are, truly, my first love."

"So, why can't we get married? I love you and you love me. Where is the obstacle?"

"There is probably no obstacle. I guess I'm scared, that's all. I'm afraid that we may be rushing into something too fast, that's all."

"Tildy?"

"Yes?"

"What if you take the ring, and we don't set a date until you're sure. As for me, I'm very sure. What's the difference if we live together and it doesn't work out, or if you take my ring and it doesn't work out? There would still be the same explanations and upheaval. And, I wouldn't want the ring back either. I would want you to always know that I wanted to make you mine for life."

"Barry? Can I have until tomorrow to think about that? What you say makes sense. I never even thought about that. I thought when you gave me the ring, you wanted to rush into marriage. If you promise not to pressure me into a marriage too soon, then maybe it would work."

"Okay. Let's wait a day or two. I'd rather you thought about it too." They hugged and Barry started to take his clothes off. Tildy surmised that all was better and that he had decided to stay, and he did. They were both too emotional about what nearly happened to make love that night, but Tildy fell asleep with her toes touching Barry's. She was very relieved. He slept with his hand caressing her shiny hair.

## Chapter Twenty-Five

Tildy had decided to work at Barry's office in the morning and pack in the afternoon. This way, she could stay in touch with Mrs. Petersen more easily, and also stay connected to the practice of law. She was especially anxious to see the game from the plaintiff's side.

She hoped that she and Ray Tobias would get along, since she knew she could learn a lot from him. She had met him once or twice when she went to court with Jason and he seemed to be a very nice young man and very competent, so the next morning she arose, showered and dressed for work before Barry awakened. She had the coffee on when she heard him stirring.

He called to her and she said she was ready to go with him to the office. He quickly showered and they sat down to a breakfast of toast and coffee. He was glad she was coming to work with him and he reassured her that she and Ray would get along. Then Barry remembered last night and wondered what Tildy was thinking about.

Again, Tildy noticed that little frown of his, but she also remembered last night's conversation. This time she knew what it was about, and she realized how very much he loved her. This made her smile. He noticed her smile and asked her about it. She just shook it off and made him feel that there are some things that he'd be better off not asking. At least, this was a happy thought, he realized.

When they arrived at the office, Eleanor jumped up from her desk to greet Tildy. She told her that she had gotten the back office ready for her, and to holler if she needed anything. She said there were probably some things she would have to get, herself, to make it personal.

Barry laughed and said, "Don't spoil her. There'll be no living with her demands, if you do." They all laughed, especially since Eleanor could see, right away, that Tildy was not that kind of person. Women are very intuitive about other women, and Eleanor liked Tildy right away. Now, here was a woman good enough for Barry. *Maybe even too good,* she thought. She smiled at the thought. She had always wished she had a daughter old enough for her great boss. No one was too good for him.

Eleanor handed Barry some messages and said, "Nothing too important." Barry then took Tildy by the arm and showed her around the office. Everyone was very cordial to her and she recognized a few faces she had seen in the courthouse, but hadn't known that they worked for Barry. Ray was especially nice and she could tell by his smiling eyes that he felt no threat from her. Barry had prepared them well. She was happy to be there.

She hoped they wouldn't treat her with kid gloves. She really couldn't stand that. Her office was not as nice as the office she had at Wright, Landwehr, and Cummings. It was small and sparsely furnished. Barry had warned her that it was just a spare they only used from time to time. It had an old steel desk and chair, a file cabinet, and no pictures on the wall. Luckily she had a window, which made the place brighter than the fluorescent light above her desk would have done by itself. One of the bulbs flickered and before she could say anything, Ray told Barry it would have to be fixed.

She was happy to be there. She had forwarded her calls from home to the office, in case Mrs. Petersen called her but, other than that, she didn't expect to hear from anyone for the time being. She told Ray that she wouldn't work on the Anderson or Foster cases because of conflict, but that she would be glad to help him with anything else that he needed help with. Ray was happy to have her aboard.

Barry left them, and Ray said he had a couple of cases she might help him with. He left to get the files, and she took off her jacket and sat down, waiting for Ray to return. He came in, plunked some papers on her desk and pulled up a chair. He spent the better part of an hour going over files and asking her questions about herself, where she went to school, what she liked to work on, what kind of experience she had, etc. He talked with her about a couple of new medical malpractice cases he had and she showed a lot of interest in working on them. He quickly took her up on it and pulled out some that needed research. He also asked if she wanted to make some calls and interview some people regarding the files. She said she would, but would rather read the whole file before she jumped in. She said it made her uncomfortable to talk with someone and not have all the facts she needed.

Ray liked her answer and his estimation of her went up even further. She asked him about the other associates and he gave a quick assessment of their various strengths and preferences. She found out that some were working on their own cases and others took a team approach. She liked this but thought, for the time being, she would rather work with Ray. He was very nice and she quickly sensed there was a great deal she could learn from him, even if she was here only for a short time.

Barry returned to his office and noted that Tildy had passed her first test with flying colors. Ray seemed quite taken with her and he hoped they would become good friends. Maybe she could fit in here, eventually. *Who knows*, he mused? Eleanor gave him a thumbs up as he entered his office. Barry grinned sheepishly but he was pleased. *A home run,* he thought. *No surprises there.*

Barry looked at his messages, and remembered he hadn't checked his home answering machine. He dialed his home and found there was one message waiting. He punched in the code and the voice of the old farmer, Jim Donahue, was on the line.

"Hullo, uh, Mr. Chandron. Jim Donahue calling. You remember me, the farm up in Vreeland? Well, I told you I would call you if anything changed regardin' this here place. Well, Mrs. Petersen passed on last night. She was a fine woman, but she was really sufferin'. I guess she's in a better place. Well, I got in touch with Mr. Davey, her son, and he's coming in for her funeral. I know him and he won't stick around too long, so if you want to talk to him about the farm, I guess it might be best if you came to the funeral and talked to him afterward.

"I know it ain't Christian to talk to him that day, but judgin' from past actions, I don't think he'll be here any too long. Sometimes you have to do what's practical. Uh, don't tell him I was the one who told you. Don't want to rock the boat.

"Call me as soon as you can. Them developer guys will be all over him soon's they hear. I'll tell you 'bout the arrangements, when you call back."

Barry called Donahue right back. He said he had gotten in late the night before. Donahue gave him the details, which he already knew, and he thanked the man. *Poor guy,* he thought. *Thinks he's going to have an easy job in his retirement.* He felt a little guilty about Mr. Donahue, but realized his brother's welfare, if not his life, was at stake. He pondered his next move. Then he picked up the phone and dialed Jake.

Jake was in court starting pretrial motions on a big drug bust the cops made last August. He was doing what he had been born to do. Jake loved this job, especially, when he got to send away the bastards who sold drugs to kids. Like most prosecutors, Jake had a self-righteous streak, but he was proud of his record and with good reason. He had the most drug convictions in the State of New Jersey, and was called by other prosecutors for his advice when they had a really tough case.

He had won a few of his motions and also lost a few. Well, this was par for the course. The judge wanted to appear fair to both sides, but Jake was up against a tough opponent. For that reason, he always put in a few of those throw away motions. The ones he knew he couldn't win. The judge reserved decision on the close ones. *Well, you can only try.* He figured though, that he had an even chance on the fourth amendment count. The cops had done a solid job on it.

He packed up his briefcase, listened to a joke from his adversary. It was old, but he laughed anyway and pretended he had never heard it. As he left the courthouse, he could hear the others laughing. He never liked to hang around with the good old boys in the courthouse. He had fish to fry and young lawyers to oversee, so he hurried back to the office.

He walked in the door and his secretary called to him. "There're a couple of messages for you." He walked by her desk and picked them up. He saw some he had to take care of right away, and some that could wait. He made the important ones, first, but held back on the call from Sandy Bishop.

Somehow, he had a hunch that the call from Barry Chandron should come first, in case he had to alert Sandy about something. Barry never called to chat. He must have some news. He dialed Barry's number himself.

"Hi Barry."

"Hi Jake, I have news for you, but you have to reassure me of your promise to me the last time I called. I think, on this, we need each other."

"Barry, I shouldn't have to reassure you of anything. We go back a long time and I've never made a promise I didn't keep. That's why I don't make too many promises. What's up?"

"Petersen's coming to town. His mother just died and word has it, that he'll be at the funeral." Jake didn't have to ask how he knew. He knew that if Barry was telling him this, he was pretty sure. Jake asked him for the time and place of the funeral and told Barry he should do nothing. He shouldn't even try to speak to Petersen, because he might tip him off.

He said he would arrange for a couple of his best officers to go and arrest him. Barry told him about his contact with Donahue and what he had been told by him. He said he wanted to be sure the farm would go to Dan's case.

Jake assured him that there were no other claimants. He took a deep breath and said, "Um, on second thought, maybe you shouldn't go at all." I'll let you know when we have him. Barry told Jake that Tildy had promised Mrs. Petersen she would be there. Jake said it was okay for her to go, just so she ducked out as soon as the service ended and didn't hang around. They would get their man as soon as he left the chapel.

"Don't worry, Barry, we'll get the bastard." He called Sandy Bishop and got all the wheels turning. He then returned to other matters, but felt good that this book would soon be closed.

Barry rang Tildy and asked how she was getting along. She said fine and he proceeded to relate his conversation with Jake. She said that she would go to the funeral alone, if he thought he shouldn't come. He agreed, reluctantly. He asked if she wanted to grab a sandwich with him for lunch. She said that Ray invited her to join him and the rest of the associates and that she wanted to have a chance to get to know them better. He told her to go, and thought, *Gee, she's smart. What a good idea!*

He wasn't sorry, either. He figured he'd like to go for a walk after lunch and think this through. Even though he trusted what Jake told him, he needed to think it all through. Barry ate lunch at his usual hangout and then took his walk. If Petersen got away, then there was certainly nothing he could do if Jake's best men were on it. As for Tildy, he could see no danger as long as she left right after the service. In fact, she could put in her appearance with Mrs. Petersen and then leave if there was a large enough crowd. He would leave it up to her judgment, which he had come to trust implicitly.

After his walk, he came back to the office and told Eleanor he was going to see Dan. Luckily, Dan lived close enough so that he could run over there for a short visit. Tildy wasn't back yet, so he told Eleanor that he would return around three.

Dan was fully dressed when he arrived. He was actually quite chipper.

"Hey Dan, you look great."

"I feel a lot better. Where's Tildy?"

"Hey man, she liked you so much, I'm afraid to bring her back here, especially since you're looking so much better."

Dan laughed and seemed to be back to his old self. He told Barry he was now walking around the block and feeling pretty much back to normal. The color in his face was better than Barry had seen in a long time, even well before the heart attack.

Dan told Barry that he had had a long talk with Alex, and that things between them were much improved. He confided to Barry that, as soon as this mess with the malpractice case was over, he was looking forward to a substantial lifestyle change. He had been looking into a possible overseas post, helping indigent children in Asia. He wasn't sure just where, but he had a colleague from India, who had been talking about a hospital in Delhi, where his services were badly needed.

"Do you think Alex would be interested in going to India?"

"She seems to want to do anything to keep the marriage together, and she said she would go. I was really surprised."

Barry resisted the urge to tell Dan that his troubles might soon be over. Anything could still happen and he wanted to have the bird in hand before he built up Dan's hopes too much. Dan told him that if he had to pay the judgment out of his own assets, he was prepared to do so. Barry said that he hoped that wouldn't be necessary, but was proud of his brother, nevertheless. *I guess the apple doesn't fall too far from the tree,* he thought, thinking of their father. *There must be a gene for morality.*

He remembered the story of his father selling his entire inventory at a loss, when the bottom fell out of the textile business. He owed a lot of money to his bankers, and he wouldn't go out of business until every last one of them was paid. He said that his good name was more important than his pocketbook, and that he had had nothing before and could make it all again. He had refused, against his lawyer's advice, to file for bankruptcy.

Barry was always proud of his father, since he heard this story. He always regretted not having known the man as an adult. He was fifteen when his father died, but he knew he came from good stock, not only from the stories, but also from the example of his big brother. Yes, Barry was proud of him, too.

When Barry left Dan's house to return to the office he thought of last night for the first time that day. He wondered if Tildy would relent and accept the ring. He knew, now, that it wasn't a question of competing with the memory of her first husband. He knew, now, that it was fear, only fear, which kept her from saying yes. *Funny, I was the one who was afraid of rushing into a relationship and now it's she who's afraid. Life is crazy, but I won't pressure her. I have to learn to be patient. I waited this long for the right one, I can certainly wait a while longer. Besides, she'll be with me. She's moving into my place. I know it's just a question of time.*

The next two days, Barry spent looking at cases soon to come to trial. He also scheduled some appointments he had been putting off, and called some clients he had been avoiding. *Yes, things are looking up, it's time to get back to work.* Ray seemed genuinely relieved to have him back full time. Tildy was settled, at least for the time being. Dan seemed on a pretty even keel, so now they just had to wait until Friday. Everything was falling into place very nicely.

On Friday, Tildy attended Mrs. Petersen's funeral. She was not surprised to see the chapel crowded with people. People of all ages, as many men as women, filled the hall. She greeted the younger Mrs. Petersen when she entered and the daughter-in-law seemed genuinely pleased she came. It was evident that she had been crying and she told Tildy how much she loved the old woman. She said that the divorce had done nothing to change her feelings for her and she went on to say what a wonderful person her mother-in-law was.

After this exchange, Tildy slipped back to a seat near the door at the rear of the room. She saw many others come up to Mrs. Petersen, and to the tall handsome man with graying hair, who stood next to her. She surmised this was the renegade son, the crook, the destroyer of other people's lives.

He was very good looking, the first attribute of a confidence man. She couldn't help but feel anger toward this man and what he had done to Dan. *How callous, and yet, there must be some redeeming value in this person who came to his mother's funeral, risking his imminent arrest.* Then she thought of the mother's estate and realized there was probably more than one reason he was there. *Greedy people never have enough, do they?*

The minister started the service and Tildy looked around the room. She wondered if she could spot the cops who were there to arrest him, but she couldn't see anyone who didn't look as if they belonged. She heard the minister's praise of this woman and realized that he knew her well, and that she was very well loved in the community. No wonder she and her daughter-in-law remained so close.

*How could that no good S.O.B. be her offspring? There are no rules, are there?* When the minister started to wind down, she carefully got up and left. She had parked a block away, and couldn't resist watching the door from the safety of her car. Just as she got into her car, she saw Petersen and another man jump into a car parked across from the chapel. The other man was driving and Tildy looked for the cops. She realized that they— wherever they were— had not seen Petersen leave the chapel. She started her car and followed them. Instead of heading for the cemetery, the car was going toward Benson. She tried to follow at a safe distance and did not think the occupants were aware they were being followed. She tried to call Barry on her car phone, but the phone showed no signal. She proceeded to follow them toward Benson. The car entered the parking lot of the Farmer's Bank in the center of town. She was sure that she was now the only one who knew where Petersen was. She had no idea who the other man was.

Tildy didn't know what to do. She parked her car and entered the bank, but there was no sign of Petersen or the other man. She was pretty sure that there were no offices in the building, other than the bank, so she looked around and saw a corridor in the back. She entered the corridor and saw restrooms. At the back of the corridor was a door that said "Private." She thought that she could leave the building and call the state cops; Barry had given her the number, but there was no public phone. If she left the building to find a phone, she was afraid they might leave.

She had to call Barry, but how? She thought of pulling the fire alarm, but the men might get wise and drive away. Just as her mind was racing, the door marked, "Private" opened and both men stepped out. She ducked into the ladies' room, and ducked out again when she heard the side door in the corridor open and close. They had left the building and gotten back into the car in which they came. Tildy had no choice but to follow them again. It was obvious that they didn't know she was following them, because they took no evasive action. They headed south toward the highway. Again, she followed but wished there was some way to contact the state cops or Barry. When they reached the highway, she followed, still worried about where they might end up. They finally stopped at an office building in one of those small towns, on the outskirts of Hamilton, a town which was beginning to show the effects of urbanization. They parked behind the building and entered a side door. Tildy parked across the street. Petersen looked her way and Tildy thought he might have become suspicious. She had been driving Barry's red Mercedes, not exactly a low profile car. If he had noticed it at the funeral, or at the bank, he would certainly be surprised to see it here again. She pulled down the mirror and pretended to be putting on lipstick. When she looked up, they had gone into the building. She was about to get out of the car, to look at the directory in the building when there was a tap on her window.

She wheeled around. Her heart started to race as she jumped, startled out of her wits. When she saw a man and a woman standing outside the car, she began to shake uncontrollably. The shaking didn't stop, even after they showed her their state police badges through the side window. She opened the door, quickly.

"Ms. Jennings—?"

"Yes, you scared me to death."

"Sorry about that. I was afraid you might try to follow them into the building."

Tildy looked bewildered.

"Ms. Jennings, we have it covered now. Just drive slowly away, and go back to your office. Mr. Chandron knows we've had you in sight since you left the funeral home." The cop grinned at her.

"We just called and told him we were relieving you of your command. We were in the bank right after you, and were worried you might do something foolish. Just as we were about to approach you, they came out of the office. There was nothing to do but just let you follow them and we followed you. We'll take it from here. We've got him, now."

Tildy took in a deep breath and let it out slowly. How did you know who I was?"

"Mr. Sommers told us the kind of car you would be driving. We had strict orders to keep an eye on you. By the way, nice car."

"Thanks guys, he's all yours."

Tildy got back in the car and drove toward Hamilton. She didn't like the idea of playing cop. She didn't even wait to see them apprehend Petersen. She knew that they would.

Instead of going on to the office, she went home, which was nearer, and called Barry.

He told her that soon after she left, he had a second thought and called Jake to be sure his people kept an eye on her. He told her he knew it wouldn't be hard to describe his beautiful redhead driving a red Mercedes. He really didn't think it necessary, but after hearing her story, he was very glad he did. He always was a cautious man and this time it paid off.

She changed from her business clothes and began packing again. She was almost finished; the movers were coming next week. She had mixed feelings about leaving this little nest she had fixed up for herself. She had been happy here, but not as happy as she had been since Barry Chandron had come into her life. She thought, *Maybe I will take the ring and announce our engagement. It would make Barry happy and we wouldn't have to get married right away. I don't know why I'm so hesitant, but I have to obey my instincts. I couldn't bear to make another mistake.*

Barry came home late. She had fixed a light dinner and they talked about their respective days. Barry wanted to know all about the funeral and Tildy was careful to tell him about all her observations. Barry told her that Jake had called to tell him that Petersen was in custody.

He seemed relieved, but still somewhat apprehensive. Somewhere in the back of his mind, there was the nagging thought that it was too easy.

Something could go wrong. He dismissed this thought with the knowledge that he was a natural worrier, and that he always worried when things seemed to be going too smoothly.

They had each had a couple of drinks before dinner, and some wine with dinner. Afterward, Barry helped Tildy with the dishes and realized she was almost finished packing when he opened the cabinets to put the dishes away. There was exactly two of everything left to pack, no more, no less. She was well organized. He couldn't wait to have her in his place and see it all fixed up. He was, actually, looking forward to helping her shop for things to complete the apartment, and to put on the finishing touches.

He knew his life had changed, but he was very content with the change. He hadn't known how lonely his bachelor life had been, until now.

Jake sat down with the prisoner. He went through all the routine questions. David Petersen answered all, directly, and with candor. Jake was impressed. Here was a clean-cut guy, well groomed, handsome in a way, and obviously from good stock. Where did he go wrong? He seemed to have had every advantage in life. A good family, strong values, a deeply religious community, tightly knit, and yet, somewhere, somehow, this good citizen got off the track.

Getting the story would have to be enough. The whys and wherefores of evil he would leave to the psychologists and sociologists. One thing that Jake knew in his heart from his fifteen years as a state's attorney, there were some people who were inherently evil. Some with no sense of conscience or compassion for the people they hurt. David Petersen, a nice, affable guy in every sense of the word, a guy you might want to sit down and have a drink with, was able to go out and cheat people without a second look back at what he had done. How do you account for it? Jake wondered, but he really didn't care.

All he wanted were the facts. Dates, times, places, victims' names. He couldn't believe how cooperative Petersen was. Ask the right question and you'll get the answer. All except one. A list of victims. Petersen said he remembered a few, but the list was in his office in Nevis/St. Kitts. Unless others came forward, or Petersen gave him the list, there was no way to know how many or for how much they were bilked of their hard earned money.

Jake needed to know how many victims and how much money Petersen took. Petersen knew Jake needed this information and that he was facing some serious time. He told Sommers he had no accomplices. He told him that the last act of fraud was two years earlier.

He told Jake that he had a secretary on Nevis/St.Kitts. He said she was a native woman, whom he trusted, and that she was an innocent party. He told him that she could send the list. Other than that, there was no one else involved.

He told Jake of his failed marriage, and that he regretted the shame these acts had brought on his mother. Jake really didn't believe him. Petersen was facing ten years on each fraud count, alone, and there were over one hundred in New Jersey. It was hard even for Jake to believe that so many doctors had been taken in.

It seems that Petersen saw a good thing when malpractice rates for doctors went sky high. He found their Achilles heel and decided to take advantage. Doctors felt put upon, blaming the lawyers who prosecuted malpractice cases for their high rates. Many, without investigating, were only too happy to find a company to insure them at a lower rate. Many, so happy to be relieved of the burdensome expense, believed what they wanted to believe, a fertile territory for a confidence man. And David Petersen was an accomplished con man. He looked good, he spoke well, and he talked a good game. He had fancy stationery printed and impressed his clients. Pretty soon, word of mouth spread throughout the medical community that there was a cheaper alternative.

Jake had seen this type before. He had seen the con men in the home improvement business and con men gigolos, romancing old ladies out of their savings, but he had never met anyone as smooth as David Petersen. This guy could have been a success in any legitimate business; why do some people just have to take the crooked route?

*Oh well, let's get through with this.* He turned to Petersen and posed the sixty-four dollar question.

"Just how much are you prepared to pay in restitution?"

Petersen, ever cagey, said, "How much will I have to pay?"

"Hey, look, you're going away forever on these charges unless you cooperate. I already have a pretty long list of your victims. In fact, one of them is facing a ten million dollar lawsuit. How's that for starters?"

Petersen looked at him blankly. "I don't have ten million dollars."

Jake looked him dead in the eye and said, "By my calculations you have a damn sight more than that and then you'll have the FBI to worry about, too. Anything less than ten million won't get you any kind of deal. You'd better go back to your cell and start counting your fingers and toes. Until you come up with that figure, there's nothing on the table." With that, Jake left the room and left Petersen with his mouth hanging open.

Tildy went to work with Barry the morning after the funeral. She had started doing some research on one of Ray's cases and was eager to get back to it. It was a medical malpractice case involving an informed consent question.

There were quite a few cases on the question of when informed consent is not really consent because the doctor didn't inform the patient about all of the possible consequences. Suddenly, the phone rang. She heard Eleanor's voice.

"Tildy, it's Mrs. Petersen." Tildy thanked Eleanor and took the call.

"Hello, Mrs. Petersen, how are you today?"

"Hi, Miss Jennings. It was very kind of you to come to my mother-in-law's funeral yesterday. Wasn't it a nice service? You know, of course, that they picked up David."

"Actually, I knew it was going to happen, but I didn't arrange that."

"Oh, I didn't think you did, but my information helped to get him, didn't it?"

"Well, yes it did." Tildy didn't know what to say, next.

"That's okay. I don't want to see him punished, particularly, but I do want him to repay all the money he stole. You know, Miss Jennings, we're very good, hard-working people in this community. We go to church and pay our taxes and are, generally, good citizens. I know you can tell that David's mother was well respected here. That was one reason I asked you to come, yesterday. David is an aberration and, truthfully, everyone is at a loss to explain his behavior. You know, he wasn't like that when I married him.

"I'm going to the lawyer's office this morning, to arrange representation for him. That's the least I can do. Besides, I have some business of my own, there. I wonder if you could meet me for lunch today. The lawyer is in Benson, and I don't expect to finish with him until twelve. Do you know the Raleigh restaurant? We could meet there at about half past twelve."

Tildy said she knew the place and would be there at twelve-thirty. She really liked this Mrs. Petersen and, under other circumstances, felt they might have been friends. Yes, she was looking forward to going, and to the drive up there. She hung up on Mrs. Petersen and rang Barry. She told him of their conversation and heard Barry say, "Uh oh." She said she didn't think anything was wrong, but she would be on her guard, anyway. She was surprised at Barry's response.

She didn't want to be late so, promptly at eleven, she left the office in Barry's car. She had left her's at home, never dreaming that she would need it. Here she was, again, going to Benson and driving this gorgeous car.

She put the top down and let the wind go through her hair. It was a warm, sunny day, and she was enjoying the scenery on this beautiful drive into the hilly northern part of the state. The air was warmed by the sun of Indian summer, but there was a cool crisp breeze as she drove, carefully watching her speed. This car had a tendency to run away from her. The last thing she needed was a ticket.

There was the smell of autumn in the air and the sky above was bluer than she had seen in a long time. The leaves had turned beautiful shades of red and gold but had only partially fallen. It was one of those special late October days that one always remembers.

She reached the charming village, turned industrial during the post war boom years only to have been abandoned later, as industry moved south in search of cheap labor. She passed the deserted plants and then up the hill to the courthouse, where she and Barry had started their search.

It seemed like ancient history, not just two weeks since they had first come here. So much had happened and so quickly. She was anxious to have another conversation with Mrs. Petersen, but was just a little uneasy after her conversation with Barry, this morning. Why did the woman want to meet her?

She arrived at the restaurant early. It was exactly twelve when she was seated. This gave her time to look around. The restaurant was old but very well taken care of. She looked up and saw the high, white embossed tin ceiling of another era. It looked as if it had been painted very recently. The chairs were all bentwood and there were sparkling white tablecloths on the tables with fresh flowers in tiny blue vases, on each. The floor was black and white checkerboard ceramic tile squares, many bearing the cracks of age, but immaculately clean.

There was a low room divider separating the dining area from the most magnificent bar she had seen in a long time. It was made of dark polished mahogany with a large mural behind it. The painting was a landscape of the village as it probably looked a century ago. It showed rolling hills and dairy farms with cows in the foreground. The barns, and there were several in the picture, all had Dutch gambrel roofs, which was the typical Dutch design of the previous century and even back before that.

The restaurant had probably been built in the early 1950s to serve the needs of the new businessmen who built the factories, but it gave the impression of being much older. Now, it was mainly patronized by lawyers on their way to court, or in the middle of trial, since it was just a block and a half from the courthouse. Tildy loved the place and didn't mind the wait.

Mrs. Petersen arrived at twenty five past twelve, and spotted Tildy right away. She was dressed in a gold, well-tailored suit, which matched her blonde hair. She was carefully made up and was carrying an obviously expensive handbag, with shoes to match. She was a very attractive woman, and Tildy saw a few male heads turn as she entered the room. She carefully made her way to the table and sat down. She looked flushed.

She shook Tildy's hand warmly, as if she was an old friend. She said, "I just love to come back here. Even with all the changes in this town, it's still home to me. I remember being taken out to dinner by my parents in this very restaurant, when I was a little girl. Now, it's run by the son of the original owners. I went to school with him. I'm so happy he didn't change the décor."

"Do you think you'll ever come back here to live?"

"That's just become a distinct possibility," she said cryptically. Tildy gave her a quizzical look, but didn't ask why. Mrs. Petersen didn't offer. Instead, she said, "Have you looked at the menu? The food's nothing out of the ordinary, but it's all very wholesome and well prepared." They both looked at the menu and ordered.

Tildy began, "Your mother-in-law's service was really beautiful. And so many people came. She must have been very well thought of."

"Yes, how often to you hear a daughter-in-law extolling the virtues of her mother-in-law?"

"Not very often," Tildy admitted.

"Well, David and I knew each other as children. We grew up on adjoining farms. He's a few years older than I and he was so handsome. I think I had a crush on him since I was nine years old. I never thought he would look at me; he was very popular. Our parents were friends and we attended the same church. Sometimes, I would walk home with him, but he was only helping my parents by keeping an eye on me. Then one day, I guess I had grown up; he asked me if I would write to him when he went away to college in Michigan.

"Of course I jumped at the chance and, when he came home to visit, it just seemed natural that we would begin to date. We had a beautiful wedding at the church we both grew up in. The whole community was there to wish us well. I don't know what ever happened to change him. He got a job with an insurance company in Michigan and we set up housekeeping in Ann Arbor. I've been there ever since.

"After our divorce, there didn't seem to be much point in coming back. My parents had both died and the farm was sold. I had my business in Ann Arbor, and was doing quite well. I still had a few friends here, but they were married, and I was single again. My mother-in-law and I remained very close, but it wasn't enough reason to live here.

"I came back to visit, but I had nothing in common with anyone here anymore. Nevertheless, I always loved this place, and I guess I always will."

They had ordered drinks and Mrs. Petersen seemed very relaxed and especially talkative. She didn't seem in any hurry to tell Tildy why she had invited her. They continued to chat as if they were old friends, catching up after a long hiatus. When they finished, Mrs. Petersen ordered dessert and Tildy indulged herself, too.

Finally, Mrs. Petersen told Tildy why she had called her. "May I call you Tilden?"

"Actually, my friends call me Tildy."

"I'm Helen, Tildy. You know, I liked you the minute I met you, and despite the fact that we really hardly know each other, I feel as if we're old friends. I hope we'll remain friends when this is over." Tildy reassured her they would.

"Well, as you know, I went to see my lawyer, well rather my mother-in-law's lawyer, this morning. The main reason was to ask him to represent David, but there was another reason." Tildy waited.

"The lawyer came back to the house after the service and told me something I didn't expect." She waited a minute for effect. Tildy had a sinking feeling.

"She told me that my mother-in-law changed her will last year and left everything to me. Her house, her stocks and bonds, her jewelry, and the farm, the whole shebang. It's all mine, now. Mr. Applegate wanted me to sign some papers while I was still in town and, if possible, to remain here for a while, while certain arrangements are made."

*Uh oh,* Tildy thought. *Barry was right. If it's in her hands, we can't touch it.* Mrs. Petersen saw the look on her face. She said, "You know, Tildy, I'm not responsible for my ex-husband's debts. These are not ill-gotten gains. Mr. Applegate assured me that these possessions are mine to keep."

Tildy managed a smile and congratulated Mrs. Petersen on her good fortune.

"That's not all, Tildy. I want you to represent me. I not only like you, but I trust you. I was very impressed at your first phone call and the way you approached me so truthfully. A lesser person might have lied to get my cooperation. You just jumped in with the truth, and I made a strong mental note of that. I have many things to take care of now, and I would like your advice and your representation should I need it. Tildy, how about it?"

Tildy didn't know what to say. As far as she could see, there was no real conflict. Even if she continued to work for Barry, Mrs. Petersen was a stranger, even with her new assets. She was out of the deal.

She said, "Helen, at the moment, I don't see any conflict of interest. I would like to talk it over with my associates, but I really don't see any impediment. If they agree, I would be most happy to represent you. How long do you expect to stay in town?"

"I guess I'll have to stay about two weeks. Then I must return to the shop and, depending on what I decide to do, I will probably come back here to attend to my business here, who knows for how long. By the way, there's no mortgage on the farm. I own it free and clear."

"It's probably worth a fortune," said Tildy.

"Yes, but only if I sell it. Otherwise, it'll take a lot to fix it up and pay the taxes. I haven't really had time to think about what I want to do. You know, I knew my mother-in-law cared for me, but I really didn't expect this. She said, right in the will, that she no longer trusted her son to use the money wisely. She left him one dollar."

"Well, this is quite a shock."

"Tildy, I'm not in a position yet to make any promises. All I can say is I always do the right thing, and let's leave it at that. I do have a responsibility to my mother-in-law's memory to protect her assets. You understand that, don't you?"

"Yes, of course."

## Chapter Twenty-Six

Dave sat in his jail cell, thinking about his meeting with Jake Sommers. He couldn't believe they had caught him. He knew that the FBI had stopped pursuing him and had thought that New Jersey had as well. But here he was. Now what to do? His employers were expecting him back in San José in a couple of days. He had told Lindy about his mother's death, since Lindy and he were both in Nevis when it happened. Lindy offered to fly him to San José from Nevis, so he could catch a direct flight to New York, right away. He had also told Marianne that he would be back within a day or two of his mother's funeral. He didn't bother to call his employers; he hoped that he could come back with good news after he met with Ron who had indicated he might be interested in assisting him in his money-laundering scheme. Dave had planned to discuss the wire transfer deals with him today. He was too busy yesterday after the funeral, meeting with the developers and pretty much striking a deal. He was agreeable to their offer, which was even more generous than the previous one. Ron was ecstatic, seeing a great opportunity for his bank. Dave knew he could give his lawyer a power of attorney to complete it all, after he went back. He never dreamed they would pick him up. He didn't even try to use his phony passport. They knew who he was, why compound his felonies?

He thought for a moment about seeing that red Mercedes at the bank and at the developer's office building, but dismissed it as paranoia. After all, cops don't drive cars like that and there must surely be more than just one car like that in New Jersey. Just a coincidence, he decided. But what to do now? He knew he had a couple of cards to play, pretty good ones, too. That damn prosecutor had spoken to him this morning, and he was so aggressive, but Dave didn't want to tip his hand. He gave him just enough information. He knew he couldn't beat the rap on the fraud cases. There was too much of a trail. That's why he left the States. He was waiting now for the right moment. He called Applegate, his lawyer, and asked him to contact Helen to arrange bail. Helen was a good soul and—in spite of all that happened—her good nature would get the better of her. She wouldn't want him to rot in jail; they had known each other too long for that. He also wanted advice from his lawyer, before he made his deal. He wondered why Applegate had told him that he also had some important matters to discuss with him. What did Applegate know? He had a few cards to play, but this hand had to play out just right. Applegate told him he would be there right after lunch.

Applegate was a good lawyer, and he remembered that he had done some criminal law before settling down to a private practice in Benson. And Applegate was smart. Dave knew he could handle a plea bargain for him. He also knew there would be no trial.

Tildy said goodbye to Helen Petersen and agreed to call her in the morning. As she drove back to the office, she no longer took stock of the scenery, the crisp air, the sun lowering in the sky casting a beautiful golden glow. These were all the things she might have enjoyed on this otherwise pleasant drive home. All Tildy could think about was Barry. What is Barry going to say? Mrs. Petersen was smart not to leave her money to old Davey, but how could she have known that he was about to be arrested. But then, maybe this was her way, too, of protecting an asset that had been in the family for generations. Why should some total stranger get the benefit? I guess if I were in her shoes, I would have done the same. No, you can't blame Mom.

She thought of Helen Petersen. *What did she mean by "I always do the right thing"? In the next breath she had said, but I have to protect the asset. What, exactly, did that mean? Would she help to make some restitution for her ex-husband's transgressions? Why in hell should she?* thought Tildy. *How could she do that and still protect the asset? Wow, what a dilemma. I just can't figure it out.* She really dreaded having to tell Barry the bad news. He was so upbeat at the thought of resolving all of Dan's problems.

About an hour and a half later, she reached the office building and drove the car into the parking garage. She hurried out and got into the elevator. When she arrived in the office, Eleanor smiled a warm smile.

"Is Barry in?"

"Yes, shall I tell him you're back?"

"Please, Eleanor. I need to tell him something." Eleanor could see the worried look on her face and knew that she didn't have good news for Barry. She rang Barry and Barry came out of the office to meet her.

"Well?'

"Barry, we need to sit down, I have a lot to tell you." Barry noted her mood and sensed that things were not good. He opened the door for Tildy and followed her in.

"It's not good."

"What do you mean?"

"Mrs. Petersen senior, left it all to Mrs. Petersen, junior. She cut old Davey out of her will."

"Oh my God! What now?"

"There's more. She wants me to represent her."

"Wow. Let's think about this. I don't know, Tildy."

Tildy proceeded to relate the whole conversation she had had with Helen Petersen. Barry couldn't make any sense of it either.

"I really don't see any problem with you representing her. After all, we don't have a claim against her. It was just an expectancy of her ex-husband's we were hoping to get our hands on. It was never legally his. I just can't believe it. Why didn't we see this coming?"

"I guess because Helen didn't either, and she's the only one with whom we were in contact. That is, except Mr. Donahue and he thought Davey would get the farm too. I guess Davey thought so too. Do you think he knows yet? He's certainly in no position to contest the will from jail, is he?"

"On what grounds could he contest it anyway? She was obviously of sound mind, according to everything you told me was said about her at the funeral; he gave her plenty of reason to do what she did, and there was no undue influence on the part of Helen. She didn't even live in this state. So that's a dead end for Davey."

"Wait a minute. They have him in jail. He's facing pretty serious charges. He's been living like a king in the islands, so he must have a pretty good stash. I'd better call Jake and tell him about this latest development." Barry called Jake right away and, as luck would have it, Jake had just gotten back to the office. Barry quickly told Jake what they had had in mind, and how that avenue was now gone. He asked Jake about Dave Petersen's assets and did Jake think there was enough there to cover Dan's claim. Jake told him that he thought, by his estimate, that Petersen had managed to bring about two million dollars out of the country, over time. He said, cryptically, there are other matters, though, that they were exploring which may account for a much larger amount hidden away. He said that there were many illicit opportunities for enhancing his stash in the islands, and he was going to pressure Petersen into "finding" more of his money. He didn't think Petersen liked the thought of spending the next hundred years of his life in jail. He tried to reassure Barry, and said that Dan's claim had been the only one in New Jersey of any substance. He wanted to make his deal with Petersen, before the Feds got wind of the fact that there was a large stash of cash and that New Jersey had him. He thought Petersen would make a deal, as soon as more pressure was brought to bear. He hoped they could get enough to solve Dan's problem.

Barry got off the phone and told Tildy what Jake said.

"There's nothing more we can do, now. Let's pack up and go home. We'll grab a bite to eat. We've got a lot of moving to do in the next two days. All we can do is sit and wait for Jake."

## Chapter Twenty-Seven

The moving truck came early Friday, but Tildy had awakened by six. Barry and Tildy had moved a few boxes at a time, and had managed to move most of the small stuff before moving day. Because of all the chaos of moving, Barry had gone home last night to move furniture around to make room for Tildy's. They planned to switch places later in the day so that Tildy could oversee the placement of the furniture.

Despite her preoccupation with moving, she was still thinking of Helen Petersen. She wondered what kind of representation she might need and what she meant by her statement, "I always do the right thing." Was she referring to her ex-husband's debts? Why should she bail him out? Tildy didn't think that that was what she meant at all. It was hard to figure this one out, but she didn't doubt the honesty and goodness of this woman. She knew somehow she meant some good, but what? She was really leaning toward representing her, since she liked Helen and did not want to end the relationship. Besides, this might help her to find a good spot with a good firm. Having a substantial client in her pocket would not hurt her.

It only took one day to move Tildy's furniture into Barry's apartment. The larger apartment somehow showed the pieces off to better advantage and totally transformed the feeling of the place. Barry couldn't believe how homey his former barn of a place looked. *That's it*, he said to himself. *Good things always look good no matter where they're placed, but if the space is large, they show off even better.*

Tildy was ecstatic, but reminded Barry that they now had to change the drapes and get some nice rugs. Barry was happy at the thought of shopping with her. He loved her taste and knew it would be fun just to see how happy she would be, picking these things out.

He and Tildy went back to her place to make sure that nothing had been left and that the people they hired had cleaned the place. Everything was in order. They were both tired and decided to eat at Jerry's, the place they had their first date. They had been back since, and Jerry had caught on very quickly that they were now a couple. He always showed them to a back table to give them privacy.

They each had several glasses of wine, fully intending to finish unpacking tomorrow and sleep in Sunday morning. It would be their first Sunday in their own home, together, and they talked about just hanging out, with no plans. It had been a busy week. Barry told Tildy that Dan and Alex seemed to have worked things out. Tildy was happy. She had no family of her own and hoped that she and Alex would become friends. She also liked the idea of acquiring a niece and nephew as well. Then she stopped herself.

*Wait a minute*, she thought, *I'm getting ahead of myself here. He wants to marry me and I'm the one who put him off. He hasn't brought it up again; he seems to be giving me the room I asked for. What am I afraid of? This man is offering me everything I ever wanted. A wonderful life with a wonderful man and a family to belong to. Why should I hesitate? I never met anyone I cared about more, or who was better suited to me, temperamentally.*

Just then, Barry looked at her in the candlelight. Her green eyes had turned a soft green gray. "Should I ask?" he said.

"Ask what?"

"What you're thinking." She smiled that wry smile that came over her when she'd been caught thinking something she wasn't ready to share. He saw a moment of hesitation. Then she said, "I was thinking about all you've offered me."

"Is this a place I want to venture into?"

"Maybe, maybe it's time we talked about it."

"Some things are better left unspoken."

"Yes, some are, but not this. I love you. I want to spend the rest of my life with you."

"Are you sure?"

"Is one ever sure?"

"That's not the answer I wanted to hear."

"Barry, are you sure?"

"As sure as I could ever be. I've never wanted another woman the way I want you. I'm only happy when I'm with you, and when I'm not, you're all I can think about. I want to know that you're part of me, so that I can get on with my life. If you keep me waiting too long, I will lose all my clients, and the reputation I've earned as a tough litigator. Tildy you've ruined me for anyone and anything else." He said this last, laughing, keeping the mood light.

"I wouldn't want to be the ruination of your career. And I would hate to think of you alone in your old age." She was also laughing, teasing him, playing him. He knew it and he loved it. He also believed he was going to get the answer he wanted.

"Barry, how does Tilden Jennings Chandron sound to you?"

Barry grabbed her hands across the table. "Really?"

She smiled and nodded her head. He saw the tears in her eyes. For a moment, he felt his eyes misting over too. Then he remembered.

"Damn it Tildy, I put the ring in the safe deposit box. And the bank is closed tomorrow. We'll have to wait until Monday to get it. Damn it!"

"Barry, do I look like the kind of woman who needs a ring to prove that you love me?"

"If you can't tell by now, you aren't very perceptive. But, seriously, are you sure you're ready?"

"Yes, I'm sure. I'm sure I love you too; it's only that I've become very cautious. I hope you understood."

"Yes, in fact, I was planning to wait until you said something, if it took years."

"That's what made me sure, your wonderful patience. I'm a very lucky woman."

"Can I call Dan and tell him?"

"There's time enough tomorrow. Let's just keep it to ourselves for a few more hours. Okay?"

"Yes, love, of course." They finished dinner and went home. The house was not in very bad shape, since the movers had moved with most of the things left in the drawers, so all Tildy had to do was go to her dresser and find the pale gray nightgown she wore in Ann Arbor. They undressed and then Barry opened a bottle of champagne he just happened to have on ice. They sat on the sofa and curled up next to each other as they sipped the champagne. They snuggled and kissed and held each other close. Before long, Tildy picked up both glasses and told Barry to bring the bottle and they went into the bedroom. Tildy never knew if it was the wine, the engagement, or their first night in their own home, but their lovemaking was the best ever. This was the night Tildy always went back to in her dreams, during their whole married life together.

The next morning Tildy awoke before Barry and went into the kitchen. She found some bacon and eggs. She found the coffee pot and the coffee. She found the dishes, Barry's dishes, and set the table. Then she went back into the bedroom and found Barry rolling over.

"I'm going to make us a nice breakfast," she said.

"Not yet you're not," he answered. He reached out and grabbed her and they made love again. Then they took a shower together. It was half past ten before they sat down to breakfast. After breakfast they both cleaned up and finished unpacking the rest of the boxes. It was just noon when the phone rang. It was Dan.

Barry told him about the engagement and Dan was ecstatic. "We must celebrate. How about we go to Rinaldo's tonight, my treat?" Barry asked Tildy, who quickly agreed. They decided to meet at the restaurant at seven. Tildy wasn't ready to receive guests with packing boxes all over the place.

The phone rang again. Barry reached for it.

"Hello? Oh, hi. Are you in the office? Don't you know it's Saturday? Glad I'm getting something for my tax dollars. Yes. Yes. That sounds great. You did what? Are you sure? I hope it all plays out that way. Boy, I guess it's true that underground money is dangerous. I'll call you tomorrow, but you can call here if something else breaks. Yes. I will. Okay."

Tildy looked at him, quizzically.

"The two million that Petersen had amassed has turned into twenty-five million."

"How?"

"He's been laundering money. It seems that Petersen doesn't want to do any jail time. He has promised restitution of all claims on the fraud charges, and he's going to work with the Feds on some big names with whom he's been doing drug business. It seems that the fraud was just the beginning. He met some so called 'business people' and he's been 'investing.'"

"Investing?"

"Yes. When he went to the Caribbean, he went first to Costa Rica and became acquainted with some people who were into drugs, big time. He quickly turned his two million into twenty-five million and going. He has his own cash reserves in Nevis/St. Kitts. He's agreed to pay Dan's claim from this money. His money is just the tip of the iceberg, though, of what he can deliver to the Feds. He's been involved in money laundering during the past year. He also made a deal with the Feds to help get and give up some of his 'business associates' in return for witness protection. It seems that he has acquired some very important friends and the DEA, especially, are very interested.

"Jake said he wasn't going to get the Feds involved, but then Petersen said he had more information about drug dealing and money laundering. He put a lot of pressure on Petersen, threatening him with a long jail term. Then all of a sudden, Petersen dangled this gem in front of Jake and Jake got hold of the Feds. They brokered the deal together. Jake said he was happy to get the pot of money to satisfy all the claims in New Jersey.

"Dan has the largest claim. The others are mostly return of premiums, and the small amounts the other doctors had settled from their own assets. The Feds will work with him, since he'll help to prosecute some "really bad guys" the Feds have been watching for years. This is the first time they actually have the goods on them. I think we'll have even more than our engagement to celebrate with Dan and Alex tonight."

Marianne awoke and looked at her clock. It was 5:00 a.m. She had slept fitfully last night. She hadn't heard from Dave in three days. He told her he would call. She wondered what to do. He hadn't left a phone number where he could be reached. In fact, she really knew very little about him. The only one she had ever been introduced to, of his many associates, was Lindy. She didn't even know Lindy's real name. In the pit of her stomach, she knew two things and they weren't good; he was in some sort of trouble, and that her life, as she had known it in the last six months, had come to an end.

It wasn't really knowledge. She had what grandmother called the *Instinct*. Even her grandmother had said it when she was a little girl. She wasn't exactly clairvoyant, but she had what had been loosely defined as a "truthful feeling." Oh, yes, she had that "truthful feeling." The *Instinct* was not something you could conjure up when you wanted it. No, it was more invasive, it was that dreaded thing that came to you when it was most unwanted. It was more than dread. It was the full understanding, the palpable feeling that disaster had struck. It was knowledge, just the same as if someone called her on the telephone and told her. Oh no, the *Instinct* told her there was trouble.

Marianne did not know what to do about it. She had no one to call, no way to find out. Ever since she first met Dave, she knew that he was involved in things she would never know about. She assumed it was for her own protection, so she blindly accepted her relationship with Dave. She also knew, that it would not last forever. There was something about Dave that said that loud and clear, even though it had never been spoken. She wondered if she knew that from plain old women's intuition, by the way he acted, or was it the *Instinct*? No matter. The day had come.

She managed to get out of bed, take her shower, dress, put on her makeup, as she did every day. She did not take her time, but acted as if this day were just like every other. She had to go to the office, she had some appointments. She knew that if Dave didn't return, she would just list the house for rent, once again, sell or keep the furniture, (some of it was hers anyway) and keep on going. She knew that she was strong. She knew she would cope. After all, this was not the first time this had happened to her and, damn it, she wouldn't let any man destroy her. She was a strong woman. She never did fall into that trap of becoming dependent on a man.

Lindy also didn't understand the cryptic call he got from Dave. Dave had asked him to set up a meeting in San José with his employers. This meant either good news; he knew about Dave's plans to arrange wire transfers from the States, or bad news that he was in some kind of trouble. Lindy had seen bad things like this go down before. He would do as Dave wanted. He would set up the meeting, but he wouldn't be there. Oh no, it was bailout time. If it was all okay, he would find out and make some excuse why he wasn't there, but if it wasn't, he knew how to protect himself. Anguilla, that was a good place to go. Yes, he was very happy he had the old Cessna. It was better than any insurance policy.

Barry was restless all day Sunday, even though they had had a wonderful dinner with Dan and Alex. It appeared that a change had come over Alex. All Barry said was that he thought things would work out for Dan, but he didn't want to tell him too much until all the loose ends were tied up. He was itching to call Ted Jernow, but Ted was, after all, his adversary in the malpractice case and he couldn't tip his hand, surely not until he had a sum certain.

He and Tildy spent all of Sunday relaxing. They shared the Sunday paper and Tildy did the crossword. At dinnertime, they were still exhausted from all the events of the previous week, so Barry went out for some take out food, while Tildy rested. Barry looked over his place and it looked great. *Nothing like a woman's touch*, he thought. When they finished eating, Tildy said, "I guess I'll have to start looking for a job."

Barry thought about how he would love to have Tildy stay with his firm, but he knew that it wouldn't work for a variety of reasons. He felt that Tildy wouldn't want that either. He still had a number of unresolved issues in his life and he knew that it was time he got back to his own cases that had been put on hold. After all, Ray was only putting out fires. There were a number of things that the clock was ticking on and he needed to get back to work.

The next morning, Barry got up bright an early and was surprised to hear Tildy in the shower. For a minute, he couldn't figure out why someone was in his shower. When his mind cleared, he smiled. *Too many years alone*, he thought. Tildy dressed quickly and made a light breakfast, while Barry showered and dressed. He put on a light gray suit that matched the streaks of gray at his temples. Tildy thought about how handsome he was. She turned away from him and smiled.

They reached the office by eight-thirty. Eleanor was already there. It was too early to go to the bank to get Tildy's ring, but he made a mental note of it. They decided not to say anything about the engagement until he got the ring. Tildy found Ray and offered to help with anything Ray was working on. Ray smiled and said he had a number of things she could work on and they walked down the hall to the rear of the office.

Barry went through the weekend mail. Monday's mail wouldn't come until ten o'clock. He put the mail back down on Eleanor's desk for her to sort out and take care of. This was a ritual with Barry. He was always looking for those small settlement checks, one third of which paid for running the office. The other two thirds belonged to his clients.

His share of the larger settlements was usually his to keep unless there was a slackening of fees for the month. The office and staff took a big chunk of his total income, but the good employees generated some of the business, too. So it usually evened out. He looked at the time and, though it was not yet nine, he knew that Ted Jernow would be in the office. He called and asked the secretary for him and Ted got on the phone.

"Hi, Barry. How are you doing as a detective?"

"Not too bad, actually. Our insurance guy is in custody and it seems there's a small pot to draw on. If you haven't already done so, file your claim and we can start negotiating." Ted knew Barry very well and assumed if he was ready there was more than a small pot. He didn't say it, but he felt that when the time came to talk numbers he would be able to get a fair settlement for his client. He had seen the young man and realized that it would take a lot of money to care for him and that he had a pretty long life expectancy.

"Barry, I was going to call you and tell you that I couldn't wait too much longer to file, so I'm glad you called. You know the facts of the case. For whatever reason, your brother malpracticed my client and he'll spend the rest of his life in a wheelchair. He'll need a lifetime of care, and who knows how much rehab, occupational, and otherwise."

Barry knew the dance was beginning.

"Okay, how much?" There was the slightest hesitation that someone less experienced would not have noticed. After all, they were both highly experienced and played the same games, usually on the same side.

"Seven million," Jernow answered.

"Seven million? Okay, what's the real number?"

"Do you have the money in hand?"

"No."

"Do you know precisely what's in the pot?"

"No, not yet, but it's nothing like seven million."

"So why are we talking? Why don't we talk further when you have your hands on the money? Right now, it's seven million."

"This might take a while, before everything is finalized, but I'll get back to you when I find out just how much we have to work with."

"Okay, bye."

"Wait a minute Ted. I have something else to tell you. Tildy Jennings and I are going to get married."

"That's great. I thought you were definitely a confirmed bachelor. Wow! She's a great gal. Jason said he was sorry he had to lose her. Is she working with your firm, now?"

"Actually, no. We both thought it would be best for her not to work here, for all the obvious reasons. Do you, by any chance, have a place for her? She was on Law Review by the way. She's one smart woman."

"Let me think about that. I'm planning some changes and I might just have something, but I can't make a commitment yet."

"That's okay. Just keep it in mind."

"I will, thanks. Oh, and good luck to the both of you." Barry hung up and dialed Jake, immediately. He was told that Jake was out of the office and would be back around two. He asked that Jake return his call. He called Eleanor and asked for his mail and went through his messages. The rest of the morning, he spent getting up to speed on his cases.

## Chapter Twenty-Eight

About an hour later, Eleanor rang to say that Jake Sommers was on the phone.

"Hi, Jake."

"You called me?"

"Yes, I did. I spoke with Ted Jernow and he placed a demand on this case for seven million dollars."

"Wow, and he gets a third of that? I'm in the wrong business."

"It'll be less than that, but close. I asked you to come in with me when I opened here, but you wanted to spend your life prosecuting the bad guys."

"I guess I was young and stupid, but I really love what I do, so I guess I made the right choice. Especially when we can get a scumbag like Petersen. God, I hate guys like that, guys who just love to prey on good guys, like Dan."

"Dan was stupid to do what he did. He almost paid with his life."

"Well, I'm happy it all turned out as it did. What do you think you can settle the case for?"

"With a lot of negotiating and hard work, about four and a half mil, but for a fast, easy, settlement, five.

"You want to get it over with, don't you?"

"I want to, and Dan needs to. He's going to make some changes in his life, and he needs to see this over."

"I'll clear it with the Feds. See what other claims there are. I'll fight for the five, seeing as our guy can give them things they want more than this small fry stuff. He has names and he will testify. He'll do anything to get out of doing time and the Feds will take care of him, if his information helps nail some big traffickers. I think I can get the five and end it fast.

Give me a couple of hours to talk to them. If I don't get back to you today, it'll be early tomorrow."

"Thanks, Jake. This will mean a lot to Dan."

"I know, and if I can pull it out for him, you know I will. Bye."

"So long."

Barry sat back in his chair and mused over the conversation. Well, it really is good to have friends and to play it straight with them. Jake's one in a million; he does it all for love. They don't make too many like that anymore. He thought that Ted would be thrilled with the five. It was a fair settlement with very little work involved. No need going through all of that discovery, and doctor's reports. Just more costs for the kid. Dan knows what he did to that kid and there's really no defense. Ted's an honest person. He wouldn't overestimate the damages when dealing with me. He knows that I know. It's not like he's negotiating with an insurance company. We've been on the same side for a long time, even had a few cases together with multiple plaintiffs. He'll be glad to settle and move on. I know I'd be.

Barry rang Tildy's office and told her about his conversations. She was happy. She told him that she had heard from Helen Petersen, who wanted Tildy to set up a trust for Jim Donahue. He had been with the family since he was a young man. He could run the place, as long as he was able, and oversee the modernizing of the house. She would, of course, pay for any permanent improvements to the barns, etc. She was thinking of selling her business in Michigan, and moving back to New Jersey. She figured that after Jim passed on, there would be plenty of time to sell the land and it would probably go up in value. She and Jim would start boarding horses and operate the farm in partnership. She wanted Tildy to help her with the partnership agreement, as well. With a small income from the farm, the securities her mother-in-law left her, and the proceeds of her business, she would have sufficient income to wait it out. She said she had heard from Dave's lawyer, and he told her there was a possibility of a deal. She was happy about that. She really held no animosity for Dave, as long as he stayed out of her life. She knew that he would.

Tildy was happy that she had some business to bring with her to another office. If Helen Petersen remained happy with her work, the potential for the big sale is there in the future.

Barry said, "You ready for lunch? We have to get to the bank."

"Yes, whenever you are. I'm so happy that things are working out for Dan."

"He and I owe you a lot for what you put into it."

"Barry, we're family. No one owes me anything."

"You're right, love, we're family. Grab your coat; we're out of here."

Barry and Tildy went out for a leisurely lunch and went to the bank. Barry got the ring from his safe deposit box, looked at it, and slipped it on Tildy's finger. She was all smiles, and kissed him lightly on the lips. She said, "Barry, it's beautiful. I just love it and I plan to wear it for the rest of my life."

They left the bank and went directly to the office where they called everyone together and announced their engagement. A couple of the associates went downstairs and bought a couple of bottles of champagne and, after work, they had a small party and toasted the couple. Eleanor was all smiles. She really liked Tildy and thought she was right for her Barry.

The couple was very noncommittal about their wedding plans, mainly because they hadn't made any. It was clear to both of them that they would have a small wedding performed by one of the local judges, probably Judge Rowland, who seemed to enjoy Tildy's company so much the night of the bar dinner. Besides, Barry had known the Judge from before he went on the bench, and he was one of the few that Barry respected and admired. He was always happy to have a case in front of him, not because the Judge would favor him, but because he knew the law, he was intelligent, and he was fair. They agreed that there would be no wedding for a while, at least until they were both well settled and could get away for a weeklong honeymoon. In the meantime, they were together and that was all that mattered to either of them.

Barry didn't hear from Jake that day, but he received a call early the next morning.

"I have your money for you."

"How much?"

"Five million, isn't that what you asked for?"

"You're a bloody genius."

"Well, you get some points for bringing the guy to justice, from me and the Feds. They got more than they ever expected, and I got all my victims repaid. I have no reason to hold him. After what he told the FBI, he's not going to come back to New Jersey, again. So, he'll stay out of our hair, and the government will give him a new identity. They're confiscating the rest of his money, which he has agreed to bring back from Nevis/St.Kitts for his freedom. I guess it's all going to work out. By the way, I heard a rumor about you."

"Yes?"

" Are you getting married?"

"I found the most wonderful woman, and I intend to spend the rest of my life with her."

"I hear it's that gorgeous redhead who worked for Jason Kraus."

"Her name is Tilden Jennings, have you met her?"

"No, but she's Judge Jennings' granddaughter, the one you went to Detroit with, isn't she?"

"Yes, that's true. She helped to get Petersen too."

"You clerked for Jennings' firm, when we got out of law school, didn't you?"

"Yes, you have a good memory. She comes from a great family. I loved the old man. He taught me most of what I know. It'll be a long time before someone like him comes around again."

"Yes, he was a good judge, too. I remember him well. To answer your question, I haven't met her, but I hope you'll bring her around, one day. I only know that she came to court a couple of times with Jason, and everyone wanted to know who the hot redhead was."

"Well she's hot all right, but she's smart and classy too. I'm looking for a job for her; she's not with Jason anymore."

"I could probably find something for her here, if she wants criminal."

"I'll talk to her, but I think she wants to stay in civil. Thanks for the offer, and if I'm wrong, I'll have her call you. And again Jake, thanks for everything."

Barry got off the phone and called Ted, right away. Ted was in the office.

"Ted, I have the number and I hope you and your client will accept. I have five million for you, but I had to squeeze it out of Jake. The FBI got back into it, and they're confiscating the rest of the money by agreement with the defendant to keep him from serving time. He's giving up some bad drug buddies he made offshore. Ted, this is it. There just isn't any more. You know if I was an insurance lawyer we would probably take a lot more time and I'd settle for somewhere around three million. Costs, alone, would put a big hole in the three. It's a good offer, and I know you believe me when I say there is no more."

"Let me make a call. I think I can sell it to my client. I think it's a fair settlement for a quick offer without any costs to him."

Five minutes later, Ted called back and made the deal. He was happy because it was probably more than he would have gotten with an insurance company, and he would have had to work a lot harder for it. Besides, if it went to trial in New Jersey, the juries lately had been very conservative. Furthermore, he would have waited years to get it before a judge. The courts were hopelessly log jammed.

Barry was ecstatic. He told Eleanor to prepare the release and he called Jake to tell him to make out the check. It was over. The next call was to Dan.

"Dan, it's over."

"What's over?"

"Your case. I just settled it for five million dollars, and the money is available from the bastard who sold you the policy."

There was dead silence.

"Dan, are you okay?"

"I'm here. Five million? I could never have raised that much."

"You are one lucky bastard. You dodged a very big bullet."

"I'm lucky to have a brother like you."

"You didn't know I was a good detective, too, did you? By the way, Tildy had a lot to do with it, too."

"I can't tell you how relieved I am. Tildy's a wonderful girl and I'm sure you'll be very happy together. Did you give her the ring?"

"Today. We told my office staff, too. They bought champagne and we celebrated."

"That's great. Barry, Alex and I had a long talk. I'm giving up my practice. I'm looking for a good VA job or university position. Maybe as Dean, somewhere. I can't take the stress. With my heart, I don't think I want to do surgery, anymore. I don't want to carry all that insurance and I don't need this damn lifestyle. Alex agreed that she could easily give it up, if we can spend more time together. We owe it to each other. Who knows how many years I have, but I know I can lengthen the time if I get rid of the pressure."

"I think you're making the right decision. You're too young to retire, but there are other options. I really think you should give up surgery. It's a younger man's profession.

"Barry, thanks for everything and also for your support. You're the best brother a man could have. I love you very much and don't know what I would have done without you."

"As you said. We're brothers. I love you, too. I think you've made some wise decisions and I'm glad you and Alex patched it up. She's really all right."

Barry called Eleanor in and told her all that had happened. He said he thought she'd be happy to know he was going to be able to work full time for the firm.

# EPILOGUE

Tildy went to work for Ted Jernow and brought Helen Petersen's business in with her. Through Mrs. Petersen's contacts, she was able to bring in many more clients from in and around Richmond County. When Mr. Donohue became old and eventually died, Mrs. Petersen sold the farm and the negotiations generated even more revenue for the firm. In a few short years, Tildy became a partner.

Dan found a job as Dean at the state medical school. He and Alex found time for weekends and vacations. They terminated their membership in the country club. Alex was very content to have a peaceful, non-competitive life. She lost herself in charity work and crafts, but she was always available to go, whenever Dan needed a vacation. They traveled a great deal and saw much of the world. Ultimately, their children married and they devoted much of their time to being grandparents.

Barry and Tildy were married in a quiet ceremony in the chambers of Judge Rowland, who kissed the bride and held her a little longer than was quite proper. Jason Kraus gave her away. She and Barry had a long and happy life together. They had two children twenty-two months apart, and then five years later, were blessed with twins. Barry was a wonderful father. He later went on the bench and became an outstanding jurist.

Ray Tobias took over Barry's firm and made a big name for himself as a first rate trial lawyer. He had several multi-million dollar verdicts over the years.

Jake Sommers ended up on the Federal bench and eventually became an esteemed member of the United States Circuit Court of Appeals for the Third Circuit.

Ted Jernow continued his fast-paced practice and ended it with a sudden fatal heart attack at the age of sixty. Tildy became the senior and managing partner of the firm.

Helen Petersen married a Dutch Reformed minister and stayed in Vreeland Corners for the rest of her life. She remained Tildy's client throughout her life and the two couples became fast friends.

David Petersen went into the Federal Witness Protection Program and started a new life in Arizona, after assisting in bringing his employers to justice. He met and married a beautiful Mexican-American woman, twenty years his junior, and they had three children. He converted to Roman Catholicism and became very devout. As far as anyone knows, he got a job as a car salesman and stayed on the straight and narrow for the remainder of his life. One of his children became a neurosurgeon.

Lindy, Dave's colorful sidekick and companion, set up a meeting supposedly between Dave and his employers. When the time came for the meeting, Dave did not attend as expected, but the San José police did and picked up Tino and Hugo. They were extradited to the United States, and gave up even more of their associates, enabling the authorities to break up a very strong and well-established cartel. Lindy escaped the net and is believed to have died in a plane crash in Honduras some months later, under questionable circumstances.

Marianne stayed in Nevis/St.Kitts and was very successful in her real estate business. She had several liaisons with rich foreign investors, the last was a Russian man she had sold a house to in Nevis. She was found dead one morning, apparently having died under suspicious circumstances. Her murder remains unsolved.

The boy who was rendered a paraplegic by Dan's surgery, went to college and became a famous writer of mystery novels.